**W9-DGX-393**

**DISCLAIMER**

**ISBN (Paperback) : 979-8-4592655-0-7**

**ISBN (Large Print): 978-1-957207-01-8**

This is a work of fiction. Names, characters, businesses, places, events, and incidents are either the products of the author's imagination or used in a fictitious manner. Any resemblance to actual persons, living or dead, or actual events is purely coincidental.

# THE STOLEN CHILD

ROBERTA KAGAN

# CHAPTER ONE

KARA PACED the floor frantically in the hotel room where she was staying in Warsaw. Her hands trembled, and her knees felt weak.

"Do you think he will find him?" Kara asked as she turned to her sister, Anka, who was sitting on the bed.

"I don't know. I only know that I blame myself," Anka said, wringing her slender white hands together.

"Dear God, Anka, not everything is about you. My son, my little Karl, is missing. He's only three and he's missing. Somewhere, he is all alone and he's looking for me. I can hear him calling out *Mutti, Mutti,* and it's driving me insane. I can't go to him because, I don't know where to find him."

"And it's my fault. I told you to leave him with a babysitter who we hardly knew. It was me. I told you it would all be all right. Oh, Kara. I convinced you to do it. I had no idea that something so horrible could happen. All I wanted was to see you finally get out of the house. I wanted to see you laugh and enjoy yourself. I wanted you to attend a party. Perhaps meet someone. You've been so alone. I never thought this could happen."

Kara couldn't bear to comfort and reassure her sister as she'd always done in the past. She was in too much mental anguish to worry about Anka's feelings. *It was Anka's fault.* Anka had convinced her to leave her son with a Polish grandmother they'd met, in order to attend a Nazi gala, the night before. *This damn party was so important to Anka,* Kara thought as she paced the room. She couldn't even look at her sister, let alone comfort her. *How different we are. She is my sister, and we were so close when we were children. But things have changed. I have changed,* Kara thought.

Anka was married to Ludwig, a man who was trying to make a good impression in the Nazi Party so he could rise in rank. And although she wasn't in love with him, she was the perfect wife for him because she wanted the same thing. Anka made no excuses for how much she enjoyed the comfort of being married to a Nazi official. She loved the parties. She loved the good food and fine clothes. And she loved the nice home she and her husband had been given by the Nazi Party when he went to work on the Wolf's Lair, a luxury entertainment center for the führer and some of his high officials.

It had taken persistence, but she had finally convinced Kara to leave her son, Karl, with this Polish woman. Kara knew Anka would never hurt her or Karl on purpose. She was just thoughtless. And because she'd been so insistent, Kara had finally agreed. Everything should have been fine. But it wasn't. The following day, when they'd gone to pick Karl up, the old woman's apartment was ransacked, and the old lady and Karl were both gone. Kara, Anka, her husband, Ludwig, and Oskar Lerch, a high-ranking SS officer who was smitten with Kara, spent the rest of the day searching frantically for the boy. They went door to door, asking neighbors if they saw anything. No one wanted to get involved. Who could blame them? After all, Kara was accompanied by Oskar Lerch, who was intimidating to anyone Polish, in his black SS uniform. Poland was a newly conquered country. And the Polish feared the Germans, whose bombs and cruelty they'd witnessed firsthand. Kara could see the fear in their eyes. She wanted to throw herself on the floor and beg them to help her. But she knew it wouldn't make any difference. They were too afraid to speak.

Finally, Kara found a neighbor who was compassionate. She lived in the same building as the babysitter, Sonia Smolak. And she admitted to having seen the child and the old lady, Smolak, being shoved into a car by the Gestapo.

Kara turned to Oskar. "Gestapo?" she said. "Why would the Gestapo take my son?" She was hysterical. And although Oskar was scheduled to leave Warsaw and head back to work, he canceled his plans and insisted on staying to help Kara find her son. "I don't know," he said, "but I promise you this: I will find out, and we will find your boy."

"I wish he would get back here already," Anka said. She was referring to Oskar who had gone to the Gestapo headquarters in Warsaw to find out anything he could about the missing boy.

Kara was flushed. She felt faint. *Everything is out of my control*, she thought. *Dear God, how I wish my Abram was here. But I can't talk to Anka about Abram because none of these people knew of his existence, and that was because he was Jewish. Abram is the love of my life, and he is also Karl's father.* Abram was arrested right after Kristallnacht. His mother, Hoda, in order to protect Karl, insisted that Kara take Karl and go to live with Anka, who had married a high-ranking officer in the Nazi Party. Hoda and Kara decided it would be safest for Karl if he hid in plain sight. No one was ever to know he was half Jewish. Kara had lied to Anka. She told her that Karl was the son of a pure German man whom she had an affair with. She claimed the man was married, and he'd gone back to his wife and left her to raise the boy on her own. Anka took her sister and her nephew into her home to live. And because of his strong Aryan features, no one suspected Karl of having Jewish blood; he was accepted into Ludwig and Anka's world. All had gone well until this gala. Kara had not wanted to go. She had a bad feeling about it before she even attended, but Anka had assured her that all would be well. It wasn't.

# CHAPTER TWO

WHEN OSKAR RETURNED LATE that afternoon, Kara was sick with worry. She ran to him as soon as he opened the door to the hotel room.

"What did you find out?" she pleaded, grabbing his arm.

"Not much, but the Gestapo has no record of having been involved in arresting a woman and child at that address. However, they were familiar with the name Sonia Smolak. According to police records, they have been keeping an eye on her. They think she is involved with the Polish Resistance. They wanted to follow her for a while before arresting her, in hopes of finding some of her contacts. I went to the apartment again to look around and see if I could find anything. I searched for the neighbor, who we spoke to when we were looking for Karl, but her apartment was all closed up, and I asked the landlady about it. She said that the woman we saw no longer lives there. She was just there; now she's gone. It's all very strange."

Kara gasped, "Where could she have gone? It's only been two days. How did she move away so fast?"

"I don't know. I tried to find out. But no one in the building will admit to ever having known her."

"This is horrible," Kara said, putting her hands on her temples and squeezing.

"I found this at the apartment," Oskar said, handing a dirty, singed stuffed bear to Kara.

"Oh, my dear God." Kara had been too upset to notice that he had been carrying a stuffed animal. She took the bear and held it up to her face. Then she began to cry. "Little bear . . ." she said, remembering Karl's face when Abram had brought Little Bear back to Karl after their apartment had burned on Kristallnacht.

Oskar put his arms around Kara and held her like a baby as she wept.

"It's all right," he whispered into her ear. "It's going to be all right."

"What are we going to do next? I can't see how we are going to ever find him." Kara's entire body was shaking as she paced the floor, pulling at her hair.

"We will find him," Oskar said calmly. "I give you my word I will do everything in my power to find him." Then he added, "I found out where

Sonia Smolak's son lives. We'll go there tomorrow and see what we can find out. We'll tell him that his mother was babysitting your son and now they've both disappeared. Perhaps he's heard from his mother."

Kara's heart sank. She didn't care about Sonia Smolak or her son right now. This was unlike her. She'd always been concerned about others. But never before had she been in such a perilous position. All she wanted was to hold her child in her arms.

Oskar saw the look on her face and said, "Kara, I am pleading with you to trust me. Please don't worry. I will stay with you and help you. I will not give up on this. I won't give up on it no matter how long it takes. We will find your son." He touched her arm, and she recoiled from his touch.

Even though he was so kind and ever so helpful, he still wore that uniform with the Nazi emblem, and it put her off. "Just to let you know, I called my office this morning and told them that I need to take some time off. I told them I might be gone for a while. So, as I said, I will be with you through this entire ordeal. You won't be doing this alone, Kara. Together we will find Karl."

She knew he was trying to be reassuring. But no matter what he said, all she could think about was her son. Then a horrific thought came into her mind, and she said aloud, more to herself than to him, "Dear God, please no. I don't know what I will do if he's—"

"He's not dead or hurt," Anka interrupted. "It's all just a misunderstanding. We'll get to the bottom of it. I promise." She tried to smile reassuringly but her lips trembled. "Why don't we do something to distract you. Would you like to go shopping or out for a drink?"

Kara glared at her sister. *Sometimes Anka can be so insensitive.* "No," Kara said harshly.

Oskar put his hand on Kara's upper arm. It felt strong, warm, and supportive. "The first thing we will do is make a trip to Mosciska. It's about eighty-five kilometers from here. We'll go tomorrow morning. Yes?"

Kara nodded.

Then Oskar continued, "You and I will have a little visit with Sonia's son and daughter-in-law. They just might have some information for us."

Kara nodded again.

Oskar could see that she was cold. He took off his jacket and put it around her arms. She thanked him. It was his uniform jacket. He meant well. But it represented the dreaded SS. Kara removed the jacket and laid it on the bed. Then she took the blanket and wrapped it around herself. Taking a deep breath, Kara turned to face Anka and said, "Perhaps it's best if you return home to Ludwig. You don't want to leave him alone to care for himself." Kara said it more curtly than she'd wanted to.

And although she saw the pain on her sister's face, she wanted Anka to go before she said something even more hurtful. After all, even though Anka didn't mean for this to happen, it was her fault.

"You want me to leave here and go home?" Anka repeated in disbelief.

"I think it's best. I'll stay in contact with you," Kara said.

"All right. I'll go. I mean, if that's what you want."

"Don't worry, Anka. I'll be here with Kara. And I promise you, we'll call you at least once a week to keep you abreast of everything we are doing and everything we find out," Oskar said.

"I understand. I'll pack," Anka said. "And I'll call Ludwig and ask him to come and pick me up."

Kara didn't say a word. She loved Anka, but right at this moment, she resented her too. She couldn't look at Anka's face. *I didn't want to go to that ridiculous party. You knew that. I told you. But you insisted. And you insisted that we leave Karl with a babysitter. Now, my son is gone. I can't stand here and coddle you like I did when we were children. I've lost everything dear to me, and you seem to need so much. Just go home.*

Anka called Ludwig to pick her up., He arrived late the following morning. And by the afternoon, Anka and Ludwig were on their way home. After they left, Kara and Oskar got into his automobile and drove to Mosciska to speak to Sonia's son and daughter-in-law.

For a while, they drove in silence. Kara looked out the window in despair. She wanted to scream, to hit her head on the window until she became unconscious. But she knew it would do no good. Inside she was raging, terrified, angry, filled with emotion. On the outside, she was silent. Then Oskar patted Kara's hand and said, "Don't worry, I've paid the hotel for the month. So, you will have a place to stay in Warsaw while we figure all of this out."

"Where are you staying?" she asked, worried that he might think because she needed him, he could take advantage of the situation and share her room.

"I've secured another room for myself across the hall from yours. Please don't worry. I would never try to stay in your room. It's not my nature to put a lady in a position that might make her uncomfortable. I am here to help you, Kara. I am a gentleman, and I will never do anything to compromise how you see me."

She managed a smile. *If there is one thing I can say for Oskar Lerch, he is telling the truth. He has always been a gentleman. I don't know anything about his past, like his family or where he was born. But from what I know of him, I would venture to say he came from educated and wealthy people. He has so much class. And even though he is a Nazi, I can honestly say he gives every indication that he was raised properly.* "Thank you. This is all very kind of you," she said.

"I know how much you are suffering, and I

don't blame you. A mother's love for her son is probably the strongest kind of love there is." He hesitated, then a little choked up, he added, "You are a good mother, Kara. I see wonderful things in you. And I plan to do whatever needs to be done to find your boy."

She nodded. Her eyes burned with unshed tears. "Oskar . . ." she said in a soft voice, "you don't think that something has happened to him, do you? I can't help but think of all the horrible things that could have happened. It's driving me crazy."

"No, of course not. Nothing has happened to him. We'll find him. Please trust me." He patted her hand. Then he added, "If it's true that he was somehow mistakenly taken by the Gestapo, then we can be sure he's all right. He's a beautiful Aryan boy. It's not like he is a Jew, after all. So, please don't worry. They would never harm him."

His voice was warm and reassuring. And she so wanted to believe. But when he said the words, *"It's not like he is a Jew,"* Kara felt the tiny hairs on the back of her neck stand up. *Is it possible that they could find out somehow? Dear God, please protect him. Please don't let them find out the truth and hurt him.* Then because she had to know—the answer to this question was nagging at her—she tried to sound casual as she asked, "They wouldn't hurt a child even if he was a Jew, would they?"

"Of course not. We're Germans, the most civilized, superior race on the planet. We don't hurt children." He patted her hand, then added, "But you needn't worry anyway. He isn't a Jew."

They drove for a little over two hours until they came to a lush green farming village.

"Nice land here," Oskar marveled as he looked around. He turned the steering wheel and maneuvered the car down a winding path. A few moments later, they pulled up in front of a modest white wood farmhouse. It was newly painted with a small flower garden in the front. Oskar turned off the motor and got out of the car. He walked around and opened the door for Kara. "Are you all right?" he asked as he extended his hand to help her out of the car.

She nodded. She couldn't speak. For some reason her throat felt raw as if she'd been weeping. And she had been, on the inside.

Taking her hand into his own, he led her to the door of the house. Her hand felt small and protected in his, and she was thankful to have him by her side. He gave her hand a tiny, reassuring squeeze. Then he knocked. A young woman with a small child at her side opened the door. Kara could see that as soon as the woman saw them, there was a look of fear on the woman's face. Kara trembled. She wasn't sure if it was because of something Sonia had done or if it was because of Oskar's uniform.

"Yes, what do you want?" the young woman asked, trying to sound brave.

"I'm here to see Hubert Smolak," Oskar said. "This is his home, is it not?" His voice was soft, but there was an underlying threat in his words as if he were daring her to lie to him and say that this was not the home of Hubert Smolak.

She was too afraid to lie. Her body was trembling. A little girl was staring wide eyed in the background. The child grabbed her mother's leg and held on. "Yes, this is the home of Hubert Smolak. But he's working in the field right now." The young woman's voice cracked as she stumbled on the words.

"All right, then we'll come in. You can prepare a cup of tea for us, and we'll talk to you while we wait until he returns," Oskar said, smiling.

Although Oskar's voice was soft and gentle, Kara could see how the woman would be afraid of him. She was a Polish farmwife with a little girl who Kara estimated at about three or four years old, confronted by an SS officer who smiled at her. But his smile wasn't sincere. Again, there was an underlying threat.

"So, may we sit down," Oskar said, taking a seat on the sofa before the woman answered.

"Yes, of course," the farmer's wife said. Her child was now hanging on the skirt of her housedress.

"And your name must be . . . Maja?" Oskar smiled again. It was that same terrifying smile. Kara saw a side of him she didn't want to see. So she ignored it.

"Yes, I am Maja Smolak."

"And that cute little girl must be Roza," he said. And Kara felt it was just to let the woman know that he knew everything about her, and not only was he threatening her and her husband, but also her child. Kara trembled. But she wouldn't stop him. He was doing what was necessary to find Karl. Although in the past Kara had always cared about others and their feelings, right now, all she cared about was her son.

Now Maja's lips were quivering. "Please, we have done nothing. I don't know what you want from us. My daughter is just a child."

"I am just here to find out the truth about a missing little boy who is very dear to my heart." Oskar smiled. "I'm sure you'll be as helpful as you can. As will your husband, Hubert. Am I correct? It is Hubert, that's his name, is it not?" Oskar said. He was toying with her.

"Yes, my husband's name is Hubert. Please, I don't know anything about a little boy. My husband knows nothing either. I beg you, please let us be."

"You may not know about the boy. But your mother-in-law should have some information. She seems to have disappeared. I am talking about your husband's mother. Sonia Smolak?"

It made Kara cringe to hear him playing with

the woman, terrorizing her like a cat terrorizes its prey.

"Yes, that's my mother-in-law's name."

"Did you know that she has disappeared?" Oskar said, his voice tilting upward at the end of the sentence.

The woman looked at him incredulously. She was clearly shaken by his words. "Disappeared? What do you mean? Arrested?"

Oskar didn't speak for several moments. He stood up and began to pace the room slowly. He was intimidating in his black uniform. A smile came over his face, a threatening smile. Kara felt sick when she saw a line of sweat form across Maja's upper lip. Still, Oskar did not speak again. When he finally spoke, his voice was even softer than before but with an even more frightening undertone. "And . . . do you happen to know of some reason why she might have been arrested?"

"No, I am just asking if she has been arrested, because I don't know why she would have disappeared," Maja stammered. Kara could see that Maja felt trapped. The child who held on to her mother's skirt began to cry. It seemed as if the little girl could sense something in the air, something menacing. Kara closed her eyes and reminded herself, *I know Oskar is being cruel and I feel horrible about it. But we must do this to find Karl.*

Kara thought of Karl as she studied the child. *He would have done the same thing. He would have held on*

*to me in terror. Even though he would not have known why or
what he was afraid of.*

"I see . . ." Oskar said, fixing his eyes on Maja.
"So, if someone disappears, you just assume they've
been arrested. Is that what you're telling me? But
doesn't it seem rather odd to you that your mother-
in-law, a helpless, old woman, would be arrested for
no reason at all?" He drummed his fingers on the
kitchen table. Then he glared at Maja. "As I see it,"
he said, hesitating for a moment, "there must be
something you haven't told us?"

Just then the kitchen door opened, and a tall,
muscular young man walked into the house.
"Maja?" he called out as he walked into the living
room. But when he saw Oskar and Kara, he
stopped talking and stared. His hands were dirty
from the soil. His overalls were dirty too. He had
the open, honest face of a man who worked the
land.

"Well, well, look who's here," Oskar said. "Let
me guess . . . you must be Hubert?"

"I'm Hubert Smolak. What do you want?" the
farmer said sternly, but even so, Kara could hear
him hiding the fear in his voice.

"I want to know what happened to your mother.
I'm sure you have some idea, do you not?"

"My mother? What's happened to my mother?"
The farmer forgot his own fears and was suddenly
full of concern.

"Haven't you called her lately? Now, every good

son should call his mother every few days. Don't you agree, Hubert?" Oskar asked in a condescending tone.

"No. I mean yes, of course. I would call my mother daily if I could. But, we don't have a phone. To call her, I have to go into town. Dear Lord. What's happened to her?" Hubert sounded frantic.

The child was crying harder now. The sound of it was unnerving Kara. *What if my son is somewhere terrified and crying and I can't get to him?*

"Why, your mother has disappeared . . ." Oskar said.

"What do you mean? Disappeared? How could that be?"

"I mean she is gone from her apartment. The apartment has been closed up. The landlady says there is no one living there anymore." Oskar's voice and facial expressions were different. In his tone of voice, he pretended mock concern, but his face was threatening. "You see, your dear mother was babysitting for this young lady's son. And this young lady happens to be a very good friend of mine. So, of course, I am very protective of her and her child. I'm sure you understand?"

Hubert nodded. He was clenching and unclenching his hands. It was as if he didn't know what to do with them.

"Well . . ." Oskar hesitated. "While your mother was watching my friend's son, both of them went missing. Can you imagine how distraught my friend here is? Just think how distraught you would be if that pretty little girl over there went missing? How distraught would you be if I took her with me today?"

The farmer's wife let out a gasp. Hubert went to punch Oskar, but Oskar pulled his gun. "Now, I am sure you don't want to leave your young wife a widow already, do you?"

Hubert dropped his hands to his sides in defeat. "What can I do?"

"Well, you can help us. We came here because you are going to tell us everything you know about your mother's disappearance," Oskar said calmly, but he still held the gun pointed at Hubert.

Maja had now picked her child up and held the weeping little girl in her arms.

"I have no idea. I didn't even know she was missing. I don't know what happened. We only speak once a month when I go into town to use the telephone. Most of our communication is through letters." He was shaking. His eyes told Kara he was genuinely worried about his mother but also about his wife and daughter.

"Hmmm . . ." Oskar sucked his lower lip and looked into Hubert's eyes. "You appear to be so innocent. But I have some inside information about you. I know that you have been active with the Polish Underground."

"NO!!!! No!!! I swear it," Hubert protested.

"And your mother? Was she active with them too?"

"Of course not. She is an old woman. She has no political views."

"I see," Oskar said. He walked around the family once and Kara saw Maja tremble. Then he said casually, "All right, then. We'll be going. Come, Kara."

They walked outside and got into the car. Hubert was standing in the walkway as they left. Oskar called out, "Lovely farm you have here. Even if it is a bit small. I am sure you've been giving the proper amount of your harvest to the Germans when they come by to pick it up for the war effort. Haven't you?"

"Yes, yes of course," Hubert said.

As Oskar backed the car out of the drive, Kara could see Hubert's knees shaking.

The car shook and rattled on the dirt road as they drove away. Oskar took Kara's hand. "That wasn't as promising as I hoped it would be. But I'll put a watch on him and see if he doesn't try to get in contact his mother over the next couple of days," Oskar said, "If he knows where she is, he'll want to tell her that we are searching for her. So he'll lead us right to her. And, of course, if we can find her, we will find Karl."

"I hope so," Kara said, squeezing Oskar's hand. Then she turned and looked out the window at the landscape. It was green and beautiful. A nagging thought filled her head. She couldn't help but re-member how easily Oskar had turned into an intimi-dating, almost monster of a man. She'd never imagined he could be so heartless to a family, especially with a small child witnessing his vicious cruelty. And yet, she had to remember, *he did it for me and for Karl. This is not the real Oskar. It's not the real him. I've seen the real Oskar. He's the kind and gentle man who is trying to help me. Isn't he?*

# CHAPTER THREE

WHEN THEY RETUNED THAT AFTERNOON, Oskar dropped Kara off at the hotel and went to the police station. He returned shortly after he left.

"I told the police what happened," he said. "They'll keep a close watch on Hubert and his family to see if any of them makes some kind of contact with his mother. Meanwhile, I found out that Sonia Smolak was a traitor. She and her son both were members of the Polish Resistance. That tells me that the son is a liar. He had to know that his mother was involved."

"Really, Oskar? I met her. She's an old woman."

"It doesn't matter. The police say they don't know what happened to her. But someone is lying. And no matter what it takes, I plan to find out every secret and every lie until we find Karl."

"Do you think the police took Sonia and Karl?"

"I can't be sure," he said. "It could have been the Gestapo."

"If they did, what would they have done with Karl? Would they have hurt him?" Kara said, her hand flying up to her mouth.

"No, of course not. The Germans are not animals. We would never hurt a child. You should know that."

She didn't know that. She remembered what happened on Kristallnacht and she shivered. "I'm terrified. What if I never find my son again?" Kara asked, tears filling her eyes.

"I promise you, Kara, we'll find him."

"But you can't promise me he'll be unharmed."

"No, I can't promise you that. But if he has been harmed, there will be hell to pay. That much I vow."

# CHAPTER FOUR

KARA TELEPHONED her sister that night. She had a few days away from Anka to rethink everything she'd said. Her anger had faded, and now she felt badly about the way she treated Anka. It was true that Anka could be foolish, childish, and thoughtless, but she was Kara's only sister, and Kara had to make peace with her.

"'Allo," Anka said.

"It's me, Kara."

"Kara! Have you heard anything about Karl?"

"Nothing solid, but we did find out that the old lady was in the Resistance."

"What Resistance?"

"The Polish Resistance."

"Do you think she did something to Karl? Oh, Kara. This is all my fault." Anka was on the verge of hysterics, and Kara was suddenly sorry she'd telephoned. Instead of making Kara feel better, this conversation was making things worse.

"I pray she didn't."

"Is Oskar helping you, or do you want me to return to Warsaw?" Anka asked.

"Oskar is here with me, and he has been wonderful. He's truly a gentleman in every way," Kara said. "I think it's best that you stay with Ludwig for now. He needs you."

"He's very nervous. They are trying to make sure that everything is perfect at the lair before the führer arrives next month. Ludwig took me to see the lair. It's really quite marvelous. He's worked so hard for this, Kara."

"Yes, I know," Kara said. She had no interest in Adolf Hitler or his lair. She could think of nothing but her son. "All right, well, I just wanted to let you know what has transpired so far. I am going to let you go now. I need some rest. We'll talk again soon," she managed to say.

"I love you, Kara. My thoughts are with you," Anka offered.

"I know. I know you do, Anka, and I love you too," Kara said honestly, but also a little exasperated.

After Kara hung up the phone, Oskar walked over to her. "You haven't eaten today."

"I'm not hungry," Kara said.

"Kara, you must eat. We'll find your son. I promise you that. But you cannot let your health suffer in the meantime. When we do find him, he's going to need his mother. And he's going to need for you to be in good health. Now, come on, eat something, please?"

"I'm so afraid, Oskar. I'm so afraid that he's gone forever." She was staring down at the floor.

"Look at me," he said, gently raising her face with his hands. "I promise you that I am going to find him."

"You can't promise that he'll be alive."

"No, I can't. But I can promise you that if he's hurt, I will do everything in my power to punish anyone who might have hurt him. But let's not think about that. Let's not dwell on it. Instead, let's try to believe that all will be well."

She swallowed hard. His eyes were shining with sincerity.

"Please, Kara. Let's go and have dinner. You must eat. Do it for me, will you?"

She nodded. "All right."

They went downstairs to the restaurant in the hotel. Oskar ordered several different dishes in hopes of enticing Kara to eat. But she only pushed the food around on her plate. Once they finished dinner, and the waiter cleared the table, Oskar ordered two glasses of schnapps. She looked at him. "I don't drink," she said.

"Have a little. It will help you sleep."

She sipped the schnapps. It was smooth and warm going down her throat.

"Do you feel a little more relaxed?" he asked.

She nodded.

"Good." He smiled. "When we get back up-stairs, you should take a hot bath and go to sleep. I'm going to go to my own room and make some calls. I must see what I can do. I am going to call in some favors."

"What do you mean?"

"No need for you to worry your pretty little head about all of this. You have enough on your mind," he said. "That's why I want you to try and relax. It's best if you just let me handle this, Kara. Please, just put your trust in me. Won't you do that?"

"All right," she said, knowing she had no other choice. He was the only lifeline she had to her son. But as they walked through the lobby, she turned to look at him. She had to ask, "Oskar, why are you doing this for me?"

"You don't know?"

She shook her head.

"I care about you, Kara. I think I am falling in love with you. I want to take care of you . . ." he said, then he stopped. "I have said quite enough. I don't want to put any additional pressure on you. Please know, I expect nothing from you. I only want to help."

She squeezed his arm. "I appreciate everything you're doing for me and my son."

When they arrived at the door to her room,

Oskar turned to her. "Are you all right, or would you like me to come in and sit with you?"

"No, thank you. I am fine. I am going to try and get some rest."

"That's a good idea," he said and waited until she went into her room.

Kara closed the door. Then she ran a hot bath and got in. The warmth of the bath soothed her. But even as it did, it brought tears to her eyes. *My son, where is my son? I would do anything, even give up my life, to find him.* She lay in the bathtub and sobbed until the water grew cold. Kara was spent; every muscle and nerve in her body was exhausted. She lay down on the bed, but she still couldn't sleep. Her mind was racing. She thought of Karl and of Abram. Memories she treasured of a past she must keep hidden. Then she thought of what Oskar had said to her earlier that night and she was confused. *How could Oskar be so kind and caring and still be a Nazi?* Because, after all, she must never forget that he is a Nazi. *The strange thing is, he is gentle and understanding. Is it possible that all of the SS are not bad men? I mean, Ludwig is a good man. I know he hates Jews. And that bothers me. But perhaps it's something that stems from things he was told as a child. After all, I used to be afraid of Jewish people too. That was before I met Abram and Hoda.* The sun had begun to rise when she fell asleep.

At a little before nine in the morning the following day, Oskar knocked on the door to Kara's hotel room. She got out of bed and let him in, not realizing that she'd forgotten to put on her robe. He didn't look at her body. Instead, he kept his gaze focused on her eyes. In his hands he was carrying a bag of sweet rolls and two cups of steaming coffee. He set them down on the writing table in the corner, then plopped down into a chair.

"I brought breakfast," he said cheerfully.

She looked down at her nightgown and gasped. "Excuse me. I was so tired I . . ."

"It's all right," he said, looking away.

She ran to the bathroom and got her robe. Quickly, she put it on.

"You do look lovely in the morning," he said. "So fresh, like a spring flower. But I know you have so much on your mind. And so, I am not looking at you in that way . . . if you understand me. No gentleman would."

She avoided his last statement. "Did you find out anything else about Karl?"

"Just that as soon as we left the farm, Sonia's son tried to call his mother at the telephone number we have in Warsaw. Of course, she didn't answer. Because she's not there, as we know. So far, he hasn't done anything else. We'll give him a couple of days. If he doesn't make contact with her, then we know he doesn't have any idea where to find her."

"Which leaves us without any direction."

"Well, that's not exactly true," Oskar said.

"There is a possibility that Karl was taken by the Gestapo even though there is no record of it."

"Which means what? What would they do with him? Dear God, help me. He's only four years old. What could they possibly want with a baby?"

"Well, I am looking into the Lebensborn."

"I thought that was some sort of a breeding factory for Aryan women and SS officers. What would they want with my Karl?"

"He's a beautiful, Aryan child. I am sure they didn't know he's a German. They probably thought he was Polish. After all, he was with a Polish woman in Warsaw. I'm afraid there just aren't enough blond-haired, blue-eyed children. So, when they see a Polish child who fits the criteria, they take the child and check him over, by measuring his skull, his nose, things like that. They do it to make sure he doesn't have any Jew or Gypsy blood. Once they're sure he's of good stock, then they Germanize him."

"What does that mean? Germanize him? You're frightening me."

"Well, it's not really all that scary. Let me explain," he said, taking a sip of coffee. "It would actually be a good thing for us if he were in a home for the Lebensborn. You see, as I am an SS officer, they would give him to me. And, of course, I would bring him back to you."

"Yes," she said, and suddenly she felt relief that he held a high position in the party. *After all, he seems to be a good person. And he told me that in his job, he doesn't have contact with Jewish people. He never talks about them. I wonder what his feelings about them are. I am sure he must have the same terrible thoughts as the rest of the government but perhaps not as full of anger or hatred. He seems more educated, more sophisticated than most of them. But why bring it up? I have asked him too many questions already. I think it's best if I just keep my mouth shut. I need to get my child back, and he might be the only person who can help me.*

"I'll return in a moment," he said, getting up quickly. "I have some things for you." Then he left her room with the door cracked just a little, so he wouldn't have to knock when he returned.

It was only a few hours, and he was back, with his arms full of bags. "I went shopping and got you some clothes. I know you had some things when you arrived here in Warsaw, but most of your clothing is at your sister's home. So, I assumed you might need these."

She looked at him, stunned. *He is so considerate. So thoughtful.* He gently pushed the bags toward her. She smiled. "Thank you," she said as she opened the bags. There were several dresses and pairs of stockings, and there were undergarments too. When she looked in the bag with the undergarments, she happened to glance up and see his face. He was blushing.

"I had the saleslady help me with those things," he said, looking away as if he were shy or ashamed.

Kara smiled. *He's charming,* she thought. Then

she said, "Thank you again, Oskar. This was very thoughtful of you."

"W-well," he stammered, "I wasn't sure how long we might be here in Warsaw, and I thought you might need clean clothes."

Her heart ached with despair. "Oh . . . I hope we can find him soon."

"I am doing my best. Please know that."

"I do," she said. "I know." But then she began to cry. He walked over to her and put his arms around her. She lay her head on his chest, and he cradled her in his arms while she wept like a child.

"Kara . . ." he said her name softly, almost a whisper. "I will put in a call to headquarters, and I'll have them search all of the Lebensborn homes for a boy of Karl's description. Do you have any photographs?"

She nodded. "In my handbag."

"Good. I'd like one."

"I have a few."

"All right. After I call headquarters, they'll begin the search. Then I'll drive over there and give them the photo. But there is no need for you to come along with me. You can wait here until we hear something substantial.

"Either something from the police concerning that Smolak woman or something from one of the Lebensborn homes. But don't you worry. You are not alone. I'll be by your side throughout this entire process. And, no matter what it takes," he reassured her, "we will find him."

She nodded. "I'm sorry I am carrying on so. I can't help myself." She straightened up and took her handbag off the writing table. Then she took out a photo and handed it to Oskar. He looked at it. Then he touched her cheek and put the picture into his wallet.

"I understand, Kara. Of course, you can't help yourself. You're a mother. A good mother. I would expect nothing less," he said. "Now, I am going to headquarters to drop off the photo. Then, when I return, why don't we go out for lunch today? Perhaps take a walk around the zoo. It would do you good. It would be a good distraction."

She shook her head, "I don't know . . ."

"I think you need the distraction. Sitting here in this room weeping and worrying won't help us find him any faster. Please, let me take you out of here for a while. The fresh air will do you good."

She looked down at the floor. Then back up at his face. He was smiling. *Just look at him. His face is wide open. His smile is one of a gentle, concerned man. Not the smile of a vicious Nazi.*

"Please . . ." he said, "you can't sit here in this room like this staring at out the window. It's not healthy."

"I know, you're right."

"So, you'll come out? At least for a short while?"

"I will," she said.

"Good. Very good. Now, you go ahead and get dressed. I should be back in about an hour. I'll meet you in the lobby then. Is an hour enough time for you to get ready?"

"Oh yes. An hour would be plenty," she said.

Oskar was waiting when she walked into the lobby. He smiled when he saw her and stood up.

"Did you drop off the picture?"

"Yes, everything is taken care of. They are checking all the Lebensborn homes. Don't you worry about anything."

He slid his arm through hers. They walked through the city. "It was a shame we had to bomb Warsaw," he said. "Poland is quite beautiful. Of course, not nearly as beautiful as our fatherland. Germany is superior in every way."

"It is going to take a great deal to clean this mess up," Kara said as she looked at the rubble.

"Yes, I suppose it will. But it will get done. We'll have the Poles do it," he said with confidence. "After all, we own Poland now."

She had no answer for him. There was nothing to say. Kara felt sorry for the Polish people. They were defeated and reduced to little more than slaves. If speaking out about her feelings toward the Nazis would have made any difference to the plight of the Jews or the conquered, she might have found the argument worth her time. But arguing with Oskar, her only lifeline right now, was foolhardy, and she knew it. Nothing was more important to her than finding her missing child. And Oskar had the connections to help her do that.

Then as if he had been reading her mind: "Sometimes I feel sorry for the Polish people," he said, "but they need the Germans. They aren't as smart or capable as we are. When we took over this country, I believe it was the best thing that could happen to them," he said as he kicked a stone on the ground. "You know our führer has a plan for the Polish people."

"Oh?" she said.

"Of course." He smiled. "Our führer has many plans. The Aryan men and women, like you and I, who are the superior race, will rule the world. But we can't rule the world without workers, can we? And that's where the Polish come in."

"That sounds cruel," she said, forgetting herself for a moment.

"But it isn't. Everyone needs to have a place in the world. The Polish aren't smart like the Aryans. However, they do make good workers as long as they have good direction. They can do what needs to be done. They just don't have what it takes to lead."

Kara just nodded. She didn't want to argue. The last thing she wanted right now was to do anything that might stop him from helping her even though he was getting on her nerves.

They walked for a while in silence. He put his

arm through hers and then patted her hand. "You know, I like it that you care about people. It shows me that you are kind. My mother was kind like you."

He'd never mentioned his family's past before.

"Oh?" she said.

"Yes, she was like you in many ways. A good mother. A kind and caring woman. Not as strong, I am afraid, as a true Aryan woman should be. But quite beautiful," he said wistfully. "My father didn't deserve her. He didn't treat her the way a man should treat his wife. I vowed that if I ever found the woman I wanted to marry, I would not be like my father. My wife would be happy. She wouldn't run away from her family with another man."

Kara looked up at Oskar's face. It was red with anger. "You don't have to talk about this if you don't want to," she said.

"I will tell you everything one day. But not now. Not on this beautiful afternoon. I wanted this walk to be a distraction for you, not a time to tell you things about my hurtful past."

She hesitated. Looking at him at this moment, he looked like a sad and angry little boy. In many ways, he reminded her of Karl. Kara squeezed his hand. "If you ever need someone to talk to, you can talk to me."

Just then they passed the wall of the Warsaw Ghetto. Kara shivered. She wondered if anyone she knew and loved was inside. Then boldly she asked,

"I've never asked you this. But I want to know what you feel about the Jews?"

"What about them?"

"I was told by a waiter in a restaurant when Anka and I first arrived in Warsaw that there are Jews who are imprisoned behind that wall." She pointed to the ghetto wall.

"That's correct," he said, carefully watching her face to see her reaction. Kara recoiled. Then he added, "But it is only Jews who've broken the law. Criminals. We Germans are civilized, Kara. We don't imprison people who aren't criminals."

"But I've been told that all Jews were considered criminals by our government. I've been told they are considered criminals for being Jewish."

"Yes, that's true in a way. The Jews have never been friends to the German people." He sighed. "It's quite sad really. But they have always taken from Germany rather than helped us to grow. And, from what I hear from my fellow colleagues who have contact with them, they are very dangerous. They are liars and thieves. I am thankful that I don't have any contact with them in my work. Still, I know that we Germans don't imprison all of them. Could you imagine what would be involved in trying to do something like that. For the most part we just keep an eye on them. So they don't cause more trouble. After all, they are the reason we lost the war."

"That's strange, because I have heard of Jews

being arrested and taken away by the Gestapo in the middle of the night for no reason at all."

"Oh, my dear sweet Kara," he said, smiling. "When a Jew or anyone else is arrested, there's always a reason." He hesitated for a moment, than added, "There are so many rumors that fly around. You can't believe everything you hear."

*Is he lying to me? But why? Perhaps he really doesn't know anything about how the Jews are being treated. Or could he actually be telling the truth.*

He glanced down at her, and she caught his eye. "Let's not talk about these sordid subjects. Let's just enjoy the beauty of the day. By the way, did I happen to tell you that you look ravishing as always?" Then smiling, he said, "Shall we walk through the zoo before lunch or after? I love animals. I had a dog for many years. When I had to leave him behind, I felt like my world was falling apart."

"Let's go now. I'm not hungry yet, are you?" she asked.

"No, let's walk a little longer."

They began walking toward the zoo.

"I've never had a pet," she admitted. "It was always too expensive for my family to keep an animal. My parents could hardly afford to feed my sister and I."

"Are you two the only siblings in your family?"

"Yes, just us. How about you?"

"I had a brother, but he died. Where I came

from, children were lucky to grow up into adults. Lots of them died early."

"I'm sorry," she said.

"It's all right. It was a long time ago. I was just a boy myself." Then he quickly changed the subject. "Do you like dogs?"

"I don't know. I've never had any contact with them. I suppose I am a little afraid of them. Some bite, don't they?"

"Some do. But if I am fortunate enough to ever marry you, I would like to have a dog. And I will make sure that he's a devoted animal who never bites. An animal you will love."

"Married?" she said, stunned.

"Yes, I hope to marry you someday, Kara. I believe you are the woman I have been waiting for all of my life."

She stopped walking. "I don't want to lead you on, Oskar. I am not looking for a husband. I don't know if I can ever marry."

"Why, are you still in love with Karl's father?"

"Yes," she said quickly. Then she was trembling. *Why did I tell him that? I don't want to talk about this with him. I am afraid I might say the wrong thing and rouse his suspicion. All I want is my child back.*

"Where is he now? Perhaps he had something to do with Karl's disappearance."

"No, he had nothing to do with it. I assure you. He didn't want his son. He is a married man." She swallowed hard, hoping he wouldn't ask any questions. "We don't speak. We haven't spoken in years. I don't know where he is. He left me when he found out I was pregnant with Karl."

"And you say that you still love him anyway?"

The lies were growing bigger. But she couldn't stop now. She said, "I don't know if it's love or fear of getting hurt again. All I know is I don't want another man in my life." She hoped she had stopped his questions.

"I can understand how you feel. But if you had the right man in your life, you just might feel differently."

"Perhaps, but for now, all I want is to find my child. That is the only thing I can think about."

"I know that. And, trust me, Karl is my priority. We will get him back. This I promise you. And, maybe once you are reunited with Karl, you will find it in your heart to look at me differently. Perhaps you might decide that it would be good for Karl to grow up with a father. There is so much I could teach him. I am a good swimmer." He hesitated, "I love to play ball. But most importantly, I care deeply for him . . . and for you. I would cherish you both, and I would take good care of you."

She looked up at him as they strolled through the entrance of the zoo, "You do care for him, don't you?"

"Yes, and I care for you too."

She looked down at her feet. "You have always

been very kind to me," she said more to herself than to him.

"And I always will be. That's because . . . I love you."

She stopped walking. "How can you be so sure? You hardly know me."

"I knew it the first time I saw you. I couldn't tell you then because you would have thought me mad."

"Yes." She let out a short laugh. "I would have. But I am beginning to believe you are telling me the truth. A man would have to have deep feelings for someone in order to take time away from their job to help the way you have done for me."

"And I will always do everything I can to make sure you are happy and safe. You and your son."

She felt a warm glow come over her. A man who would love her Karl the way she did would be a good father. And this one seemed to really want to be a father to her son. "You do care for us, both of us, don't you?" she said. *I should be happy*, she thought. *I don't know where Abram is. I wish I did. I wish he and I were raising our son together. The way it should be.* Kara looked into Oskar's eyes. His face was open. She could see the glow of love all over him. *Well, I can't say that I love him. My heart belongs to Abram. But at least if I allow him to, Oskar will be a good husband to me and a good father to our son. I have to think about this more. I can't make any promises to him.*

"Yes, I do care for both of you very much," he

said, and then as if he were reading her mind, he added, "I don't expect you to say you love me. I don't expect you to agree to marry me. All I ask is that you let me help you find your son, and during the time we spend working on this together, I hope that you will give me a chance to show you how much I am willing to do for you."

She patted his hand. Then, changing the subject, she said, "Look, over there is the lion house. When I was a child, I loved to see the lions. They are so majestic; don't you think so?"

He nodded.

# CHAPTER FIVE

OSKAR WAS RIGHT; it was a good distraction for her to go out for the day rather than spend more time in the hotel room feeling anxious about Karl. The weather was lovely, warm, but not hot, with just a slight breeze. The sky was bright blue with powder-puff clouds. And for a few hours she relinquished control to the strong man at her side. She allowed herself to believe, because she wanted so much to believe, that Oskar would find her son and return him to her. Then all would be well. But when she returned to her room, alone, late that afternoon to dress for dinner, she began to feel the panic set in again.

They met in the restaurant in the hotel lobby for dinner. Oskar was very alert to her feelings. He saw immediately that she was anxious again. He ordered a bottle of wine. Then he took her hand and said, "I received a message from the police this afternoon. I returned their call as soon as we got back. The officer told me that they have arrested Sonia."

She put down her fork, stunned, and looked into his eyes. "What did she say about Karl?"

"I don't know yet. They asked her about Karl, but according to what the officer told me, she was evasive."

"Oh, what am going to do? She was the last person to see my son, and she won't tell the police where he is. I'm so scared, Oskar. Karl is just a child. He is so defenseless."

"I know. Don't worry. Please. Tomorrow morning, first thing, you and I are going to go to the police station. We'll talk with the old lady. We'll find out everything she knows. I promise you. I'm sure she will have some information for us about Karl's whereabouts."

"Where do we have to go to see her?"

"The police headquarters. We can't go tonight. It's too late. But I promise you we will go at the crack of dawn."

"Yes." She took a deep breath and sighed. "Yes, this is encouraging. I am hopeful," she said, but the tears began to form behind her eyes. "Oh, Oskar, I can't stop worrying," she said. "I won't be able to stop until Karl's home. Until he's back in my arms. I'm so afraid for him. He's so little and he's all alone."

"Shhh, I promise you . . ."

"Why can't we go now?"

"Because I have a friend there who is going to allow us to see Sonia. But he has left for the day. So, we must wait until tomorrow.

"All right." She nodded, but she was unable to eat.

The following day, they drove to the German police headquarters in Warsaw. Kara was trembling so badly that when she got out of the automobile, her legs almost gave out. Oskar saw her sway and put his arm through hers to hold her up. Then he led her inside the building. They were met by a policeman who greeted Oskar warmly. "Come, follow me," he said. "I am holding the Smolak woman in a cell in the basement."

Oskar nodded. He held tightly to Kara's arm as they descended the stairs into a dimly lit basement. *This looks more like a dungeon than a police station.* The air was damp and chilly. Kara shivered as they walked down the long dark corridor until they came to a small cell. Inside, the old woman lay curled up on a cot without a blanket. When Sonia heard them approaching, she fell off the cot and huddled in the corner cowering in fear. Kara looked at Sonia and gasped. The old woman was savagely beaten. There was blood all over her housedress and a deep cut that ran from her forehead back through her hair that looked as if it were becoming infected. Sonia tried to walk to the bars of the cell when she saw

Kara, but she could hardly stand up straight because her ankle appeared to have been twisted leaving her foot in an unnatural position. She stumbled. "Kara. Help me, please," she said, then fell back down, defeated. For a few moments no one spoke, but Kara heard Sonia's raspy breath. "Why are they doing this to me?" The old woman extended her hands toward Kara, trying to grab Kara so she would listen. "Please help me. I don't understand what is happening. I don't know why the Nazis came and took Karl and then they arrested me. You know I am not a bad person. I am only an old grandmother who was babysitting your son. I'm begging you to please help me, Kara. Tell them I didn't do anything wrong."

"Who took Karl?" Kara said.

"Nazis. Nazis took Karl. They beat me. I was afraid, so I hid in a church basement. Then once I thought it was over, I went to my son's house. But when I got there, I saw that he was gone. I don't know where he is. Arrested? Dead? I don't know. But it was there at my son's farm that I was arrested. The police brought me here. They beat me again. My life has taken a dark turn since the day I met you, Kara. And I don't know why. I've done nothing wrong. I don't know who you are or why this is happening to me. But I wish I had never laid eyes on you or your sister, or the little boy."

"Shut up, old woman. You are a traitor to the fatherland. You can't fool me. I know that you are a member of the Polish Underground. That's why you are here," Oskar said, then he turned to Kara. "She is an enemy of the Reich. She would say anything to save herself."

"No, Please, no! I am an old woman. I am not a member of an Underground. I was babysitting her son, and that night the Gestapo came and took the child. I don't understand why. All I know is that I am begging you, Kara. Please make them let me go. Please, I am old, and if they keep me here, I will surely die."

Kara was shaking so hard that she grasped the bars of the cell to steady herself. "I'll do what I can for you," she said, "but please, you must tell me all that you know about Karl. Who were the men who took him?"

"Gestapo. They came in a black automobile."

"Liar!" Oskar screamed. "Shut up. You have no more to say."

"I am not lying; I swear it. It was the Gestapo. They almost broke the door down to my flat. When they came, Karl was playing on the floor. They grabbed him and took him away. I screamed. I begged them not to take him. I told them the truth that he was a German boy and that I was only his babysitter. That's when the young one beat me up. He hit me with his fists until I fell, and then he kicked me in the head."

"I told you to shut your mouth. Do you want to

lose the few teeth you still have. I wont have you lying to us."

"I swear, this is not a lie. Karl was scared. I begged them to leave him with me. I told them his mother would be returning soon. But they took him anyway."

"All right, then." Oskar smiled a wicked smile. "So, if, as you say, you are not lying. Then let's see . . . you said after the Gestapo left, you went to hide in a church? If you did nothing wrong, why would you need to hide?" Oskar asked.

"I was afraid. I was so scared and wounded. I didn't know what else to do," she said pleadingly.

"And then you went to your son's farm? Perhaps he was involved in all of this?" Oskar asked in a sly, condescending tone.

"No, my son didn't even know that I had taken a babysitting job. He knew nothing about any of it. When I thought things were safe, the first thing I did was go back to my apartment. It was de-stroyed. The Gestapo had torn everything inside apart, and my landlord was angry. He told me I couldn't live there anymore. So, I left. I had no other choice, no place else to go. I went to my son's farm. But when I got there, the place was ransacked, and he, his wife, and my granddaughter were gone. Oh, sweet Lord, help me. My family and I did nothing wrong. Please, Kara, my grand-daughter is just a child, a child, like Karl. Help her. You must help her."

"Come, Kara. This old woman has no more to say to us. She is obviously lying," Oskar said.

Kara didn't believe that Sonia was lying. She had a feeling that if Sonia had any information at all, she would have told them in hopes of saving her granddaughter. Kara felt badly for the old woman, and even worse for the child. But there was nothing she could do. She couldn't even find her own son, so how could she hope to help Sonia. She looked into Sonia's eyes and said, "I'm so sorry. I don't know what is happening. I wish I could help you. I want to believe you. I really do. But I can't. My son is gone. He is out there somewhere all alone. You were supposed to be caring for him and now he is gone." Kara began screaming. She was becoming hysterical, tears flooding her cheeks.

Oskar put his arm around Kara's shoulder and led her away. Then he took her outside and turned to take her into his arms. "It's all right," he said. "We'll find your son."

"What if we can't find him? What if we never find him," she said, her voice still high pitched with terror.

"I promise you. I will find him. I am a superior being. You can depend on me. And I promise you, Kara, I will do whatever I must do to find him."

Oskar walked Kara to the car. He opened her door. But after she got in, he turned to her and said, "Are you all right if I leave you for a few minutes? I have an idea."

"Yes, I am fine," she said, but she was still shaking. "I need a minute to collect myself."

"I'm going to go and talk to the police. I want to see if they got any other information out of her or her son. I'll be right back."

"I don't believe she would hide anything. After all, she has lost her family. I think she would do anything to get them back."

"Perhaps, but you don't know these Poles. They're a stubborn lot. I'll just go and see if she might have given the police a clue that she failed to tell us. It's worth a try, yes?"

"Yes, of course," Kara said. "Shall I come with you?"

"No, please, just relax here. You've been through enough already. Besides, the officer won't talk to you. But because I am an SS officer, he'll tell me everything."

Oskar walked into the police chief's office and closed the door behind him. Then he turned around and smiled. "Good job, Herr Muehler."

"Thank you, Oberstrumführer Lerch. I did everything as you requested."

"Good, very good. And how about the old woman's son, Hueber, or something like that, is his name?"

"Dead."

"His wife?"

"Dead too."

"The child?"

"Dark hair, dark eyes, not of any use to the Reich. She's been disposed of. A necessary evil, I'm afraid."

"Yes, I agree. But you've done a good job thus far. Now, get rid of the old lady."

The police chief nodded.

# CHAPTER SIX

## 1941

FIVE MONTHS HAD PASSED. Because of his rank, Oskar was able to secure the rooms in the hotel for as long as necessary. The owner was happy to accommodate him in exchange for good standing with the Reich. November came; it brought with it the promise of a cold winter. But for Kara it also brought memories of Karl's birthday and of Kristallnacht. How she wished there was someone she could talk to. The memories clutched her heart, and she needed to speak about them. But she knew that her secrets must never be revealed. *Oskar is a good person. But even so, I dare not tell him the truth.*

She and Oskar were having breakfast at the hotel restaurant on the morning of November 8.

"Today is Karl's birthday," she said softly as she watched him butter a piece of toast.

He put the bread down on his plate and looked up from what he was doing. His eyes met hers. His face was filled with concern.

"I know he is too young to know it's his birthday, but it is. And if he is alive, whoever has him doesn't know or care." She was trembling.

"He is alive, Kara. You must keep believing. Karl is alive. And we'll find him, and we'll celebrate his birthday. This birthday and all the ones to come." He reached out and took her hand, squeezing it gently.

"Oh, Oskar, I am losing hope." The tears began to run down her cheeks.

"You mustn't. You must remain strong. And you must trust me. I will find him."

"I pray he is still alive."

"He is still alive. I know he is. Stay strong, Kara."

Oskar made copies of the pictures of Karl and had them posted all around the city. He paid to run ads in the newspapers in search of the little boy. And he offered a hefty reward for anyone who could help in finding Karl. They received plenty of calls in response to the ads. People who thought they had information or, in truth, just wanted the reward money. Kara and Oskar exhausted every lead. Time ticked by. Morning came followed by endless night. Kara felt as if she were on a roller coaster. Someone called and said they saw a child that looked like Karl living with a young couple. Oskar and Kara drove over to the couple's flat immediately only to find that the child, although he looked like Karl, was not Karl. Another caller said Karl was being held by strangers in an abandoned building. But when Kara and Oskar arrived at the address, all they found were homeless children huddled together in a broken-down building. When shown Karl's picture, none of the children knew anything about Karl. Then in late November, the body of a young boy fitting Karl's description was found dead in an alleyway. When they received the call asking Kara to come down to the police station to identify the body, she could hardly stand. Oskar helped her to walk to the car. Then he held her hand as she sat stunned and pale faced on the drive to the police station. Kara didn't speak until the car stopped in front of the station.

"What if it's him," she said, hardly able to get the words out.

Oskar squeezed Kara's hand.

"We have to go inside and find out," he said gently.

"I would almost prefer to go on searching forever," she said. "If I find out he's dead, my life is over."

"We don't have to go if you don't want to," Oskar said. "I'll do whatever you want. We can get back into the car and go back to the hotel."

Kara sat silent for a moment. Then her voice broke as she said, "No, I have to know. It will haunt me if I don't find out the truth. Let's go inside."

The bright overhead lights cast a green garish hue over everything. A police officer walked over to escort them to the room to show them the body. Kara felt her tearstained face grow hot as a rush of heat coursed through her body. Trying to follow the officer, she trembled, nearly falling to the floor. But Oskar, whose eyes had not left her for a second, saw her stumble. He caught her before she fell. Then he put his arm around her to help steady her. And then they walked into the morgue. The police officer led them to a small, covered body. Kara was trembling so hard, and her heart was thumping so wildly, she thought she might be having a heart attack. The room seemed to go dark. Then it seemed to be spinning, and she was afraid she might vomit.

"Are you ready?" the police officer said before removing the covering from the dead child.

Kara gripped Oskar's arm. He held her tightly. "I'm here. I'm right here with you," he whispered.

"I'm ready." She was breathing heavily as she squeezed the words out. Then she caught her breath and held it in terrible anticipation.

It seemed like forever, but it was only a few seconds before the officer peeled back the covering. The little boy's face was peaceful. His blond hair was short. And his eyes were closed. There was no doubt he was a beautiful child. But to Kara's relief, it was not Karl. She let out a cry and bent at the waist holding her face in her hands. Then she turned to Oskar, and tears of relief ran down her cheeks. "It's not him," she said.

"No, it's not," Oskar whispered in Kara's ear as he wrapped her in his arms. And for several moments he held her as she wept, thankful that her son was not dead.

# CHAPTER SEVEN

KARA HADN'T SPOKEN to Anka in a while. It was hard to talk to her sister, who seemed so disconnected during all of this. In fact, she'd told herself that she should have telephoned Anka to find out how things had gone when the führer had visited the lair. But she just couldn't bring herself to call. There was no doubt in Kara's mind that Anka was angry with her, because Anka had not telephoned her either. *Sometimes my sister can be so insensitive. Her problems are monumental to her. Meanwhile, she doesn't even recognize that I am searching desperately for my child. Still, she is my only sister, and I don't want to lose her,* she thought as she dialed the operator to have a call connected to Anka.

"Hello," Anka said.

"Anka, it's Kara."

"Kara, nice of you to telephone," Anka said in a cold voice.

Kara could hear the quiet anger in Anka's voice. "I'm sorry," Kara said. "Oskar and I have been going mad trying to find Karl."

"I thought you would have at least telephoned me to keep me abreast of it all. I mean he is my nephew too. A call only takes a few minutes," Anka said.

"I know. And I should have called. But it's been such a terrible nightmare." Then she told Anka about the dead child that she'd gone to identify. "I was so terrified that it was him," Kara admitted.

Anka was quiet for a few moments. Then she said, "You know, I still blame myself for what happened. If I hadn't made you go to that party, Karl would not be missing. That's why you haven't called, isn't it? I mean . . . you would be right to blame me."

"Anka, can't we please just let this whole idea of blame go. It doesn't do either of us any good. All I want is my son back. I don't blame you. It's just that sometimes I can't bear to talk on the phone. My heart aches too much."

"I understand. But I blame myself. I don't know what I can do to help you. Kara . . . I am so, so, sorry."

"I know," Kara said.

There was silence for a moment. Then in an effort to lighten up the conversation, Kara said,

"There is nothing you can do. I will try to keep you updated on everything Oskar and I do. But for now, please, can we stop talking about it." She was tired of trying to comfort Anka. It was exhausting to constantly reassure her sister that she didn't blame her when, in fact, she sort of did. Then Kara added in a forced jovial voice, "So, how was the führer's visit to the lair?"

"It went well. He liked it. Ludwig was so pleased. When this is all over. I mean, once you've found Karl, you and Oskar will have to come and see the lair. Ludwig took me to see it. It's really quite marvelous, with plenty of comfortable bunkers. The men outdid themselves in the designing and building of it. It's well hidden in the forest, which makes it very safe, so our precious führer can stay there without being threatened. The builders thought of everything, even put trees on top of the buildings so it could not be spotted by enemy planes. I must say it has everything you could possibly want. You know what, Ludwig told me that two thousand people are employed there. I asked him if any of them were women. He wouldn't say. So, I am assuming they are. I don't care. Who would want poor old Ludwig anyway? Would you believe that there is a cinema and a casino right on the grounds? What an exciting place. They've also installed a lovely quaint tea-room, where the führer can go to relax or work on military matters. I hear that the führer plays

Beethoven, operas, and Wagner on his gramophone in the evenings. I would love to attend something like that. "

"I'm sure it is magnificent," Kara said, trying to fake enthusiasm for her sister's sake. "Well, I have some things I have to take care of. So, I am going to get off the phone. But it's been good to talk to you, Anka. Let's talk again soon."

"Yes, let's."

Kara placed the phone back into its cradle. Then she stared out the window. So much had changed in her life. There was an emptiness in her soul that made her feel old and tired. *Is it really possible that I don't have the same feelings toward my sister as I once did? How could that happen? I suppose I do blame her for what happened to my son. How could I not? But I don't want to. I have lost so many people that I love: Abram, Hoda . . . Dear God, I can't bear to think it, but maybe even my son. I couldn't bear to lose her too. There are so many memories she and I share. There is so much about me and my past that only Anka could understand. Losing her, in a way, is like losing a part of myself.*

# CHAPTER EIGHT

WEEKS PASSED, and soon it would be Christmas-
time. Kara and Oskar were still staying at the hotel
in Warsaw. She wondered how he was paying for it.
She thought perhaps that they weren't being
charged because of his position in the party. Either
way, she didn't ask. He was taking care of the bills,
and for that she was grateful. She needed to stay in
Warsaw, and she could not have afforded to do so
had it not been for Oskar. Each day, she waited for
a phone call or a telegram. But nothing came. And,
for what seemed like a lifetime, there was no new
information. Kara thought she would go mad with
worry. She couldn't eat because she found it hard to
swallow. Her throat was always raw and dry. Every
bite of food made her wonder if her son was eating
or if he was starving, or worse.

On the first of December, there was a snow-storm. The white powder covered everything. And even though the hotel was heated, Kara felt the cold more deeply than she'd ever felt it before. It was almost Christmas. When she and Anka were little, they had loved this time of year. Although the family never had money for gifts or special food, sometimes the people who attended the church in the neighborhood brought over a Christmas basket. Inside, there would be food and something small for each of the girls. Anka and Kara would wait in excited anticipation for the arrival of that basket. And, when it came, they were so thankful for the gifts and the meals that they sometimes wept with joy. The years that it didn't arrive were the saddest. They couldn't tell their parents how disappointed they were. Not with their father's alcoholic rages and their mother struggling to keep a roof over their heads and food on the table. During those hard years, they had leaned heavily on each other. In fact, the closeness they shared had been every-thing to Kara. "Anka," she said her sister's name aloud, "life has certainly changed both of us."

Tears burned her eyes. It was early morning, and it would be at least an hour before Oskar awoke and knocked on her door. She washed and dressed, then sat down in the chair at the window to wait. Her thoughts began to drift again, and this time she remembered Hanukkah. That little apart-ment behind the bookstore where she lived with

Hoda and Abram when Karl was just an infant. It had been such a joyous time filled with life and love. She thought about how close they had all become over the time they'd spent together. She remembered the songs they sang at Hanukkah. How they had managed to take care of each other. The immense love she'd felt in those rooms. In her mind she could hear Karl's laughter. It was baby laughter, innocent, full, and pure.

Now the tears came. They ran down her cheeks like the rain on the window in Abram's room. She remembered how the two of them would lie in his bed cuddled together under a blanket and watch the raindrops on the window. Kara began to whisper aloud to Abram as if he were sitting beside her in this strange hotel room in Warsaw. "I can't bear to go on, Abram. I don't know what's become of you or of our son. It's been so many months since I last held him. And . . . you . . . where are you? Are you alive? Oh, how I pray that you are. Every night I ask God to watch over you. Abram, I miss you. I still and will always love you with all my heart."

She hesitated for a moment, then she said, "If you are watching over me, I know you see Oskar, and, of course, you can see that he is a Nazi. We hated the Nazis, but he is not like the others. Oskar is a good person. He is helping me to find Karl. Right now, this man and his connections are my only lifeline. And from what I can see, he bears no ill will toward Jews, although I am still cautious. Something tells me not to trust him completely. I don't think I would ever tell him the truth about Karl being half Jewish. I can't say how he would react. But I am not willing to find out."

# CHAPTER NINE

## Christmas Eve

*Nothing could make me feel more hopeless than sitting in a hotel room without my son or Abram on Christmas Eve. I sit in this chair at the window most of the time now. It makes me feel like an old woman waiting to die,* Kara thought as she watched the snow fall outside her window. It wasn't a storm this time, just a light dusting. Soft flakes fell on the already snow-covered ground.

Oskar said he wanted to do something special for her, so he had made reservations at a fine restaurant to celebrate the holiday. *I should be grateful to him. I know he means well by this. He wants to distract me from my pain. And I know he's trying his best to help me find Karl. But going out to eat doesn't help. Nothing helps. The only thing that would make my life worth living is if I could find Karl and Abram. Still, it is Christmas, and perhaps it would be a good idea to call Anka and wish her and Ludwig a Merry Christmas.*

Picking up the telephone receiver, she dialed the operator.

"Operator, how can I help you?" a female voice said.

Kara didn't answer. The phone receiver felt cold in her hand.

"Operator? How can I help you?" the operator repeated, sounding annoyed.

"I'm sorry, Operator. I don't need anything. I accidently knocked the receiver off," Kara apologized. Then she hung up the receiver. *I can't talk to her tonight. The truth is I just really want to be alone. I don't want to talk to anyone. I wish I didn't have to go out with Oskar, but I can't disappoint him. And I should call my sister. Perhaps I will have the energy to talk to her tomorrow.*

Kara spent a few minutes putting on makeup. She hadn't worn it since Karl disappeared. The idea of taking time to put on rouge and lipstick had seemed futile to her. But this evening was important to Oskar, and so she was forcing herself to try to look her best. Reaching for the prettiest frock in the closet and the silk stockings that Oskar had given her, in the dresser drawer, Kara began to dress. A wave of guilt came over her. She dropped the dress on the bed and put her head in her hands. *How can I be going out for a nice dinner and pretending that everything is all right while my son could be in danger.* For a moment she considered calling the hotel operator and asking to be connected to Oskar's room. *I could tell him I don't feel well, and I can't go out tonight.* But just as she was about to pick up the phone, there was a knock on the door. *He's here already? He's early. But, I suppose I will have to go.* She quickly picked up the dress and tossed it over her head. Then she went to answer the door.

"Yes? Who is it?" Kara asked.

"Hotel staff with a delivery," a male voice said.

She was surprised. Why would someone from the hotel be at her door. *It must be a surprise gift from Oskar. He is always doing kind things like that.*

Kara opened the door. The man handed her a box. "This is from Herr Lerch."

"Thank you," she said and closed the door. Then she opened the box. Inside she found a beautiful emerald-green silk dress even lovelier than the one she had chosen for the night. She picked it up and looked at it. It was one of the prettiest things she'd ever seen. There was a card in the box: *I thought you might like a new Christmas dress to wear to dinner tonight. I hope you like it, Oskar.*

*This man is so good to me. He has found a way to keep us in this hotel for all these months, and he has paid for all this food too. What kind of person would I be if I stood him up on Christmas Eve?* She changed her dress to the new emerald-green one. *It is such a pretty Christmas dress, and he means so well,* she thought as she looked in the mirror. *I wish I could be happy, for his sake. But I can't, not with Karl missing.*

There was another knock on the door. Thinking it was the hotel staff again, Kara opened it without looking through the peephole. Two men wearing long, black leather coats grabbed her. One put his hand over her mouth before she had a chance to scream. Her heart was pounding. *Who are these men, and what do they want with me? I have done nothing wrong. This must be some mistake. If this man would take his hand away from my mouth, I would tell them that I am here with Oskar Lerch. Once they know he is an SS officer, they will surely realize that they've made a mistake. Or . . . perhaps they've found out about Abram or, even worse, about Karl. Maybe they know that Karl is half Jewish. Maybe they have him and they're hurting him. Or worse.* She let out a deep, heartfelt groan like a trapped animal.

# CHAPTER TEN

KARA FELT the sweat running down her face as the men took her outside and then pushed her into the back of a black automobile. She looked around for Oskar, praying he would come out of his room and see what was happening. But he was nowhere in sight. *Oskar, I need you. Where are you?*

Once she was in the back seat of the automobile, the door was slammed shut.

"Please, I am here with Oskar Lerch, Oberstrumführer Oskar Lerch," she said. But they weren't paying any attention to her. They were talking among themselves. "Please, please, listen to me. I am here with Oberstrumführer Lerch," she shouted. "I am the sister-in-law of Ludwig . . ."

One of the Gestapo agents turned around in his seat, leaned over, and slapped her across the face. "Shut up. Or I will really hurt you," he said. She felt something running down her face. She touched her nose and saw blood on her hand. Kara was silent, but tears slid down her cheeks.

When she arrived at the Gestapo headquarters, Kara was thrown into a small, dark room. Fear pulsed through her body as she lay on the cold floor waiting, wondering. *How much do they know? They must know something, or they would not have arrested me. I am praying they don't know about Karl. If they only know about me and Abram, then perhaps my son will be safe. I don't know what they plan to do with me, and I am scared. But, no matter what they do to me, I would rather die than let them hurt Karl. I will tell them that he is not Abram's son and beg them to believe me. Does Oskar know everything too? Does he know about Abram and Karl? Is that why he didn't come out of his room when he heard the commotion in the hallway?*

For what seemed like a lifetime later, a young woman, no more than twenty-five years old, walked into the room. Kara felt a strange sense of relief. The woman was slender and by some standards would be considered pretty. Kara studied her. *She doesn't look mean or rough. In fact, she looks like a young mother. I would say she is probably a secretary here at the Gestapo headquarters. And my only hope is that the officers have sent her to tell me that they've realized they've made a mistake and arrested the wrong person. Oh, dear God, please make it so.*

"Kara Scholz?"

"Yes. I am," she answered, her voice cracking.

"We have reason to believe that you are involved with the Polish Resistance and that you are an enemy to your own people. You have been disloyal to the fatherland, and for that, mark my words, you will be punished."

"Polish Resistance? No!" Kara shouted. "No. You are terribly mistaken."

"We have sources," the woman said. Then she took a whip from her belt and cracked it across Kara's back.

White-hot pain surged through Kara. She let out a cry. "Oh no, please. Please call the hotel where I was staying and contact Oberstrum . . ."

Another crack of the whip. Kara screamed again. "Please, wait. Please, I am begging you to listen to me. Please contact the hotel and ask for SS Oberstrumführer Oskar Lerch. He will tell you all about me. He knows I am not in the Polish Resistance."

"SS Officer Oskar Lerch?" the woman said, looking at Kara. "How do you know him?"

"He is my friend. Please, call him. He will tell you everything you want to know."

"Did you not have dealings with a woman by the name of Sonia Smolak?"

"Yes, but not like that. I mean my sister and I hired her to watch my son when we went to a party. I know nothing of her affiliation with the Resistance. And I am not a sympathizer."

"Hmmm, interesting," the guard said, tucking the whip back into her belt.

"Yes," Kara spoke quickly, the pain still surging through her. "Yes, please, call the hotel and ask for Oberstrumführer Oskar Lerch. And, also, my brother-in-law is Ludwig Brunner. He is working on the lair for the führer. You can contact him too."

"For your sake, Kara Scholz, I hope you're not lying."

The woman left the room. Kara touched her back. The beautiful green dress that Oskar had given her was torn where the whip had cut through it, and the lashings were covered in blood.

It was less than a half hour before Oskar arrived. He came racing down the hall. Kara could hear the footsteps outside and she trembled. But when he entered the room accompanied by the woman who had whipped her earlier, Kara began to weep. She ran into his arms, and he held her tightly.

"What is the meaning of this?" Oskar said in a strong, angry voice to the female guard.

"It has come to our attention that Fräulein Scholz has had dealings with the Polish Underground."

"Are you mad? I know this woman. You are sadly mistaken."

"She has been in contact with a known member of the Underground. A woman by the name of Sonia Smolak."

"You idiot. You fool," Oskar said. "Smolak babysat for her son, and now the child is missing. I have been with the Fräulein from the beginning of all of this, and I can assure you that she has not had any dealings with the Polish Underground. What I cannot assure you is that you will still have a job tomorrow. How dare you lay a hand on this woman. I will speak to your superior. But first"—he turned to Kara—"let me help you into the car. You don't need to be subjected to this nightmare for even a second longer."

Kara was weak in his arms, and he practically carried her to his car. "Are you all right?" he whispered in her ear as he helped her into the automobile. "You're covered in blood. Your back. Your lovely face. They hurt you. They will pay for this. I will see to it."

"I think I am all right. But that horrible woman hit me with a whip, and my back is killing me." Kara was still crying as she laid her head on his chest.

"Shhh," he soothed her, "I'm here now. I'm with you, and nothing will happen to you. I promise. I swear it, my love."

She wept in his arms for several moments. And he held her gently, like a baby. Kara felt herself softening toward him.

Once she'd calmed down, Oskar gently lifted her face to his and kissed her. She closed her eyes and felt safe.

"Now, you stay here in this car with the doors locked. You will be safe here. I am going back into the station to speak to that woman's superior officer. You can be sure that she will be punished for what she's done to you, my love."

Kara looked into his eyes, and then she kissed him again. *I think I am falling in love with him.*

# CHAPTER ELEVEN

OSKAR WALKED into the Gestapo headquarters. His face looked angry. The others stared at him, frightened by his very presence. The agents tried not to make eye contact. They were afraid that they were going to suffer severely for having made a grave mistake by arresting a woman who was a friend to an SS officer. The thick smell of sweat and fear permeated the air. No one spoke; there was no sound except the loud clicking of Oskar's bootheels as they hit the floor. "Heil Hitler." The agents saluted as Oskar passed them on his way down the hall. He did not even glance up at any of them, and he did not return their salutes. When he got to the end of the corridor, he entered an office in the back of the building. The woman who had whipped Kara was there waiting for him.

"Oberstrumführer Lerch," she said.

For a moment there was an eerie silence. Then Oskar's face broke into a smile, which was followed by a quick laugh. "We did it, didn't we?" he said.

"I did exactly what you told me to do," the woman said.

"It's good to see you again, Zelda. How is Georg?"

"He's doing well, thank you. We both are. I can't tell you how much I appreciate your getting me this extra job. I wasn't earning enough teaching."

"Are you still teaching kindergarten?"

"Yes, of course. I love working with the children. I feel so productive teaching them everything they will need to know to grow up to be good Germans."

"Well, good. I am glad to hear it. You did a good job tonight. You followed my orders perfectly," Oskar said.

"I hit her twice, just enough to let her know that she was in serious trouble, but not enough to really damage her permanently in any way."

"Good. I am glad you were able to follow my instructions."

"Yes, of course, Oberstrumführer. And I think your plan worked. She saw how important a man you are and how you are able to protect her. And, well, she seemed to fall right into your arms."

"Yes, she did, didn't she?" he said, taking an envelope out of the breast pocket of his uniform and handing it to her. "This is for you and Georg. A little bonus, shall we say." He smiled and then left.

# CHAPTER TWELVE

Oskar climbed back into the car. Kara was lying against the window still shaking.

"I took care of it. That horrible woman won't be working here anymore," Oskar said to Kara. "Now, let's get you home, so I can clean up those cuts on your back. And we'll wash that blood off your face." He touched her arm. She managed to smile at him.

"I don't know what I would have done without you. You saved my life tonight."

"I'll always protect you. I'll always be here when you need me. And don't you worry about that dress. I'll buy you a new one."

# CHAPTER THIRTEEN

WHEN THEY ARRIVED BACK at the hotel, Oskar took Kara up to her room. He helped her out of her dress and then handed her a robe to put on over her slip. He looked at the cuts on her back, and she could see the pain in his eyes. *He cares so much about me*, she thought.

Oskar studied the open flesh on Kara's back. "I don't think you need a doctor," he said thoughtfully. Then added softly, "You wait right here. I am going out to the store to purchase some bandages and some medicine to apply to those open wounds, so they don't get infected. I'll be right back."

She nodded. Tears welled up in her eyes. He saw them and turned around. "Are you all right to stay here alone?"

"Yes, I am. I'm fine," she lied. *I am not fine. I am terrified and in terrible pain.*

Oskar shook his head. "No, you're not. I won't leave you and go out. I'll just go down to the front desk and pay someone to go out and buy what we need. You stay right here, love. I won't be a minute."

She nodded.

After Oskar left the room, Kara picked up the emerald dress that lay on the floor. She almost vomited when she saw where it had been shredded by the force of the whip and how her blood had stained the fabric. It hurt her heart to think of how Oskar had given it to her to make her smile in hopes that the night would go well. She sighed. There was no use in looking at the dress. It made her feel even worse than she already did. Defeated, tired, and in pain, Kara threw it in the trash. Then she plopped down on the bed and put her head in her hands. *How has my life become such a mess? Abram is gone. My son is missing. And I am in terrible pain. The only bright light in my world is Oskar. How is that even possible?*

A knock on the door made Kara jump. She was nervous and edgy. "Who is it?" Kara yelled from across the room. She held her breath until she heard Oskar's familiar voice.

"It's me," he said.

She got up and looked through the peephole just to reassure herself before she opened the door.

It was Oskar. She let him in.

"I sent one of the desk clerks to the store. He'll be back soon. How do you feel?"

"I've felt better." She tried to smile.

"I know, love. I went to my room and got you two aspirin. They should help with the pain." He stood up and brought her a glass of water and the pills. "Come on. Take these," he said.

She obeyed.

"Good girl," he said, taking the glass from her and setting it down on the writing desk.

Next, he wet a towel and began to gently wash the blood from her face.

There was a knock on the door. Kara trembled. Oskar saw her and touched her hand. "It's all right. No one will hurt you. I'm here," he said.

Oskar rose and walked to the door. He looked through the peephole, then turned to Kara and smiled reassuringly. "It's the clerk from the front desk, with the things I asked him to purchase."

Oskar let the clerk inside. He had a bag of bandages, a jar of medicine, and a bottle of Jägermeister in his hands.

"Here. This is for you." Oskar took a reichsmark out of his pocket and gave it to the young man. Then he took the items and said, "Thank you, that will be all."

"I can't believe all of this has happened," she said. "Why would they come and arrest me like that?"

"Kara," he soothed her, "I understand you must be unnerved. You've done nothing wrong. It was their mistake, not anything you did. My poor love, you have been through a horrible ordeal tonight. But don't you worry. I made sure that monster of a woman will never have another job where she has any authority again. In short, her career is over," he said, putting the items the clerk had brought down on the table next to the bed.

Kara nodded. She didn't care about that woman's career. All she knew was that she never wanted to see her or the Gestapo headquarters again.

"Before I begin, why don't you take a swig of this Göring-Schnapps. It will help with the pain." Oskar handed Kara the bottle of Jägermeister.

Kara nodded and took a long drink from the bottle. Then she took another one. "That's strong," she said.

"It's good. It will help. Now, sit down on the bed and turn your back to me," Oskar said. He went to the bathroom and washed out the towel. Then he returned and said, "May I take your robe down just far enough so I can clean these wounds? I must clean them and take care of them, or you could get an infection."

She nodded and reached for the bottle. After she took another swig, Oskar began to work on her wounds. It felt strange to have a man other than Abram touching her. But Oskar was so gentle that she allowed herself to relax.

Oskar tenderly cleaned the tears in her flesh where the whip had sliced through her. Every time

CHAPTER 13 | 89

she flinched from the pain, he would stop for a moment and wait while she took another drink. Then he would ask, "Are you all right? May I continue?"

"Yes," she would answer.

Once he'd finished cleaning, medicating, and bandaging her wounds, he called down to the hotel desk and ordered hot tea, bread, and soup to be brought to the room. Then he sat down beside her on the bed.

"How do you feel?"

"Shaken up, but better since you put that medicine on my back. The pain is subsiding a little."

Oskar smiled gently. "Good. I'm glad." He pulled her robe back up over her shoulders.

*He is such a gentleman,* she thought. *I am so lucky to have him in my life.*

The food came. At first, she didn't want to eat. Her stomach was upset, and she felt too nauseated to put anything in her mouth. But Oskar insisted she at least take a few bites of bread.

Once she got some food into her stomach, she felt better. "I think I can eat," she said, amazed that the bread had calmed her stomach. The food was delicious. "I didn't realize how hungry I was," she said.

"I am so sorry that all of this happened to you tonight. I was hoping we would have nice quiet dinner. I mean, it's Christmas Eve."

She nodded. "I know. I know you meant so well by sending me that dress."

"I don't care about the dress. Like I said, I'll buy you another one. Two, if it would make you happy."

"Oh, Oskar, I am just so afraid that the police or the Gestapo will make another mistake and come for me again. They were so brutal. So scary. I kept telling them to call you. I begged them to call you. But they wouldn't listen to me."

"Shhh, I know. I know. And don't you worry, my love. I will see to it that nothing like that ever happens to you again. I give you my word," he said.

"But what if they did something like that to my son, my little boy? If these were the same people that took him, they are capable of terrible cruelty." She was trembling.

"But they would never hurt a child. I promise you."

"I don't know. I have never in my life met such terrible people."

"You have to trust me, Kara. You have to believe me that he will be all right."

She nodded. Then her voice cracked as she said, "Oskar, I can't thank you enough for everything you have done for me."

"You must not concern yourself with thanking me. I want to help you find your son," he said. Then his voice grew husky. "Kara, I have told you many times that I care for you. I . . . more than care for you. I am in love with you." He hesitated. "I was going to give you your Christmas gift tomorrow. But tonight seems so much more appropriate." He took a small box out of his pocket and handed it to her.

The box was neatly wrapped in paper that had been adorned with swastikas. She looked at the gift in her hand and then into his eyes. "I don't have anything for you. I am so sorry. I wasn't thinking. I've been so inconsiderate. All of my attention has been on finding Karl. Please forgive me."

"There is nothing for me to forgive. I don't want anything from you, Kara. I am just happy to be able to help you." He hesitated. Then he smiled his warmest smile and added, "Well, there is something I would ask of you. It is that you would accept my gift to you."

She cocked her head, "I don't understand . . ."

"Just open it, please?"

She nodded. "All right." She tore the paper off the little white box. Then she took the top off. Kara gasped when she saw the ring. It was a large diamond in a shiny gold setting, surrounded by smaller diamonds.

"Will you be my wife?" Oskar asked nervously.

"I don't know. This is all so sudden," Kara answered, her face flushed.

"You don't have to decide right now."

"Yes, I would need to think about it. Can I tell you in the morning?"

"Of course. I would never want to push you."

She smiled and took his hand. "You're a dear man, Oskar. I know I am fortunate to have you in

my life. I want you to know that I appreciate everything you do."

"So, you like me, then?" He sounded so much
like a little boy that she had to smile.

"Of course I like you," she said.

"So, then, what would stop you from saying
yes?"

"I am not sure."

"I'll be a good husband. You just have to give
me a chance. I promise you I'll do whatever I can to
find little Karl. Then once we have found him, I'll
adopt him, and love him. I will raise him as my own
son. I will give him everything a boy needs to get
along in life. He will never want for anything. Neither will you. We will be a family, Kara. A happy
family."

She studied his face. His eyes glowed with sincerity. *He does love me. Only a man who loves a woman
would have stayed here and put his own life on hold to help
her find her child. I remember how good he was with Karl.
Karl liked him. He would be a wonderful father. I have to
face facts. My Abram, my first and truest love, is gone. I
don't know where, but I do know he would want me to have a
partner in my life who treated me kindly, and who loved and
cared for his son.* She looked into Oskar's eyes. "Yes,"
she said.

"You will marry me?"

"I will."

"Oh, Kara. You don't know how happy have
made me in this moment."

She smiled at him. He took the ring from the box and placed it on her trembling finger. "My future wife." He beamed. "The future Frau Lerch." Then he kissed her gently. "I'll file an application for us to marry as soon as I can. I'm sure we will have no problem being granted permission."

Then he kissed her. She felt a shudder go up her spine. It felt like a snake was slithering up her back. But she ignored it thinking she was only nervous because she had not been intimate with a man since Abram.

Oskar reached over and touched her face. "Get some rest. It's been a long night," he said. "I'm going to my room now." He took her hand and kissed it. Then he smiled and got up to leave.

"Oskar," she said, "am I safe in this room now?"

"Would you like me to stay? I will sit in the chair and watch over you while you sleep."

"No, that won't be necessary. I'll just be careful not to open the door without checking through the peephole."

"You will be safe, my love. That terrible woman and the officers who dared to arrest you will all be fired. I'll see to it."

She gave him a weak smile. Then he said, "Come on, get into bed." She did as she was told. He gently placed the blanket over her. "Now, please, try to rest."

"I will, and I can't thank you enough for taking care of me."

"That's what people do for those they love," he said.

"You don't think they'll come back, do you?" She got up on one elbow and asked him again just to reassure herself.

"I know they won't. But as I said, I would be happy to sleep in the chair here and watch over you. I promise you that I would be a gentleman."

"I know you would. But I wouldn't ask that of you. Go and get some rest. It's been a rough night for you too. I'll be all right," Kara assured him.

He turned off the light and left the room. Once he was outside, she heard him rattle the doorknob. She knew he was double-checking the door to make sure it was locked. Then once he was sure she was safe, she heard the heels of his shoes click as he walked down the hall to his own room.

Kara was alone and still a little unnerved from the whole night. She took a deep breath. Her face hurt, and the cuts on her back still stung. But the alcohol had helped to dull her fears, and the aspirin had taken the edge off the pain. She thought that if she lay there for a while, she could sleep. Kara thought about how eager she'd been to make love with Abram. *Why don't I feel that way with Oskar? I don't find his looks unappealing. He is handsome. I just don't feel passion toward him. Perhaps I just need time*, she thought.

She lay in bed for a few minutes, reliving the arrest. Then she got out of bed and placed a chair in front of the door. It wasn't cold in the room, but she was shivering. There was an extra blanket in the closet. She took it down from the shelf and put it on the bed. Then she turned off the light again and climbed in. She closed her eyes, but when she did, she saw that horrible woman's face and heard her terrible voice. "Abram," Kara whispered softly into the darkness, "I'm so afraid. Tonight made me realize the danger that could easily befall me. And it also made me think of you. Oh, dear God, what you must have gone through when you were arrested. I can't even fathom the horror of it. They are so cruel. When I think about it, I feel your pain and your terror. Every day that passes, I am more certain that you are dead. And, oh, how I miss you. I don't know if I did the right thing accepting Oskar's proposal. However, I know he will continue to use every connection he has to help me find our son. He is the only person I can count on to help me. And I must find Karl and bring him home. I've lost you, my love, but I can't bear to lose him too. I know that what I am doing, this tightrope I am walking, is pure madness because Karl is half Jewish. But no one knows. And if Oskar adopts him, he will be safe. I must admit that it does bother me that he is a Nazi and although he has never really discussed his feelings about Jewish people, I am sure he had the same Hitler Youth training that I did. Which means he believes that Jews are the enemy of all good Germans. Still, right now, I need him.

And he has always been kind to me. I have to over-look his affiliation with the party if Karl and I are to survive this terrible regime. How I wish you could speak to me. How I wish you could tell me that the choices I've made are the right ones and that you know I have never stopped loving you. And, most of all, I wish you could tell me that you forgive me for agreeing to marry Oskar. It would mean the world to me to know that I have your forgiveness."

The cuts on her back were painful and raw, and every time she moved, she winced. But she was very tired, and sometime during the night, Kara drifted off to sleep. She slept hard and long. She slept the sleep of someone who had endured a terrible ordeal and was now safe. It was almost eleven in the morning when Oskar rang her on the phone.

"Hello," Kara said, still half asleep.

"Are you all right? It's very late. I knocked on the door to your room, but there was no answer. I was getting worried," Oskar said.

"What time is it?"

"A quarter to eleven. I'm sorry to have awakened you. And I don't mind if you want to sleep a little longer. I just wanted to be sure you were all right."

"Yes, of course, I understand. I'm fine." She shook herself awake and sat up in bed. "Have you heard anything about Karl?"

"No, dear. I am sorry. But, of course, it's

Christmas day. I didn't expect to hear from any of my sources this morning."

"Yes, that's right. I almost forgot."

"Would you like to sleep a little longer?"

"No, I'll get up now. I can meet you in the hotel restaurant for breakfast in about a half hour. Would that be all right?"

"Of course. Take as long as you need. Would you like me to come to your room and change your bandages?"

"No, I'll be all right," she said.

"I'll see you in a half hour, then . . . my darling. My fiancée."

# CHAPTER FOURTEEN

THE HOTEL where Oskar and Kara were staying served very few Polish citizens. The owner was German, and his guests were primarily German and mostly SS officers; therefore, he had access to better food than the Polish establishments. A tall, decorated Christmas tree stood in the lobby beside a perfectly framed oil painting of the führer. The napkins in the restaurant were white and had been embroidered with small gold swastikas. The rims of the dishes had tiny Nazi flags painted on them. When Kara entered the restaurant, the maître d' smiled at her and said, "Heil Hitler." She returned the salute unenthusiastically. Then she looked around until she found Oskar already seated at a table and sipping coffee. He was reading a German paper when she walked up.

"Good morning," she said.

"You look ravishing as always." He looked at her approvingly and smiled. Then more seriously, he added, "How are you feeling?"

"Better, but sore, and still a little tired."

"It's understandable, love. You went through quite an ordeal yesterday. And if I were the sort of man who would strike a woman, I would have killed that bitch at the police station who hit you."

"I know you would have. I saw it in your eyes."

He looked down at the ring on her finger, then took her hand and kissed it. "My future wife," he said softly, "no one will ever hurt you again. Not as long as I am alive."

She shivered. *As long as I am alive. The world we live in is so uncertain. I am always afraid. I never feel secure. After all, I thought that Abram and I would be together until we were both old. I was so idealistic. I loved him so. And even though I was aware of how much people hated the Jews, I didn't believe that anything this terrible would ever really happen. I thought it would pass. I knew that throughout history people had always persecuted the Jews. I was willing to fight for what we had. I assumed we would face some problems because our relationship was illegal. But I never thought that things would become violent. I was naïve I guess, because, until he was taken away, I refused to believe he would be. I thought we would somehow be together forever. Abram with his gentle eyes and soft voice. I will always love him. He helped me to have faith in men again after what my father did to me. But then, he was gone in an instant. My poor Abram. The father of my beloved son, my Karl, who is now missing too. And who's to say that something might not happen, and Oskar could be gone too. If the truth is ever discovered about me, Karl, and Abram, Oskar could face punishment along with us. Or, God forbid, he could be the one to administer it.* She looked up at Oskar and he smiled at her. His smile was so warm and filled with love that she wiped the thought of him ever turning on her, out of her mind. *I know he loves me. I can see it in his face and in everything he does. He's such a kind and gentle man. Sweet Oskar. I am so afraid to face tomorrow. After all, in an instant, Oskar could be taken from me too. And how can I go on living if I never find Karl?* Her hands began trembling. *There is no telling where our lives are headed.*

"Are you cold?" he asked. "You're shivering."

"Yes, perhaps I am." She wished she could share all of her fears with him. But she still dared not.

He removed his jacket and put it around her shoulders. Then he motioned for the waiter. "Turn the heat up higher in here," he commanded. "My fiancée is cold."

After they finished breakfast, they sat by the roaring fire in the fireplace in the lobby and sipped on cups of hot coffee. Not the ersatz coffee she'd grown used to, but rich, real coffee, filled with thick, heavy cream and real sugar.

"I have a surprise for you. I considered canceling it last night after the incident. I wasn't sure you would be up to it. But then I reconsidered. I thought perhaps it would be good for you."

"I don't know what you're talking about." She looked at him.

"I realize that"—he laughed a little—"I'm not making any sense, am I? But when I am around you, I turn into a schoolboy. I become flustered."

She smiled at him. "You're charming," she admitted, "but I still don't know what you're trying to tell me. What is good for me or not good for me?"

"Ah yes, the surprise. I arranged for Anka and Ludwig to come to Warsaw to spend Christmas day with us. I hope that's all right with you. I arranged it last week . . . before what happened last night."

"Yes, of course it is all right. It will be good to see my sister again."

"I purchased gifts for them from us. Nothing too fancy."

"Oskar, you think of everything."

"I try. I want to make you happy, Kara."

"And you were so good with Karl. He likes you so much."

"I'm glad because I am going to be his father."

A vision of Abram's face flashed through Kara's mind. *His father*, she thought. But she said, "Yes. His father." Then she added, "I wish we could find him already. No matter where we are or what we are doing, Karl is always on my mind."

"That's only natural. You are a good mother. You're the kind of mother that our führer is referring to when he says that motherhood is the most important job in our fatherland." Then he continued, "I don't know if you realize this, but I, too, am always thinking of Karl. I want to bring him home to us as much as you do."

"I know that," she said.

"And I will."

"I believe you."

# CHAPTER FIFTEEN

THREE HOURS LATER, Anka knocked on the door to Kara's hotel room. Kara opened the door, and as soon as the two girls saw each other, any anger they felt toward one another disappeared. For a moment, they were both transported back to being two little sisters, who were as close as two people can be.

It was late afternoon. Ludwig stood behind Anka, holding a bag filled with gifts for Kara and Oskar. Each gift had been wrapped in the same swastika paper that Kara's ring box had been wrapped in the night before.

Kara glanced at the gifts and the swastikas on the paper. *Everything is centered around Hitler*, she thought, but she said nothing.

Anka hugged Kara tightly. But when Kara winced in pain, she let go of her. "What's wrong?" Anka asked.

"Oh, Anka, I wasn't going to tell you because I didn't want to worry you, but something happened last night. Something terrible. My back is all cut up. I'm sorry, I didn't mean to push you away."

"Let me see."

"No, I'll be all right."

"I want to see," Anka said, getting up and standing behind Kara. She pulled up Kara's blouse and let out gasp of fright. "This is horrible. Absolutely horrible. Who did this to you? Was it Oskar?"

"Oh, heavens no. Oskar has been like an angel to me."

"So, who did this? This didn't happen by accident. Someone did this to you."

"Yes, you're right. It happened last night. I was falsely arrested and whipped by a Gestapo agent."

"What?" Ludwig asked, his eyes wide with disbelief. "Falsely arrested, why? What did they think you did to deserve such inhumane treatment? I will get in touch with them and take care of this. I will tell them who you are and see to it that the agent who did this to you loses their job."

"No need for you to do that, Ludwig. Oskar has already taken care of it," Kara said.

"So, please, tell me what happened," Anka said.

"All right. Both of you, sit down. I'll tell you what happened." And she did. Kara told them everything. She even told them about her and Oskar getting engaged.

"Congratulations That's wonderful news!"

Ludwig said. He was enthusiastic but still stunned by the story of her arrest.

"Yes, congratulations. I've always liked Oskar," Anka admitted as she tried to smile. But then she shook her head and added, "But I am so upset to hear about what happened to you last night."

"I know. But the good thing is that Oskar was there for me. He came as soon as they called him, and dressed my wounds, so I'll be all right," Kara said.

Then there was a knock on the door. Ludwig opened it.

"You must always look through the peephole before you open the door," Kara said quickly, but she was relieved to see that it was Oskar. Then she took a deep breath and forced herself to smile at Ludwig. "You'll have to excuse me. I'm sorry. But after last night, I think I will always be careful before opening the door to my room."

"Understandably so," Ludwig said. "I'm sorry. I wasn't thinking."

Oskar walked in the room. He was smiling warmly and carrying gifts for Ludwig and Anka. "Merry Christmas to you both. I'm so glad you came," he said.

"Heil Hitler," Ludwig said, saluting.

"Heil Hitler," Oskar answered, and after saluting, he gave Ludwig a quick embrace.

Anka stood up and hugged Oskar tightly. "It's so good to see you again," she said.

"Yes, it's good to see both of you." Oskar smiled, then he walked over and put his hand on Kara's shoulder.

"We brought these for you," Anka said, taking two small, wrapped boxes out of her handbag and handing them respectively to Oskar and Kara.

Everyone opened their gifts. Kara tried to keep a smile on her face, but her lower lip trembled. Only Oskar noticed. And he took her hand and whispered, "It will be all right. I promise you. We will find him."

Kara managed a trembling smile. *He can promise me all he wants, but he doesn't know anything for sure. And my son is not here with me on Christmas Day.*

Anka was delighted with the cashmere sweater that Oskar bought for her. "This is lovely," she said.

Ludwig complimented Oskar on having brilliant taste when he opened the box containing a bottle of Russian vodka.

"I do so hate the Russians, but I must admit their vodka is the finest," Ludwig said.

"I know. I must admit that it's true. I got it from one of our soldiers who had just returned from the front."

Kara received a pair of pearl earrings. She tried to be gracious and excited, but she could hardly manage any form of enthusiasm. Neither Anka nor Ludwig noticed.

Oskar smiled when he opened the gold cuff

links with the tiny engraved swastikas. "Very nice," he said. "Thank you."

After they finished opening their gifts, Kara asked, "How long are you staying in Warsaw?"

"Unfortunately, only a couple of days. Ludwig can't stay any longer. He must return to work. But I have a surprise for you tomorrow."

"A surprise?" Kara said.

"Yes! You're going to love it!" Anka answered excitedly.

"Oh yes, I am sure I will." Kara stood up and looked away. She couldn't meet Anka's eyes. She wondered how her sister could be so glib while Karl was still missing.

# CHAPTER SIXTEEN

EARLY THE NEXT MORNING, Anka knocked on the door to Kara's room. Kara woke up startled by the knock on the door. Her heart was beating fast, and she had to take a moment to catch her breath.

She got up and, forgetting to put on her robe, her voice cracked as she asked through the door, "Who is it?" Then she looked through the peephole and saw Anka. Kara sighed with relief. Her hand went to her heart as she began to calm down. Opening the door, she said, "Come in."

"You had to know it was me. After all, who else would be awake at this hour? I was just too excited about today to sleep."

"What time is it?"

"Six."

"Six in the morning?"

Anka laughed, "Of course in the morning, silly."

Kara felt stupid. She was still half asleep and also still reeling from being awakened. Although Anka knew what Kara had gone through, she didn't seem to understand why a knock on the door early in the morning would have flustered her sister the way it did.

Kara noticed that Anka was fully dressed.

"You are never dressed this early. What's gotten into you?"

"You know how I always keep you waiting for me?"

"Yes. You always have."

"I have decided to make a change in my behavior. You know how you have always gotten angry with me because you think I am selfish? Well, I am no longer going to be so selfish. I got dressed early because I wanted you to see that I am trying to be more considerate."

"That's very nice," Kara managed to say. *But you are still selfish.*

"You're still mad at me for convincing you to leave Karl with that woman, aren't you?"

"No, Anka. I'm not angry. Anger won't do either of us any good. And it certainly won't bring Karl back. But, I am not like you, I just can't snap back the way you can. My son is missing. It's all I think about day and night."

Anka sank down into the chair. "There's nothing we can do but wait for Oskar to take care of it. He told me he is doing everything in his power to find Karl."

"Yes, he is. And I am grateful to him. But even so, I can't just put my thoughts of Karl away like folding a sheet and putting it into a closet. I am fearful for my son. Every minute of every day. I can't enjoy Christmas not knowing where my little boy is. I wish you could understand."

"I do understand, Kara. But being miserable doesn't help the situation. Whether you worry yourself to death, or you try to be happy, the outcome will be the same."

"What does that mean exactly, Anka?" Kara felt the anger rising in her chest. *Anka and I get along so much better when we are far away from each other.*

"It means . . ." she stammered, "well, it means that when Oskar finds Karl, then Karl will come home. And everything will be all right again."

"How simple," Kara said sarcastically.

"Please, can't we just have a nice visit? It's been months since we last saw each other. And I have missed you so. Don't you think I blame myself every day for what happened? But I can't change the past, Kara. So, I have no other choice but to put my trust in Oskar. And hope and pray that he will find Karl soon."

Kara nodded. *She's right. I am still angry with her.*

*But she's my sister and I love her. I must do my best to try and enjoy our time together.* "I'll get dressed, and then we can go down to the restaurant and get some coffee. We'll meet the fellows there for breakfast."

"Good. I'll stay here in your room until you're ready, then I'll go and wake Ludwig and Oskar."

# CHAPTER SEVENTEEN

ONCE KARA WAS DRESSED, Anka went back to her room and woke Ludwig. He agreed to wake Oskar. Then Kara and Anka went downstairs and got a table. They ordered coffee. Kara still found it so strange and sad that she and her sister had nothing to say to each other. They stirred their coffee. Anka told Kara about a recipe she tried and a new dress she'd purchased. Kara nodded and smiled while looking out the window. She was glad that Oskar and Ludwig arrived within a half hour. Oskar ordered platters of eggs and sausages with rolls and thick slabs of butter for breakfast.

Kara forced herself to eat a little of the scrambled eggs and a slice of toast. Then she sipped her coffee quietly while Anka talked excitedly about her meeting with the führer. "He came to the lair. I couldn't believe it was really him," she said.

*Sometimes she is so animated, like a child,* Kara thought.

"I do wish you could have been there, Kara. It was so exciting. He is like a god. I must admit that his pictures don't do him justice. In person, he is so handsome, and charming." Anka's face was lit up and beaming.

"I made sure that Anka met our führer when he came to see the lair," Ludwig explained to the others. "I arranged it because I knew how much she would treasure that meeting."

"So, how did he like the lair?" Oskar asked.

"He did. The other fellows and I were holding our breath until he said he thought it was marvelous."

"That had to feel good," Oskar said, smiling sincerely. "After all the hard work you put in to it."

"It certainly did."

Kara sipped her coffee. It was dark, hot, and rich with flavor. Anka was telling a story about a man at a party she attended. He'd worn a funny-looking suit that she'd found amusing. Her hands moved; her face was animated. But Kara's mind drifted. She couldn't listen to Anka's nonsense, and she began to wonder how she ever had. *I suppose I was different then. That was before I had a child, before I lived with Abram. It's me who's different, not Anka.*

She took another sip of the coffee. Anka had both of the men laughing. The flavor of coffee brought back the memory of the ersatz coffee she'd had every morning with Hoda and Abram. Even though the ersatz coffee had not been rich or very flavorful, she had warm memories of drinking it. The table filled with food stood in contrast, in her mind, to the single slice of unbuttered bread she'd shared with her Jewish family. It seemed a lifetime ago, and yet she would never forget it. Kara tapped her finger on the handle of the coffee cup. Everything suddenly felt obscenely opulent. *I would trade all of this, the fine china, the delicious food, the prestige and respect shown to the Germans in the East, to return to that little apartment behind the bookstore with the man I still and will always love.* She sighed softly but no one noticed.

Once the two couples had finished eating, Anka said, "I have a special surprise for my sister today. I am taking Kara shopping. You boys can go to a pub or something for the afternoon, can't you?"

"Of course. We'll be fine. Don't you worry about us," Ludwig said. Then reaching into his pocket, he took out a roll of bills. "Let me give you some money for shopping."

Anka put her hand out, and Ludwig placed several reichsmarks into her palm. She turned and winked at Kara. "We're going to have so much fun," she said.

"I'd like to give you some money to shop as well, Kara," Oskar said, taking an even larger pile of reichsmarks from his own pocket.

"I don't need anything. Thank you. I am just

grateful to you for paying for this hotel and food so we can stay here in Warsaw until we find Karl."

"Nonsense, don't even think about it. I am more than glad to give you a few reichsmarks to go shopping. Now, here is some money." He tried to hand Kara the money, but she shook her head. Then he turned to Anka. "Won't you please hold this for her in case she finds something she wants to buy?" Oskar asked.

"Of course," Anka said, taking the bills and stuffing them into her handbag along with the money Ludwig had given her. "So, then, gentlemen, we're off. You have a wonderful time today, and we'll see you tonight for dinner?"

"Sounds perfect," Ludwig said. He stood up and kissed Anka, who pulled away from him just a little too quickly.

Before they left, Oskar caught Kara's hand and put it to his lips. "I won't kiss you publicly because I don't want to embarrass you," he whispered, "but I just wanted to let you know . . . I love you. You look stunning as always. Have a good time today."

Kara's lips trembled. She didn't know why she felt like crying. There was no reason for it, and yet she felt like weeping. Controlling her emotions as best as she could, she said, "Thank you."

# CHAPTER EIGHTEEN

IT WAS COLD OUTSIDE, frigid actually. Kara shivered and wished she were back in her room at the hotel. *Walking around in this weather is pointless, especially to go shopping for things I don't even need.*

As they walked down the street, heads turned to look at Anka, who looked smart in her new blue wool coat with the white fox collar. Her bright blonde hair picked up the rays of sunshine, and her blue eyes twinkled with delight. Kara had not purchased a new coat in years, and the wool one she owned was well worn. It hardly sheltered her from the bitter winter winds. Her hair was straight and pulled back into a no-nonsense twist at the nape of her neck. *Anka looks so young, and I look so old*, she thought.

As they walked through the streets of Warsaw, careful about patches of ice on the walkway, Anka slid her arm through Kara's and talked excitedly, "We are going to have so much fun today, and I was also thinking about your wedding. Why don't you and Oskar get married at the lair? Wouldn't that be wonderful. Or do you think it's too wild of a place for a wedding? Would you prefer something more romantic?"

"I don't know," Kara said, trying to match her sister's excitement and pulling her scarf tighter around her head and neck.

"Either way, I just can't wait until you see the lair. It's magnificent. And I wonder if we have the wedding there, if the führer might even attend. Can you just imagine!"

Kara turned to smile at Anka. *How different we've become. The last person I would want at my wedding would be the führer. Our lives have taken us both down such different roads. Sometimes I hardly recognize her as the little girl who I tried so hard to protect from my father. Yet, every once in a while, I still see my baby sister in her smile or in her eyes. I love her. I always will. And sometimes I am so sad when I think that we will never be close like that again.*

"Just think, what if Oskar could find work at the lair? What fun it would be if you and I were able live in the same area. We could see each other all the time. We could laugh at everyone we didn't like." She squeezed Kara's arm and winked at her. "I would absolutely love that."

"Yes, me too," Kara offered, "but we'll have to wait and see what happens."

"You know, the führer is really insistent about the importance of good Aryan families moving east. We need more land, and the land in the east is so fertile."

"What about the people who are already living there?"

"You mean, like the Poles?"

"Yes, exactly."

"Of course we will let them stay," Anka said, nodding her head, her voice filled with righteous conviction, "but it's our right as Aryans, superior Nordic people, to eventually rule the entire world. Our führer knows what is best for everyone. Including non-Aryans. The Poles and the other people who live to the east, would still remain on the land. Their jobs would be to serve us. It is the way things should be."

Kara forced herself to remain quiet. *My sister is only going to be here for a few days. I must try not to fight with her. It's pointless anyway. When we argue, it doesn't change her way of thinking, and it certainly doesn't change mine either.*

When they arrived at the wall of the Jewish ghetto, Kara looked at Anka. Her heart began to race. She wondered if perhaps the surprise her sister had in store for her was that she'd found Abram. *But how would she know about Abram? I never told her. How could she have found out? If this is why she's brought me here, I can forgive anything and everything she's ever said or done. But wouldn't she have said something when*

*I told her that Oskar and I were getting married? Maybe she couldn't because Ludwig was there. And maybe she didn't say anything this morning because she wanted it to be a surprise. Either way, I dare not ask. I dare not trust her to ask. I have to wait and see what she has in store. Dear God, what if she's found Abram. Could it be that I am about to see him? That I am only minutes away from his arms?* Tears began to form in the corners of her eyes.

But Anka didn't notice that Kara was crying. "Wait here," Anka told Kara. Then she had walked ahead of Kara, leaving her waiting for her to return. Anka walked up to the guard at the gate. Kara could see the admiration in the man's face. *My sister is so beautiful. She thought this man is taken with her.* From where she stood Kara could see Anka laughing and flirting with the guard. She didn't want her sister to see her tears, so Kara took her scarf and quickly wiped her face. She was nervous and anxious. She wished Anka would stop wasting time talking to the strange man. Then Anka turned and motioned with her hand for Kara to come forward. Kara walked over to her sister.

"Have fun today, ladies," the guard said as Kara and Anka entered the ghetto. "And . . . do be careful. These Jews can be problematic. As I am sure you know. They can't be trusted." Then he tapped Anka on the arm and added, "If you have a problem with any of them, you can come and speak to me. I'll take care of it."

Anka tilted her head and gave the guard her

prettiest smile. Then she put her arm through her sister's, and she and Kara entered the ghetto.

Kara looked around her at the people. Their clothes were ragged, and they were far too thin. *Abram, are you here?* she thought. Then turning to Anka, she carefully asked, "So, what's the surprise?"

"You'll see." Anka winked.

*Could it really be that she knows about Abram, and she's brought me to him? I want to ask her, but I can't, just in case I am wrong. But what other reason would she have for bringing me to this horrible place.* Her heart was racing; her palms were wet with sweat, and even though it was cold outside, she felt hot all over with anticipation.

They passed two little children, a boy and a girl, who were sitting on the ground together. Their eyes were large, but their bodies were small and thin. In their tiny faces, Kara saw reflections of her son, and it made her ache for the children's suffering. The little girl wore a coat, but the boy only had a light jacket. They were holding hands. Kara wanted to take them in her arms and shelter them. But she knew if she did, it would frighten them, so instead, she turned to Anka. "I'll be right back," she said. Then she walked over to the children and reached into her handbag and took out a coin. She handed it to the little girl, who smiled at her.

"You're such a good soul," Anka said, walking over and weaving her arm through Kara's. As they continued on their journey, Kara stopped and turned back for a moment to look at the children. She thought of Karl again and said a silent prayer that wherever he was, people were being kind to him.

"Wait just a moment," Anka said. "I have to find the address of where we're going."

Anka rummaged through her handbag until she located a sheet of paper. She took it out and read an address. Then she turned to a woman who was coming out of a shop a few feet ahead of them and asked for directions. The woman looked at her with wide, frightened eyes. She shook her head as if she didn't understand as she walked away quickly.

"These people are idiots," Anka said under her breath. Then she turned to Kara. "Don't worry, we'll find it."

"What exactly are we trying to find?"

"You'll see."

Kara's heart leapt. *Abram? Is it Abram? If I am right, my sister has found him and, in a few minutes, I will see his face again. I would trade ten years of my life to hear his voice and to feel the comfort of his arms around me.* They walked a little farther. As they passed a scrappy-looking young man who stood against the building, Anka walked up to him to ask for directions. He looked at her challengingly and unafraid. Kara shivered.

"I need to get to this address," Anka said.

"So, you want to buy some furs?" the young man said.

"Yes."

"Sure. All right."

"Furs?" Kara asked, still hoping that she was not wrong. But fearing she might be.

"Yes, shhhh. I'll handle this," Anka said.

*Furs? Could it be a code word? Dear God, please, let it be a code word. I don't need furs. I need Abram,* Kara thought.

"Come on. Follow me," the young man said. He led them to an apartment building a couple of streets away. "Third floor, three-sixteen. Tell her Billy Rosen sent you. Got that?"

Anka nodded.

"Where are we going?" Kara asked again. But Anka didn't answer. Taking Kara's arm and pulling gently, Anka led her sister into the building. The odors in the hallway were overpowering. They were a combination of food, vomit, feces, sweat, and illness. Kara gagged as they climbed the stairs to the third floor.

"I know it stinks in here. Jews are so filthy," Anka said. "Breathe through your mouth."

Kara didn't answer. She was trying hard not to vomit.

When they got to the third floor, Anka followed the apartment numbers until she found 316. "This is it," Anka said to Kara as she knocked on the door.

"Yes?" a painfully thin young woman wearing a cotton housedress answered.

"Billy Rosen sent me," Anka said.

"Come in." The young woman nodded in acknowledgment.

Kara followed Anka into the apartment. It was crowded with people. There were five dirty, young children playing on the floor. And at least five adults, including the young woman, that Kara could see.

A wrinkled old woman stepped up to Anka and said, "So, what are you looking for?"

"Furs."

Kara heard the word *furs,* and her heart sank.

"Are you willing to pay?"

Anka sucked her teeth. "How dare you ask me that? If I wasn't willing to pay, I would have gone right up to someone on the street and taken the fur right off their back. I am an Aryan. I have the power to do that, you know. But I came here, because I chose to be fair and try to do right by you people."

Kara's mouth hung open. *What is going on here?* There was a deep, empty ache in her belly. It was pain from disappointment. She'd hoped; she'd prayed; she'd believed that her sister was taking her to see her beloved. She had been so hopeful that she wanted to cry. And now she felt the anguish of losing Abram all over again.

"All right," the old woman said, sighing. "All right. I have an ermine coat. Good condition. What will you give me for it?"

"Let me see it," Anka said, then she turned to Kara, winked, then smiled.

The old woman pulled a white fur coat out from under a cot. Anka looked it over. "It's nice." She nodded her head. Then she held it up to see if she thought it would fit. "Yes, this coat should do very well."

"So, how much?" the old woman asked again.

Anka opened her handbag and drew out two apples, a half of a loaf of bread, and a cube of hard yellow cheese.

Kara gasped, remembering the breakfast they'd eaten only a few hours earlier. *This is all she wants to offer this poor woman for such a coat?* Kara thought.

Suddenly, when the others saw the food, the room grew quiet. It was like being in a den of hungry wolves. The children stared at the food. "I'm hungry, Mama," a little girl said. A young woman, who appeared to be the child's mother, picked her up and held her. "Shhhh," she whispered.

"Can I have one of those apples? Please, Mama. Please?"

"You know better. The fruit is not mine to give, Mamala. And Mrs. Fine isn't going to give you one of her apples. Not if she trades her precious fur coat for it. She'll save it for her grandson."

"But Mama? I'm so hungry."

"I know. I'm sorry. I have nothing left to sell, or I would get you an apple. You know that."

The little girl leaned her head on her mother's knee.

The old woman frowned at Anka. "This is all you have to offer? Do you know how much that coat is worth? It's all I have. It was my sister's. She died from typhus in this hellish place. Please, madam, I am begging you to be generous. I have nothing else of value. And we are all starving here. This is my daughter." The old woman grabbed a younger woman's arm and pulled her over to where they stood. "This little boy is my grandson. Look how skinny he is. If he doesn't get more food, I am afraid he will die. He is so weak, and there is so much disease here. Help us, please, won't you?" she said, pointing to one of the little boys sitting on the floor. "I don't care for myself. I am old. I will be dead soon. But the children are hungry. Can't you maybe spare a few reichsmarks too?"

"You are greedy. What if I chose to give you nothing? What if I just take the coat? You have no power to stop me. You can't do a thing to me."

"Anka!" Kara said, shocked at her sister's cruelty. "Anka, please. Stop."

"I'm doing this for you, Kara. Look at that coat you're wearing. It's a disgrace."

"I don't want the coat," Kara said, taking the last two reichsmarks she had out of her purse and putting them on the table in the middle of the room.

"Thank you, madam. God should bless you,"

the old woman said to Kara. Kara wished she had taken the money that Oskar had offered her that morning.

"Give me the money Oskar gave you for me this morning," Kara demanded.

"I will not," Anka said. "I won't stand here and watch you throw away money foolishly. These people are trying to manipulate you. They are Jews. That's what Jews do, Kara."

"You are making me sick. My stomach is turning," Kara said to Anka.

"Please, lady, take the coat. It's all right. We need the food. I'm sorry I said anything." The old woman looked into Anka's eyes.

Anka put the food down on the table.

*If I had known, I would have taken food from our breakfast this morning.* Kara thought of Hoda.

"Keep your coat and the food too. I just wish I had more money to give you," Kara said.

"Kara, that's not the way we bargain. Now, you gave this woman far more than anyone else would have. Your generosity is clear," Anka said sarcastically. "Now, either you take the coat, or I am going to take back the food."

"Anka!"

"I mean it, Kara. So many of the women who live in our German settlement outside the lair come here to shop. Most of them never even pay. You are paying more than this woman deserves. This is more than she would ever get from anyone else.

Food, and two reichsmarks? Come on, Kara, don't be a fool. Either you take the coat, or I am leaving and taking the food with me."

"Like you need that food. You will only throw it away," Kara said, glaring at Anka.

"I'd rather throw it away."

"I don't know you. I don't know who you are anymore. I can't understand this person you've become," Kara said.

The old woman looked at Kara and said, "It's all right, please. Won't you take the coat. It will do us good to have this food, and may God bless you for your kindness."

Kara's hands were trembling as she took the fur. She shook her head. "I can't."

Anka went to gather the food up off the table.

"Anka, please. Please don't do this."

"Then take the coat."

The woman nodded and forced the fur into Kara's arms. Then she pushed Kara and Anka out the door.

"Shall we do some more shopping? I have some more cheese and a full loaf of bread in my purse."

"And you didn't give it to them?" Kara asked, shocked. "You had more food, and you saw those children, and you still didn't give it to them?" Kara's face was red with anger.

"Why would I? You don't understand. All of their things are ours anyway. We are like German pioneers who have come east to claim our rightful land. We must be strong. These Jews are enemies of our Reich. It is our right to take whatever we want from them."

"Our rightful claim? It is our right to steal other people's valuables. Oh, Anka, what has become of you?"

"You continue saying you don't know me. But it's not I who has changed, Kara; it's you. You are a German. You should love your fatherland. It's you who I don't understand. What is this strange love you have for Jews? It's not good for you. Not at all."

Kara shook her head.

"Listen to me," Anka said, then she continued, "Our movement east is bigger than you and I, Kara. Germany must take her place as a world power. If we are to do this, we need to clear the Slavics out of this land and get rid of the Jews."

"Clear them out? What do you mean? Where is all of this coming from?"

"I mean that we Germans must claim our land. And if some Slavic people must be removed in the process, then so be it. It's for the good of the fatherland. And the fatherland must come first. The Slavics that still remain after the clearing of the land will be servants to the Aryans, who are superior in every way. It is the way things should be. Our führer says that eastern territory, including Russia, belongs to us, and that these lands will be to Germany as India was to England. But before Germany can rise both in the east and at home, the Jews must be eliminated."

"Eliminated. You mean killed? Murdered?"

"Kara, why are you ruining a beautiful afternoon? We could be having such fun here. There are so many nice things we can purchase for little or nothing."

"Did you see those people? Did you see those children?"

"They are not people, Kara. That's what you are failing to understand. They're Jews. That's all they are."

"They are people, Anka. They are people. You should have looked into the eyes of those children when you put those apples on the table. They are hungry. We were poor when we were children. I know you remember how it was. I know you could not have forgotten what it was like to go to bed with your stomach empty and crying for food. Where is your compassion? And now you tell me that you had more food in your handbag, and you didn't give it to them? I wish I had known we were coming here. I would have brought plenty, and I would have given it away. I don't need this fur. I have a coat. This fur might have saved that woman's life, or her grandson's life. She might have been able to sell it to someone else, and it might have helped them to buy more food. But you made me take it. And now it's burning in my arms like something out of the fires of hell."

"Stop talking like that. It's treason. What is wrong with you, Kara? Haven't our lives been better since our führer has come to power? Earlier, you mentioned how it was when we were poor. So, I know you haven't forgotten. It is only because of our führer and his regime that a girl like me, who came from a poor family like ours, can live the way I do. I love the Third Reich and all it's done for me. And, believe me, I have seen it firsthand." Her face was blood red, and her fists were clenched as she continued talking, "Our führer knows what is best for Germany and for our people. He saved us after the Jews ruined us. They were the reason we lost the war and all of our territory. You should know this. You were in the Deutsche Madels. We learned all of this. What's happened to you, Kara?" Anka shook her head. "Would you like to go back to our lives the way they were when we were children, and Father had just returned from the Great War, angry, defeated, and drinking constantly? Is that what you want, or would you rather we rid ourselves of the Jews and live a life where we have every comfort in the world?"

"I am not going to argue with you, Anka. I don't feel the same way you do, and I can't stand the cruelty."

"But you must love the party? You must? Look at all we have now in comparison to what we had as children. Never in my life would I have thought things could be so good for me. And, besides, as far as Karl is concerned, if Oskar weren't so high up in the party, you wouldn't be able to find Karl. It is good to have influential friends. It's good to be a part of something bigger and more important than just your own righteous ideals," Anka said.

"Oh, please. There is nothing good about the Nazi Party. And if it weren't for the Nazi Party, my son wouldn't be missing in the first place, and I wouldn't need a high official to help me find him," Kara retorted.

Anka looked away. Then she said, "We don't know that for sure. Do we? You can't blame our government for Karl's going missing," she growled, "and you should know that I don't like cruelty either. But it's necessary. You have no idea what I have been through and just how necessary it really is. We all must do things we don't like, Kara," Anka insisted. "This business with the Jews is a necessary evil. If we don't keep the Jews locked up, we can't keep an eye on them."

"And, of course, that means that we put them in a place like this without enough food. We steal anything they have of value. Is that what we do, Anka? Is that the right thing to do?"

"It's necessary. They took everything they have from the German people. All of this . . ." She held the fur coat up in her trembling hands. "All of this, is rightfully ours."

"I don't agree with you," Kara said, then she added, "I miss my sister. I don't know who you are anymore. Do you remember when we children, and I told you the story of *The Ugly Duckling*? Do you remember?"

"Yes, and I am the same person. I haven't changed. I could say the same thing, Kara; I don't know who you are. You've become a Jew lover."

Kara shook her head. "Oh, but you have changed," Kara said. "Do you remember what the moral of *The Ugly Duckling* was?"

"I don't remember. It was a long time ago."

"Well, because you don't remember, I am going to remind you. In that little tale there was a group of ducks. In their midst was a duck who didn't look anything like the others. And because he was different, they thought he was ugly. They treated him badly. And then he grew up to be a beautiful swan."

"All right. So what does this have to do with anything?"

"I am going to tell you," Kara said. "The Jews are like the ugly duckling to the Germans. The German people think the Jews are different because they were raised to believe that. But they don't really know any Jews. If they got to know them, they might just find that some of the Jewish people have beautiful hearts, Anka. They might just have beautiful hearts, and inside they might just be like the beautiful swans," Kara said. Her eyes were tearing as she continued. "I'm tired. Let's go back to the hotel. I need to lie down."

"There are a few more things I wanted to get while I am here in Warsaw."

"Here in this ghetto? There are more things you want to steal from these people?" Kara asked.

"I have a list of things I need to acquire for some of my friends. I am not stealing anything, Kara. And I resent the way you speak to me."

"I'm sorry if I hurt your feelings, but I can't do this anymore. If you want to continue this so-called shopping that you are doing, why don't you come back here with Ludwig tomorrow. I've seen enough."

"Kara!" Anka stamped her foot.

"I'm going back. Stay if you'd like." Then she stopped walking and turned around to look into Anka's crystal-blue eyes. "Here," she said, thrusting the coat into Anka's arms. "This belongs to you. I don't want it." Then, trembling all over, Kara turned and walked toward the exit.

"Well, I'm staying here. I'm going to finish shopping," Anka called after her, but Kara did not turn around.

# CHAPTER NINETEEN

ANKA STOOD and watched Kara as she walked out of the entrance to the ghetto. *You ruined everything,* Anka said to herself. *I wanted this to be such a nice day.* Then she turned away from her sister and headed deeper into the ghetto.

Kara wrapped her scarf around her head and hurried back to the hotel. It was cold outside, but the weather was not nearly as chilled as she felt inside. It felt as if her heart was frozen. If there had not been so much ice on the walkways, she would have run all the way back, but she had to be careful not to slip. When she saw the door to the hotel, she was relieved, but she was in no mood to talk, so she was hoping to avoid seeing Oskar or Ludwig before going to her room. When she entered the lobby, she saw the two of them sitting together in the bar.

Their backs were to the door so neither of them saw her. She sighed, glad to be alone, as she went up to her room. When she got into her room, she locked the door and took off her coat. Then she wrapped a blanket around her shoulders and sat looking out the window. A few minutes later, a light snow began to fall. Tears threatened to fall as she watched the tiny flakes of lace drifting down from the sky. *Has Anka really changed, or is she the same and I just didn't see it before? I know I have changed. I've seen another side of life. My love for Abram led me to another world. Can I blame Anka for what she believes? She doesn't know any Jews, not the way I do. If I had never met Abram, wouldn't I be blinded by all the propaganda too? I wish I could talk to her honestly and tell her about Abram and Hoda and how welcome and loved I felt when I lived with them. If only I could make her understand. But I can't. And I know that it's all the secrets I hold so tightly in my heart that are wedging a wall between my sister and me. I miss her. I miss the closeness we had. I feel like Anka is another person Hitler has stolen from me. The great führer.* She shook her head. *I wish someone would assassinate him. But, of course, that won't happen. They all love him. And so, I know there's no solution to this. All I can do is hope that someday my sister and I will find a way to be close again.*

Kara called downstairs and ordered some hot milk and biscuits to be brought to her room. But when they arrived, she couldn't eat, because every time she took a bite, she saw the faces of the starving children she'd seen earlier that day in the ghetto. And she was certain that if everyone knew the truth about Karl, he would be sitting on the floor along with the others. She wondered if someone had learned the truth about Karl and had taken him and sent him off to the ghetto, or worse. A shiver went through her. She wrapped the blanket around her more tightly. Then she put her head in her hands and wept.

Once she'd spent all of her tears, Kara began to pray. She begged God to watch over her son. She told God how much she missed Abram. And she prayed until she fell asleep.

It was late afternoon, almost evening, when there was a knock on the door. Kara woke abruptly. The knock on the door brought her back to the night she was arrested. Her heart pounded. She felt a wave of heat come over her. But then she heard Anka's voice, and she relaxed.

"Kara, it's me. Please, let me in."

Kara opened the door, and Anka walked in, her face still red from the cold. Her azure eyes were glistening as if she might have been crying. *She is still so beautiful*, Kara thought.

"I'm sorry, Kara. I was a louse. Please forgive me. I didn't finish shopping. It was no fun without you. So, I came back to the hotel right after you left and went to my room. I knew you were angry with me, and I was afraid to come to you. But I love you, Kara. I hate it when we fight."

"I know." Kara took her sister into a hug. "I

know."

"I just took you to that place because I wanted you to have a good time. I never wanted to upset you."

"It's all right."

"It's not. You don't understand," Anka said, looking down at the floor.

"What don't I understand, Anka?"

"It's our right as Germans."

"What is our right, exactly?"

"To control the lesser species. Not only the Jews, because they are not even human. But all of the lesser species. It is for their own good. Now, don't get me wrong, the Jews must be watched and controlled. They are dangerous. You don't know because you have only had limited contact with them. But Ludwig told me. I understand that when you see their children on the floor playing, and they look like children. But believe me, Kara, they are not ordinary children. They are Jews, and they will grow up to be treacherous, just like their parents."

"I know you believe that."

"I wish you could talk to Ludwig. He is so much better at explaining all of this. I only know what he has told me. And it seems right. He said that it's not only the Jews we need to control. We have to take charge of the Poles and the other Slavic people as well. We need to colonize them. Once this fighting is over, and Germany has conquered the East, the Slavics will take their rightful place as slaves to the Aryans."

"Slaves?"

"Yes. That's what Ludwig said. He explained that Germany lost so much land when the treaty of Versailles was signed. The Germans don't have enough land to stretch and grow. So our führer is sending us east to colonize the land that is rightfully ours. And, like the Americas did with redskins, we have the right to take the spoils."

"Anka, that's horrible."

"I don't understand how you could say that. You are a German. You should be glad that we are no longer at the bottom. It's been too long that Germany has been kept down. If we are to rise to our rightful status as the greatest of world powers, then sacrifices must be made. It's just that simple. Ludwig says it's always that way in a war."

"The sacrifices must be made by the Slavics, the Polish, and the Jews?"

"And anyone else who is not an Aryan."

"What would happen if you were personally asked to make sacrifices in the name of the fatherland? What would you say?"

"I have been asked, and I made them," Anka said, hanging her head. "I made them because it was necessary. But it was hard. Believe me, I paid a dear price to be where I am."

"Oh, you made sacrifices? And how is that? By marrying Ludwig, because he was a good party member even though you were not in love with him? It seems to me that he turned out to be a good husband to you. He treats you well. You have everything you need or want. You never go hungry . . ."

"Shut up, Kara. Stop talking. Please." Anka slammed her fist on the writing table. "There are things you don't know." Anka stood up, walked over to the window. She turned away from Kara and looked outside.

"Then tell me . . ." Kara persisted.

"All right. You want to know? I'll tell you," Anka said as she whirled around to face her sister. Her face was flushed, and her hands were clenching and unclenching as she went on. "Do you remember when I told you that I miscarried?"

"Yes, of course I remember."

"Well, I didn't. I didn't miscarry at all. My son was born. He let out a cry. I heard his voice. I'll never forget that sound. He was alive. I looked into his tiny face, and I touched his little hands. The fingers were tiny, ever so tiny." She swallowed, and tears formed in her eyes, then she steeled herself and looked directly at Kara. "But you know what? He was deformed. A deformed child is doomed to suffer. My little boy was born with a hair lip." Anka put her head in her hands. "You see, you must understand. It wasn't her fault. You must understand that. The midwife was a good German woman who was only doing her job. When I saw the baby, I knew she had to report it. And she was kind. She stroked my hair as she explained to me that it was for his own good."

"What are you talking about?" Kara felt sick to her stomach. "What are you trying to say?"

"I'm telling you what happened, Kara. I'm telling you why my son had to be euthanized. Why I had to place him in the arms of that woman and watch her carry him away, all the while knowing I would never see him again. He whimpered, Kara, he whimpered, and he looked at me. I wanted to scream. But no one would listen. I knew no one would listen. After she, that midwife, disappeared carrying my little boy, I got up out of the bed and tried to chase her, but I fell. Blood ran from my womb onto the white tile floor. I tried to get up. I wanted to stop them, but my body was too weak. Even so, even as I lay there on the floor bleeding, I knew that they would not stop. That is because my child's death was for the good of the fatherland. It was a sacrifice I had to make for the good of the future of our Aryan people." Anka was weeping. "I will never forget him, Kara. Never. I will never forget how it felt to hold him in my arms, and to inhale his essence. He was so small and helpless. My heart ached. I wanted to take him and run away. But when it was over, I knew I had done the right thing." Anka was trembling. "As I lay on the floor bleeding, the midwife called out to me. She was already down the hall, but she called out to me from the hall and said, 'You are doing the right thing, Anka. And don't worry, he won't even feel it.' After that, I knew that I never wanted to get pregnant again because I was afraid my child would be born with a defect, and I couldn't bear to have another child of mine euthanized."

"How could you do it?" Kara looked at her sister, stunned by what she'd just heard.

"Because it was the right thing to do. I am loyal to the Reich. I know what a woman's responsibilities are, and sometimes we must suffer in silence for the greater good of our country."

Anka was then wailing in great sobs, coming from deep in her throat. Kara felt the blood leave her face as she got up and went over to her sister. She took Anka into her arms the way she did when they were children and Anka was scared. "Oh, Anka, I had no idea."

There was a soft knock on the door.

"Who is it?" Kara jumped a little.

"Oskar."

Kara let him in. She wondered if she would ever get over that terrible night. She wondered if she would be alarmed every time someone knocked on the door, and if it would last for the rest of her life.

"Did you girls have a nice day?" Oskar asked. But then he saw that Anka was crying. "Oh, I am so sorry for interrupting," he said.

"It's all right. Really," Anka said, wiping her tearstained face with the back of her hand.

"Shall I go?" Oskar asked Kara.

"Are you sure you're all right?" Kara asked Anka.

"Yes." Anka forced a smile, then in a high voice she said with fake enthusiasm. "And . . . I'm hungry. Is anyone else hungry?"

"Yes, I'm starving as matter of fact!" Oskar tried to sound glib, but Kara knew by his tone of voice that he was concerned. Then he asked, "So, let's all get dressed and go for dinner. Kara, what do you think of that little German place around the corner, the one with the excellent schnitzel? Do you think Anka and Ludwig would enjoy it?"

"Yes, absolutely," Kara forced herself to sound cheerful.

"Well then, let's get ready," Anka said.

Anka stood up and looked at Kara. There was so much gratitude in Anka's eyes that Kara felt almost guilty for having ruined her sister's visit.

"Yes, let's get ready." Kara smiled at Anka.

After Oskar and Anka left, Kara washed up and changed her dress. She was so perplexed. Her heart ached for Anka, but she was angry at her too. *How horrible it must have been for her to condemn her own child to death. But I don't understand how she could do it. How could she hand her baby over to a stranger knowing that stranger was going to kill him? I would never have done it. No matter how Karl had been born, I would not have let them hurt him. They would have had to kill me first. How is it that my sister, my dearest Anka, believes in these Nazis so much that she let them have her son? She just handed them her child, her own flesh and blood. And now she tells me that it was for the good of the fatherland? Who has she become? Dear God, who has my baby sister become?*

# CHAPTER TWENTY

THE TWO COUPLES stood outside the hotel. Anka was wearing the fur coat that she'd bought for Kara that afternoon. It was a beautiful full-length, white ermine. But when Kara looked at it, all she could see were the Jewish children sitting on the floor telling their mothers that they were hungry. She saw their faces, dirty, and bony, and she felt sick.

"Shall we take the auto?" Oskar asked. "It's about a four-street walk from here to the restaurant. However, it's quite cold out tonight."

"I don't mind the walk, but it's up to the ladies," Ludwig said.

"I don't mind either," Anka said.

Kara nodded. "Let's walk, then."

Oskar linked Kara's arm through his as they walked to the German restaurant. The wind blew an icy chill through her, but she didn't say a word.

She knew if she mentioned the cold, Anka would bring up the coat. And that was the last thing she wanted to discuss. Instead, she just watched her breath form white clouds as they strolled down the streets of Warsaw.

When they arrived at the restaurant, they were seated at a table in the back with a red-and-white tablecloth and a single handmade paper flower in a vase. Anka and Ludwig were telling Oskar how much they missed Germany and how much they loved going to authentic German restaurants. "Well, this one is very authentic," Oskar said with a smile. Kara didn't speak. It made her sad when she considered that a German restaurant was able to acquire so much food, even during the winter, while just a few kilometers away Jews were starving.

"So, what shall we have for dinner, my love?" Oskar broke through Kara's thoughts as he turned to face her. A tall, slender waiter had come over and was handing them their menus. Then Oskar turned to Ludwig and Anka. "The schnitzel here is the best I've found in Warsaw."

"Then it's decidedly schnitzel for me," Ludwig said.

"I'll have the same," Anka added, closing her menu.

"And you, love? The schnitzel?"

"Yes, perfect." Kara nodded, handing Oskar the menu.

"Schnitzel all around. And a pitcher of beer. Everyone like beer?" Oskar asked.

Ludwig and Anka nodded.

"I'll have a tea," Kara said.

After they ordered, Ludwig turned to Oskar. "You really should take a few days away from here and come to see the lair. I'm quite proud of it."

"And well you should be. I've heard that the führer was impressed."

"He seemed to be." Ludwig smiled. "So will you come? Perhaps I might get a day or two off. We could leave the girls and go on a hunting trip."

"I haven't been hunting since I was boy," Oskar said.

"I went a couple of weeks ago. We weren't able to find any animals. So, one of the fellows I work with had a brilliant idea. He had a friend who lived on an estate right near one of those "centers," if you know what I mean."

Oskar looked at him and frowned. But Ludwig hardly noticed.

Then Ludwig continued, "A center," he said again. "So, we went to stay with his friend at the estate, and his friend arranged to have a few Jews set free so that we could hunt them. Three of them were old and not much of a challenge. But two of them were teens, a boy and a girl. We took the girl down first. The boy was rather crafty and more fun. But in the end, we got him."

Kara dropped the piece of bread she was buttering and stared at Ludwig in disbelief. But he went on talking as if he had no idea that what he'd just said was appalling.

"Anyway, they were all a bit slow because of the snow, even the boy. But it was rather fun. They were more intriguing than deer or rabbits. And like I said, in the end we got them, all of them. It didn't matter to them because if we hadn't shot them, they were scheduled to be shot in a mass killing the following week. So, we relieved them from their misery a week early." Ludwig took a hunk of bread from a basket on the table and bit off a piece. Kara watched him chew and felt disgust. Then Ludwig said to Oskar, "You just let me know when you're coming, and I'll have my friend make the same arrangements for us. I think you'll enjoy it. You'll find it to really be quite exhilarating."

"I'd love to, Ludwig. However, I am quite busy here in Warsaw with Kara. We are on an important mission, trying to find Karl. I am sorry, I don't have the time."

There were a few awkward moments of silence. Then Kara said, "You hunted and killed people? Human beings? Ludwig?"

"Jews. Not humans. Jews, Kara," Ludwig corrected her.

"Ludwig. I am appalled. You shot and murdered people? I can't believe you did that." Kara was shaking.

"It's sport, Kara. And you shouldn't worry yourself. I know you are the sensitive sort. Anka doesn't like me to hunt either. However, you must understand it not people we are hunting. I would never do such a thing. These are untermenschen. Subhumans. There are so many of them, and they are like a pestilence. The Jews, the Gypsies, all of them. They're swarming like insects through the eastern lands. We Germans must rid ourselves of these vermin one way or another. They will either be shot by a firing squad, or we can use them for sport. In the end, it's all the same."

Kara stared at her brother-in-law, unable to speak. *How could a man who is so kind to his wife and who had always been kind to me and Karl, be capable of such senseless murders?* Then she thought of Abram. *He had killed a man. But that's different, isn't it? He did it to protect me. Ludwig believes he is doing this to protect the fatherland. Hunting and killing human beings. Dear God, what horrors will these people think of next?*

The food arrived. Kara couldn't eat. She stared at Ludwig in disbelief as he finished his plate with pleasure, sopping up the sauce with a hunk of bread. Anka was her jovial self. She was laughing and telling jokes to Oskar. Kara was amazed that she didn't seem at all phased by what Ludwig had said. But Oskar caught Kara's glance and he nodded. "I know you're upset," he whispered in her ear. "What he said is horrible. Don't think about it, love. There is nothing you can do." He took her hand and kissed it. "Please . . . eat," he said. Then he whispered in her ear, "I want you to know that I can't stop others from doing what they do. But I am not Ludwig. I would never do such a thing. You must know that."

She nodded. She believed him. But she still couldn't eat.

As they walked back to the hotel, Ludwig and Oskar walked together, behind the girls.

"Let's let them talk," Ludwig said. "Anka misses her sister so. I was really glad we were able to come."

"Yes, I think it's good for both of them to have time together," Oskar said. "This ordeal is very hard on Kara."

"Do you think you'll find the boy?" he asked.

"I hope so. I am trying my best," Oskar said.

"If you don't, it will take time, but I think she'll get over it."

"I doubt that. Kara is devoted to her son. I understand her. She is a good mother. She will be a good mother to our children too."

"Yes, well, let's hope you find the child. He was a nice boy. I liked him. And it's really a shame what happened," Ludwig said.

Oskar nodded.

"Is she always so sad?" Ludwig asked.

"Yes, she is."

"Have you tried to distract her while you are searching for the boy?"

"I've tried. We've gone to the zoo and, of

course, to restaurants. But I can understand her. I know that all she can think about is her child."

"Perhaps you should take her to a film where she has something to concentrate on rather than her own problems."

"A film?"

They continued to walk. "Yes. It might be a good distraction. Have you heard about the new film that is in the theaters? It's called *Karl Paytas*. I think it came out last week. I took Anka to the theater to see it. It was bit brutal for her, lots of blood and that sort of thing. It didn't bother me, but she thought it was crude. Even so, it was entertaining. And during the film it was impossible to think of anything else."

"Oh?" Oskar said.

"Yes, it was about an Aryan man who went to Africa and had to beat the Black natives into submission in order to gain the dominance that was rightfully his. It was a powerful film with a powerful message. You and Kara should go and see it if you can."

"It doesn't sound like a good film for Kara."

"I suppose you're probably right. I only thought that if she went to a film, she would have a few hours to forget her own troubles. But she is quite sensitive right now from losing her son. However, she comes from strong pure blood. Kara and her sister are good German women. You'll see, she'll regain her strength. No matter what happens, she will be the strong, Aryan woman she was born to be."

"Yes, she is a good woman. And I know that she is strong too. But she is also a gentle soul. That's one of the things that I find so endearing about her," Oskar said.

"Yes, and I suppose it's all right that she leans on you rather than her own inner strength. That is as long as she adheres to our motto of women, children, kitchen, and church," Ludwig said, his breath flowing out of his mouth like white smoke from a chimney. "And, in many ways, I do applaud her courage. You do realize that before she met you, she came east. She was a woman alone, without a man. But she still traveled into this unknown territory to meet the demand of our führer. He wants women to leave Germany and to come and settle in the east, you know. So, there is much to be said for that."

"Yes, I agree." Oskar cleared his throat, then he added, "I realize that she is strong. And when she is not, I will be her strength, no matter where we live. Whether it be in the east or back in Germany."

"Poor thing. I really do hope you find her boy."

"I hope so too," Oskar said.

After dinner they all returned to the hotel and went up to Ludwig and Anka's room. Ludwig ordered a bottle of schnapps to be brought up to his room. While they were waiting for the schnapps, Ludwig suggested, "Why don't we all play a board game? It's our last night here. Let's have a few drinks and play. We don't need to go to bed so early."

"That would be fun, wouldn't it?" Anka chimed in. "Ludwig loves to play board games. So he suggested that we bring one of the more popular board games with us when we came to Warsaw. It's lots of fun. We play it all time with our neighbors."

"All right," Kara said, wishing she could go back to her room and be alone. At the same time, she knew that Anka and Ludwig would be leaving in the morning, and she didn't want to disappoint Anka again. *It's only a few more hours. I know I am not good company, but I can do my best.*

The four of them gathered around a table in the corner of Ludwig and Anka's room. Anka took a leather suitcase out of the closet. Inside was a board game. She laid it out on the table. Kara studied the pictures on the board. There were German settlers dressed up like American cowboys. In the center of the board, it read "It is the duty of the Aryan race to Germanize the east the same way the Americans had to clear out the savages in order to claim the land that was rightfully theirs."

"So, the object of the game is to move the Aryans into the fertile eastern territory. You must clear out the Slavics on the way," Ludwig said.

"Oh," Kara said. Then she added, "Don't you do any game that is just a game? I mean, something that isn't a part of Goebbels' propaganda machine?"

"Kara!" Anka said. "Can't we just play this simple game without you making everything into a problem? Everyone loves this game. It's just a board game, Kara, not a contract you're signing. You needn't be so serious." Then she laughed a little. "Ludwig and I hardly expect you to dress up like a cowboy and conquer the eastern territories."

Kara glared at her sister.

Then Anka glared back and said, "Besides, I don't know why you aren't more grateful for everything our führer is doing for us. I really think you would be wise to try and appreciate all of the efforts our führer is making on our behalf. Every German will benefit. He will see to it."

"Efforts at everyone else's expense," Kara huffed.

There was a knock at the door. It was the desk clerk with the schnapps. Kara and Anka were both turned away from each other with their arms crossed over their chests. Ludwig took the bottle and tipped the clerk. Then he closed the door.

Once they were alone, Oskar said, "Girls, please don't fight. This is Anka and Ludwig's last night here. Let's try to enjoy it."

"He's right," Ludwig said. "It's not necessary that we play this silly game. Let's all have a glass of schnapps and toast to Kara and Oskar's engagement." Ludwig poured them each a glass of schnapps. "To a beautiful future. May you both live long and happy lives together."

"Prost! Ein Toast!" Ludwig said.

They all drank.

"Let's talk about wedding plans," Ludwig suggested. "I really think you should consider getting married at the lair."

"Yes, you mentioned that before," Oskar said, then he continued, "There is no doubt that the lair is an impressive venue; however, it's not quite what I had in mind for the wedding. I was thinking of possibly taking a trip to Munich, or Cologne, or even to Wannsee to get married. I thought it would be nice to enjoy a relaxing week or so away from Warsaw."

"How is it you are able to get so much time off from work? I can't always get as much time as I would like," Ludwig asked.

"I'm rather close friends with the reichsführer."

"Really, how impressive. Himmler is quite the man. In fact, I don't know if you are aware of it, but they say he is the reincarnation of King Henry Fowler. The first king of Germany."

"Yes, I know," Oskar said, trying to hide the sarcasm he felt. But Kara knew him well enough to know what he was feeling. Then Oskar continued, "I've been to his home. It's actually decorated to look like the home of King Fowler."

"I would love to see it. Perhaps you will take me one day?" Ludwig asked.

"Perhaps. I would have to get his permission, of

course." Oskar smiled. Then he reached for Kara's hand and said, "Kara . . . what do you think? Would you prefer to have our wedding at the lair, or would you like to get married in a quiet ceremony in Wannsee perhaps?"

"I don't know. I can't think about a celebration right now. I won't be able to think about getting married until we find Karl."

Anka looked at Kara. "I'm sorry about the way I acted before. I don't know what gets into me sometimes. But I am sorry. I should be more understanding. Of course you don't feel like playing a board game," she said. Then she stood up and walked over to Kara. She put her hand on Kara's shoulder. "Children are so important to a woman," Anka said to Oskar. "You must find Karl."

Kara glanced up at her sister. Anka had tears in her eyes. And Kara thought about all that Anka had told her about euthanizing her own child. *She is hurting. But her belief in all of this Nazi rhetoric is so strong that she did what was expected of her. My poor sister. My poor dear sister.* Kara reached up and put her hand on Anka's.

# CHAPTER TWENTY-ONE

## Warsaw 1942

KARL HAD BEEN MISSING for several months already. And with each day that passed, Kara was falling deeper and deeper into depression. Oskar received a call demanding that he return to work for a while. "I'll only be gone a week or two. Why don't you ask your sister to come to Warsaw to stay with you while I am gone? Or perhaps you would prefer to go and stay with her."

"If cost isn't a problem, I'd prefer to stay here at the hotel. Alone."

"It's no problem. You know that. But it concerns me to think of you here in the city all by yourself. I know how miserable you've been, and I would feel better if someone were here with you."

"I would rather be alone, Oskar. I'll be fine. I'll just stay in the hotel and wait for you to return."

Kara wondered if Oskar was being charged for their stay or if the Polish-owned hotel was accommodating them for free because he was in the SS. The hotel owner had spoken to them many times when they were in the restaurant, asking them how they were enjoying their stay at the hotel. He knew of Karl's disappearance, and he offered to be of help in any way possible.

"Kara, I must tell you that I am truly worried about you. I really don't want to leave you here alone."

"Then take me with you," she suggested. "I don't want to see Anka. Not now. I mean, I love her, yes. But it's too hard to be around her the way I am feeling."

"I can't take you with me. I wish I could. But it's work, my love. You know I will return as soon as I can."

"What are we going to do about Karl? I am losing hope, Oskar."

"I know. I know," he said. "But please don't lose hope. I am going to speak to the reichsführer. I will ask him if he can help us in any way."

"What exactly do you do, Oskar?"

"Top-secret work, my love. I can't discuss it. But I promise you it has nothing to do with the sordid business of Jews or Gypsies."

"So, will you see Herr Himmler when you go back to work?"

"Yes, he is coming for a visit. That's why I must return. I must be there when he arrives. It's important."

"I see. When are you leaving?"

"In the morning."

She nodded.

"Are you sure you'll be all right here all alone in this hotel?"

"Yes, I'll be fine."

Kara thought her nerves would shatter. She remembered the night she was arrested, and she shivered. Now, Oskar was leaving, and she would be alone. If she needed Oskar, she would have no way of reaching him. Still, she would rather be alone and frightened, then have Anka come and stay with her.

# CHAPTER TWENTY-TWO

IN THE MORNING when Oskar and Kara were having breakfast, he handed her an envelope. "Here are some reichsmarks. This should hold you until I return."

"Thank you," she said, taking the envelope. "I hope you know how much I appreciate all of your efforts to help me find Karl."

"I wish you didn't look so sad," he said. "I'll be back soon."

She smiled wistfully. *It's not that you're leaving that is making me sad. It's Karl. I am terrified that he is gone forever. And even though there is no logical reason that the Gestapo would return while you are gone, I am fearful anyway.*

Oskar gave Kara a respectful, modest kiss in front of the hotel before he got into his automobile and drove away. She waved as she watched him leave. After he had turned the corner and was out of sight, she went back upstairs to her room and locked the door behind her. She set a chair in front of the door to help her feel more secure. Then she sat down on the bed and thought of Abram. *Oh, Abram, I wish I had one of your forbidden books to take my mind off everything. It drives me crazy when I think that our little Karl is all alone without either of us. If you are gone, if you are in heaven, I hope you can see him and that you are keeping him safe. I can only pray that wherever he is, someone is taking care of him, feeding him, nurturing him. When I think of those children in the ghetto, I feel such fear for our little boy. I can see their hungry faces. Is Karl one of them now? Or is it even worse, is our child dead? I've heard that as a mother I would feel it if my child had left this world. But I don't know if that's true. And the thought of it all being final with Karl is so terrifying to me that I feel like screaming or hitting my head against the wall. Sometimes I am sure I am going mad. I don't know how much longer I can hold up. Abram, I wish you were here with me.*

Two days passed. Kara did not leave the room. She forgot to eat because Oskar wasn't there to force her to do so. But she did finish the bottle of schnapps that Ludwig and Anka left behind. It helped her to sleep.

On the fifth day after he left, Oskar telephoned.

When the phone rang, it startled Kara. She was almost afraid to answer. It rang again, and she forced herself to pick up the receiver.

"Hello," Kara said.

"It's me. How are you?"

"I'm fine," she answered, relieved to hear his voice and not the voice of a Gestapo agent. "How is your visit with the reichsführer going?"

"It's over. He left. But it went very well." He cleared his throat, then he continued. "I have some good news. He gave me some information about where we might find Karl."

"Oh!" She sighed loudly. "You do?"

"Yes, and it's promising. Very promising."

Kara began to cry.

"Are you all right? I can hear that you're crying," he said.

"Yes, I'm fine. I am just hopeful. Hearing you say that you might have a good lead as to where we can find my son, gives me hope."

"Yes, my love, I do have a very good lead. And because I do, I won't need to be away as long as I originally thought. I'll be returning to you and to Warsaw tomorrow night. So we can start following these leads as soon as possible."

"I can't wait," she said.

"I can't wait to return to you. I've missed you."

"Yes, I've missed you too."

Kara hung up the phone. She was breathing heavily. *I have to pull myself together so we can go and find Karl.* She pushed herself to get up from the bed. Then she went into the bathroom and took her first shower in several days. . *I haven't been out of bed or taken a shower since Oskar left.* As she washed her hair, she felt a surge of hope pulse through her like a transfusion. *Could this be it? Is it possible that Reichs-führer Himmler knows where Karl would have been taken? I don't like Himmler, but right now I feel grateful to him. My entire body is tingling, and I feel closer to finding my son than I have felt in months. This will be a long night, because I can't wait for Oskar to return so we can start looking again.* Kara let the hot water run over her head. It was rejuvenating, cleansing. Then she wrapped herself in one of the white towels from the hotel that had been embroidered with tiny red swastikas. She combed all the knots out of her hair and then picked up the phone and called room service to order a bowl of soup. For the first time in a week, she was hungry.

# CHAPTER TWENTY-THREE

OSKAR RETURNED EARLY the following morning and knocked on the door to Kara's room. She was already awake and dressed. "Who is it?" she asked, still careful, still affected by that horrible night.

"It's me," Oskar said.

Kara flung open the door. "I have such wonderful news," he said as took her into an embrace. She returned his embrace with an enthusiasm she'd never shown him before. His uniform was pressed; his black shoes were shined; his hair was neatly combed, and he smelled of expensive cologne. But his eyes were weary, and his shoulders slumped. She assumed he'd worked hard while he was gone.

"Tell me everything," she said as he walked in, and she closed the door behind him.

They sat on chairs opposite each other in front

of the window. Oskar took Kara's hand and kissed it. "Did you miss me?" he asked.

"Yes, of course," she said, a little too impatiently. Then she added, "Please, Oskar, won't you tell me what you learned from the reichsführer about where we might find Karl?"

"Well," he said, hesitating for a moment, "I brought you a gift."

"Oskar . . . please. Don't make me wait. I am not interested in gifts. I am sorry, I don't mean to be ungrateful, but please. You must tell me what you know."

"All right, all right," he said, smiling. "I explained your situation to the reichsführer, and he told me about a program that is called the hay harvest."

"Hay harvest?" she said. "What is that?"

"Well, it's program where SS officers take Polish children who appear to have German blood, and, shall we say, they Germanize them."

"How does this have anything to do with Karl? He's not Polish."

"He may have been taken by mistake."

"Taken where?"

"To a resettlement home. Perhaps, we think he might have been taken to a home for the Lebensborn."

"Taken by SS officers or the Gestapo by mistake?"

"Exactly. He is a beautiful blond boy. He looks

like a perfect Aryan child. Of course, that is because he is a perfect Aryan child. However, the officers who took him probably thought he was a little Polish boy who looked German."

"Where is he now? Is he all right? I don't know what it means to Germanize someone. All I know is that I want my son. He is just a child, and he is alone. Where is he? Her voice was raised; she wanted to scream. Kara was shaking. Her nerves were pulled taut.

"Shhh, it's all right. I've made arrangements for the two of us to go to a youth custody camp in Litzmannstadt. We'll leave first thing tomorrow. We could very well find our little boy there."

Kara wanted to beg him to leave immediately. But he'd just returned from a long trip, and she could see that he was exhausted from traveling. As she looked into his eyes, she realized that she'd never even asked him where he had gone, how far from Warsaw his job was. *How rude I am. He does so much for me, the least I could do is show an interest in his work.*

"You never told me where you were going. Was it far?" she said. "You see, I didn't mean to ignore your work; it's just that I didn't want to pry by asking."

"You could never pry, my love. But I assumed you had enough on your mind. I didn't want to bother you with my work."

"So, where *did* you go?"

"Nuremberg. I had meetings to attend. Nothing to trouble your pretty little mind about. Just lots of men talking." He smiled. "You know how those things go."

She didn't know how those things went. She'd never attended a business meeting. And she had no idea what he did exactly. Whenever she asked him about his job, he was always evasive. But the truth was, she didn't care. In fact, she was glad. Kara didn't care what he did for work. She was not interested in listening to him as he told her all about his week. It would have been impossible to concentrate anyway because her heart was aching to leave for Litzmannstadt. It was all she could think about, and although she was sitting beside Oskar and trying to appear excited to see him, inside she was counting the hours until morning.

They had a quick dinner in the hotel restaurant. After they finished eating, Oskar presented Kara with a gold necklace he'd brought for her. She thanked him and he kissed her hand.

"How I have missed you," he said.

"I missed you too."

"I hope you like the necklace."

"I do, it's beautiful."

"I'm glad. I want so much to please you." Then he touched her cheek gently. "Oh yes, I forgot something. I'll be right back." Oskar went to his room and returned with a large box with a pink bow. "This is also for you."

"Another gift, Oskar? It was really not necessary."

"I didn't get it for you because it was necessary. I got it for you because I think you'll like it." Then he smiled, and for a moment she thought he looked like a little boy who had just given his mother flowers. Her heart grew soft. "Open it," he said excitedly.

She slowly removed the ribbon and opened the box to reveal a magnificent mink coat with a champagne-colored silk lining. "Oh, Oskar," she gasped.

"Anka mentioned that you needed a coat. I agreed so I got you one. I hope like it."

"Of course I do. It's beautiful."

"I'm glad," he said. "The woman on the arm of an SS officer should have all the wonderful things that life has to offer."

"Anka mentioned that she took you to that horrible ghetto to buy a used coat from a Jew. If I had known she planned to do that I would never have approved. So, I went to a furrier and bought you a coat."

She leaned over and planted a quick kiss on his lips. "You are so kind and good to me," she whispered.

"I love you."

Kara took his hand and kissed it. Then she smiled. "We should get to sleep. You must be exhausted after traveling all day."

"I am, but I could spend all night just looking at

you." Then he added. "But I suppose you're right. We should both get some sleep. We have a long drive in the morning."

She nodded. He motioned the waiter over and paid the check. Then he walked her back to her room.

"Good night, my love," he said.

"Good night."

He kissed her passionately and held her tightly. Then he whispered in her ear, "Sleep well. Wouldn't it be wonderful if, once we have Karl back home with us, we could get married and be a real family."

# CHAPTER TWENTY-FOUR

OSKAR WENT BACK to his room. He sat down on the bed. A smile came over his face.

*I am truly superior, he thought. Kara loved the coat. I was smart enough to set my superior officer up with my young secretary so he wouldn't be around. If he had been, I would never have been able to steal a necklace and a coat. But as luck would have it, I got into the supply of goods that the Reich has stored, the stuff they take from the Jews who arrive at Auschwitz and go directly to the gas. There is no doubt that there are some beautiful and valuable things in there. And my darling Kara, who would never think of shopping in the Jewish ghetto, will never know that her gifts came from that special place. That place the prisoners call Kanada.*

# CHAPTER TWENTY-FIVE

KARA DID NOT SLEEP at all. She was far too excited and couldn't wait to be on her way to Litzmannstadt. All night she prayed, "Please God, let Karl be there."

Kara was out of bed and dressed before sunrise the following day. She tapped her fingers on the desk as she waited for Oskar to knock on her door. He would want breakfast before they made the drive to Litzmannstadt, and she wished she could just wake him up so they could get started. But she knew he was tired, and it would be insensitive to wake him. She looked at the clock. It was almost 6:00 a.m. Soon the sun would rise, and she hoped the light shining through his window would wake him. Now that she felt she was so close, the anticipation of seeing her son was heightened. Every minute that she waited seemed like forever. Her mouth was dry; her palms were sweaty. Again, she looked at the clock. It was after seven. Her heart raced. Then finally there was the knock on the door. She jumped. "Who is it?"

Oskar's familiar voice announced, "Kara, it's me."

She flung the door open.

"My goodness, you're ready to go," he said with a wide smile.

"Yes, I am. You're all dressed too."

"So I am," he said. "Let's have a quick breakfast and be on our way. How does that sound?"

"Wonderful. I can't wait." Then she added, "Oh, Oskar, could this be it? Could it be that we have found Karl?" she asked as they walked down to the restaurant in the hotel lobby.

"It could be," he said. "It could very well be."

Kara was a bundle of nerves. She couldn't eat anything. Oskar tried to entice her with eggs and sausages, but her stomach was in knots, and all she could manage was black coffee.

Before they left the restaurant, Oskar asked the waiter to pack some bread and cheese for them to take with them. Then he turned to Kara. "Just in case you get hungry on the drive," he said.

"You do think of everything."

"I try. It is my greatest wish that someday soon you will come to the realization that you love me."

Kara studied him for a moment. He smiled, but his eyes were sad. Taking his hand, she lifted it to her lips. "You are a wonderful man," she said. "I am very fortunate to have you in my life."

"I try to be a good man." He hesitated for a moment, then let out a long sigh. "Still, you don't love me. I know that. And still, more than anything, I want to be your husband." He glanced over at her as they walked to the car. Then he added, "I am afraid you are still in love with Karl's father, whoever that may be."

There was a lot of truth to what he'd just said, and there was no denying it. "I care deeply for you," she said. "You have been wonderful through all of this."

"I don't know how to ask you this. But it often plagues me so I must ask."

"Go on, please feel free to ask me anything," she said.

"It's rather personal. I hope I won't offend you, but . . . well . . . Kara . . ." His voice was shaky. "Do you ever want to feel me close to you? Have you ever wanted to wake up in the morning with me beside you? I don't mean to be crude. But you are my fiancée, and I have never tried to make love to you because I am afraid of upsetting you."

"Oh, Oskar," she said, "you aren't offending me. I know you are in love with me. You are kind and good, and the answer is, yes, I have often wanted to feel you close to me. But I can't think about romance right now. My mind is so focused on Karl." It was lie. She'd never wanted to feel his skin against hers because it would feel as if she were being unfaithful to Abram. *Abram is not here. He is a memory now.* She looked into Oskar's eyes. *You must live for today, not live in the past*, she reminded herself.

"It hurts me to know that you do not give your affection to me freely. And, of course, I would never force you," Oskar said.

"I do feel affection for you. And it is very real. It's just hard for me to think about making love right now with my son missing."

"Perhaps once we find him, you will reconsider your agreeing to marry me. Perhaps you will change your mind and decide you don't want to be my wife. I have often been afraid that might happen."

*Will I change my mind? I don't know. I need a partner in my life. And my son will need a father. If he is alive. Dear God, please let him be alive.*

"What are you thinking, Kara?"

She shook her head, unable to speak, unable to share her thoughts with him. *What will I do if Oskar loses interest in me before we find Karl? What will I do if he decides to walk away because we don't have anything physical between us? He knows, somehow, that I am still in love with someone else. He senses it.* She looked at Oskar, studying him as if it were the first time she'd ever seen him. He was tall and strong in his SS uniform. And it surprised her to realize that over the last few months she'd grown used to seeing the uniform. It no longer offended her as it had in the beginning. Oskar was handsome too. Charming and kind. *I wonder, if I had never met Abram, would I have fallen in love with Oskar?*

Instinctively, she knew what he needed. Just before they got into the car, she went over to Oskar and put her arms around his neck. They were standing outside surrounded by people who were walking by. Kara didn't care. She kissed him, letting her lips linger on his for a long time.

He sighed.

"I am going to marry you as soon as we find Karl. I will not change my mind. And we are going to be happy together," she whispered. Then she got into the car.

Oskar got behind the wheel and they headed out.

"How far is the drive to Litzmannstadt," Kara asked as they pulled out of the parking space and joined the procession of cars on the street.

"It's about two hours from here to the children's center."

Kara's lips trembled as she smiled at him. Then she reached over to touch his hand. Still watching the road, he took her hand and kissed it. He glanced over at her and smiled.

Kara could feel that the kiss she'd given Oskar had brightened his mood. And she was glad. As he drove, he talked about buying a home for the three of them. Kara listened, but inside she was a bundle of nerves, counting the minutes until they arrived.

Two hours later, they were in Litzmannstadt.

Oskar turned a corner and pulled into the parking lot of a large government building; he double-checked the address. Then he turned to Kara and said, "This is it. This is the children's welfare office." Kara was shaking but she managed to nod. Oskar got out of the automobile, then he walked around to open Kara's door. He saw that she was trembling, so he helped her climb out of the car. Taking her arm, he squeezed it gently and said, "It's going to be all right."

They entered the building. It looked like any other office building that was German run. It was immaculate, and there were Nazi flags and pictures of the führer everywhere. "Sit down, love. I'll find out where we should go from here," Oskar said, indicating a group of chairs in the waiting area.

Kara did as he asked. Her eyes were glued to his back as she watched him walk up to the desk where he was greeted by a pretty, young secretary. Even from where she sat, Kara could see the admiration in the girl's eyes when she looked up to see Oskar. It was apparent to Kara in way the girl gazed at him as she put down the papers she had been working on. And in the way she cocked her head and smiled. Then when the sweet, flirtatious laughter rose from her, Kara thought, *He must be so flattered.* And for a moment, she felt a pang of jealousy as she wondered if she was as pretty as this young blonde secretary who was carefree and vivacious. *I have been miserable for so long that I am beginning to look like an old woman.* Kara sighed; *It doesn't matter. The only thing that really matters to me is that we find Karl.* All the same, Kara couldn't help but feel relieved when she saw that Oskar gave no indication of flirting back.

A few minutes later, Oskar returned to Kara. "Follow me. I know exactly where to go," he said, taking her arm as she stood up.

They walked through a long hallway filled with offices on either side. *There seem to be so many of them. They look like ants, or mice,* Kara thought. Secretaries, wearing skirts and blouses, carried piles of papers as they rushed by. SS officers in uniform stood around talking to each other. When the officers saw Oskar, they saluted: "Heil Hitler."

"Heil Hitler," Oskar said.

Kara, unenthusiastically, repeated the greeting: "Heil Hitler."

The officers gazed at Kara and smiled at Oskar approvingly.

He nodded at them, and Kara thought she could see his chest swell with pride.

When they arrived at a door at the end of a corridor, Oskar knocked. A woman with wiry gray hair opened the door.

"Heil Hitler," the woman said.

"Heil Hitler, and good day, Frau. I'm Oberstrumführer Oskar Lerch, and I am here because I am looking for someone."

"This is the verification area. The adoption area is just a few doors down from here."

"Verification area?" Kara asked.

"Yes, Frau Lerch," the woman said, assuming Kara was Oskar's wife. "This is where we test to make sure that the children we accept for adoption are of Aryan blood, and therefore suitable for adoption by pure German couples."

*My son is part Jewish. He is alone with these people, and he has Jewish blood. Is there any chance that they can tell by their tests? Is that even possible? Dear God, protect my little boy.* "Oh." Kara tried to sound casual. "How do you do that? I mean what kind of tests do you perform?"

"It's quite a process. Come in. If you would like to see what we do, I would be happy to show you."

"And who are you?" Oskar asked, annoyed.

"I am Frau Kraus, Oberstrumführer. I am employed by the children's welfare agency; I am a brown sister."

"A brown sister?" Kara asked.

"Yes, I work for the welfare agency, but because I don't have the right coloring. As you can see, my hair and eyes are reddish brown, so I cannot be a part of the breeding program in the Lebensborn. Only blonde-haired, blue-eyed women are acceptable."

"I see." He nodded as they walked in. "I'm looking for Frau Moller."

"I'm sorry. I don't know her," Frau Kraus said.

"She is employed here," Oskar insisted.

"I don't doubt you. However, there are so many employees here."

When they walked into the examination room, Kara gasped. It was a large room, painted white. There were blond-haired, blue-eyed children of all ages, most of them wide eyed and frightened, sitting on chairs that looked far too big for them. Some of the children were crying. Others just looked around the room terrified. Doctors, nurses, and more women wearing the uniform of the brown sisters were everywhere. They were measuring the children's skulls, and their noses, checking their eye color against a chart of some kind.

"I want my mother," one little girl of about five or six said to Kara as they walked by. "Do you know my mother? Please, bring me to her. I know she is looking for me. Please, I want my mother."

"Shut up. I can't measure you when you're talking," a young, heavyset brown sister, who was measuring the child's nose, reprimanded the child, then she continued. "Don't ever speak unless you are spoken to."

"Excuse her, she was just brought in. She has not yet been Germanized," the brown sister said, speaking directly to Oskar then glancing over at Kara and nodding to include her.

Oskar returned the nod. Kara glanced up at him. He gently squeezed her arm. "It will be all right," he said.

Then Oskar turned to Frau Klaus. "My fiancée

brought a picture of her son. We would like to know if he has come through here."

"Let me see the picture," Frau Klaus said, looking at Kara.

Kara's hands were trembling as she took a photograph out of her purse. "I am afraid the picture isn't recent. It's about a year old. But perhaps you might recognize him?" Kara said hopefully.

Frau Klaus took the photo and stared at it for a moment. "He has long hair like a girl," she said, laughing a little. "I must tell you, that I don't know if I have seen him or not. So many children pass through here, and it's hard to recall each one of them."

"How can I find him?" Kara's voice was cracking. She was holding back the tears.

"Try the adoption room. He may be there. Just walk down the hall; it's the last door on the right. If he's not there, they may know where to send you."

Kara nodded; her lower lip quivered.

"Thank you, Frau Klaus. How silly of me. I thought this was the adoption room," Oskar said, putting his hand on Kara's shoulder and leading her out of the room.

She was dizzy, and for a moment she had to grip the wall. Oskar put his arm around her waist to steady her. "Are you all right? If this is too much for you, we can go and have some coffee and then come back later."

"I have to find out if they have Karl," Kara said.

"All right, come with me, then." There was a black sign on a white door down the hall that said, Adoption Room.

Oskar knocked on the door. A freckled woman with red hair and eyes that were so light blue they looked almost white, opened it. "Yes? Are you a couple looking to adopt?" she asked cheerfully.

"I would like to see Frau Moller. I am Oberstrumführer Lerch; the reichsführer sent me."

The redhead's eyes opened wide at hearing the mention of the reichsführer. "Of course. I'll get her for you right away. Please, won't you have a seat? Would you care for some tea or coffee?"

Oskar looked at Kara. "Would you like something?"

"No, thank you," she said.

The redheaded brown sister left them and walked to an office in the back. A few minutes later, a sturdy-looking woman came up to Oskar and Kara: "Heil Hitler," she said.

"Heil Hitler," Oskar repeated. Then he looked at Kara.

"Heil Hitler," Kara said weakly.

"I'm Frau Moller. You wanted to see me?" She looked directly at Oskar, then her lips formed a half smile.

"Yes, my fiancée and I have come here searching for her son. There is a possibility that he may have been taken by mistake. He is a pure Aryan child. This is his mother, and as you can see, I am an SS officer, and I would be his father. We are hoping that you might have seen him come through here. Perhaps he is still here. We have a photograph. Let me show you," Oskar said, then he turned to Kara, who handed him the picture of Karl. Oskar handed it to Frau Moller. She was silent for a few moments.

"Yes," she said, nodding her head. "He looks very familiar. We don't often have little boys come through here with such long, curly hair."

"He's a little older now. The photo was taken a year ago," Oskar said.

"Yes, the more I look at the picture, the more I am sure I do recall this little boy coming through here. We had to cut his hair, of course." She let out a short laugh. "But other than that, he passed all of his physical exams beautifully. There is no doubt that he is a pure Aryan and a perfect child for the Reich."

Kara was shaking. "Where is he? Please, tell me. Is he here? Can I see him? Please . . ."

"He isn't here. I'm afraid that we only work with older children at this location. If I recall correctly, this little boy was sent to a home for the Lebensborn in Munich, where he will be put up for adoption. He may already have been adopted."

Kara let out a moan.

"Don't worry too much. We only release children to parents of pure blood. SS officers and their wives mostly. There is plenty of paperwork, so you might be just in time."

Kara felt the room begin to spin and grow dark around her. It was hot in the room, and the heat was making her nauseated. "I feel sick, like I might faint," she said. Then she felt Oskar's arm at her waist, steadying her, holding her up. *Thank God for him. I don't know what I would do without him.*

Oskar turned to Kara and said, "Let's go outside so you can get some air. Then I'll leave you in the car, and I'll come back inside to get all the information and paperwork we'll need to find Karl. As soon as I have everything we will need to take him home from the institution, we'll head straight for Munich. I promise you we will be on our way to your son within the hour." Then he turned to Frau Moller and said, "I'll be right back."

Oskar helped Kara outside. She gulped the fresh air for a few moments. Then he opened the door to the car and helped her inside. "I know it's cold out here. But I think that heavy heat in the building was making you ill. Continue to take deep breaths."

She sucked in the cold air greedily.

"Now, I am going back inside to get the paperwork. You stay here in the car and breathe deeply. I won't be gone a minute," Oskar said.

·  ·  ·

SHE NODDED. He was right. The cold air helped with her nausea. "Oskar . . ."

"Yes, love."

"I don't know what I would do without you."

He kissed her forehead. Then closed the car door and walked back into the building.

# CHAPTER TWENTY-SIX

FRAU MOLLER WAS WAITING for Oskar to return. When he walked into her office she whispered eagerly, "So, did it work? Did I do a good job? Does she feel completely dependent on you?"

"You did very well. And yes, she does. Just as I was hoping she would when I arranged for the child to be taken from that old Polish woman's flat," he said.

"She seems quite smitten with you."

"I know. That's what I have been aiming for." Oskar smiled as he reached into the breast pocket of his uniform. "Here. As I promised. This is for you." He handed her an envelope. She took it and quickly put it into her handbag.

"I'm going to buy myself a new bicycle with this," she said, smiling.

He nodded. "Is the paperwork for the child all ready and prepared for me?"

"Of course. And I know you've been to the Lebensborn home in Munich before. So I am certain that you won't be needing directions," she said.

"I have, and I know how to get there. But all of this must look legitimate for Kara's sake. So, won't you quickly write up some directions for me."

"Of course. Give me a moment and I'll type them up."

"Hurry, please. It's cold outside. Kara is sitting in the car, and if she gets too cold, she might come back inside."

"I'll only be a moment."

Frau Moller returned in less than five minutes and handed Oskar a large envelope. He looked inside and found a sheet of directions to the home. And several photos of Karl, his face puffy and his eyes red from crying. Oskar saw that his hair had been cut very short. But his bright-blue eyes sparkled. "He is truly a perfect Aryan boy," Oskar said, more to himself than to Frau Moller.

"He cried constantly when he was here. He's soft. Not a strong German boy. He's been coddled. Someone must break him. You're going to have your work cut out for you with him. It was easy to see that he has been held and pampered his entire life because he kept reaching for someone to pick him up and cradle him. As you know, such treatment is not good for a child. It sucks their strength and independence. It is best for a child to be left alone when they are crying. They must learn to cry it out on their own so that they can come to depend on themselves. This one never cried alone before he got here. And his weeping was so loud you could hear him all the way down the hall. Pathetic really."

"His mother adores him," Oskar said, "but don't you worry. I'll work with him once we're married. He'll grow up to be the good German I know he can be. It's in his blood, after all."

"I know you will, Oberstrumführer," she said.

Oskar took the envelope and walked quicky back to the car. He got in and handed the envelope to Kara. She was shaking from the cold. But she took the envelope, her eyes fixed on Oskar. "What's inside? Just directions?"

"No, my love." Then he squeezed her cold hand and said, "We've found him. Take a look inside."

Kara gasped. She opened the envelope so quickly, she almost tore it. Her hands were trembling when she saw the pictures of Karl. "It is him. Dear God, it is him." She held the pictures to her chest. Tears began to run down her cheeks. "It's him."

"Now all we have to do is get to Munich. And of course you know I'll get you there as fast as I can."

Kara lifted Oskar's hand to her lips and kissed it. "God bless you. God bless you," she said as her tears fell onto her new coat.

# CHAPTER TWENTY-SEVEN

IT WAS a long drive from Litzmannstadt Poland to Munich Germany. Kara stared out the window thinking the drive was never-ending. Oskar explained that it would have been better if they had started in the morning. Then they could expect to arrive by early evening. But Kara couldn't wait another minute, let alone a full night. So they began their journey in midafternoon and drove straight through the night.

Oskar suggested that Kara try to sleep during the drive. He gave her a blanket that he kept in the back of the auto to use as a pillow. She rolled the blanket up and put it under her head, then she lay against the window, but she was unable to lie still. They hardly spoke. Hours passed, and then in a small and broken voice, Kara asked, "Oskar, what are we going to do if he has already been adopted?

What then? Will his new parents give him back to me? What will I do if they refuse?"

"You mustn't get ahead of yourself. We are on our way now. We will know more when we arrive. However, never doubt that I will do everything in my power to ensure that your son is returned to you."

Oskar didn't press Kara to talk. But every so often he would reach over and pat her hand and say, "Don't worry, my love; everything will be all right."

It was still dark outside when they arrived in Munich. Being so close to finding Karl made Kara even more on edge. Her patience was gone, leaving her a bundle of nerves.

"The home won't be open yet for adoptions. If you would like, I'll rent us a room so we can get a few hours of sleep before they open. I am awfully tired."

Kara nodded. "Yes, I know you are. You've been driving for hours. I'm sure you could use some rest." *I wish we could just break into that place and take him. Of course, I know that we can't. I must wait. I must find a way to stay sane for a few more hours. And, dear God, I pray that he is still there.* Her heart was pounding, but she tried to smile at Oskar. He was doing so much, and he looked so worn out.

Oskar pulled into the parking lot of a nice hotel. They went inside, and he rented a room while Kara sat on a chair and waited in the lobby. Once he had the key, he went to Kara. "Because we arrived here so late, they only had one room available. I promise you I didn't do this out of disrespect. Please don't feel obligated in any way. I just assumed we would only be here for a few hours. And I am sure, you know that I am too tired to do anything but sleep. However, if you would prefer your own room, we can try to go to another hotel where I can get you one."

"It's all right," she said. "One room will be fine."

They went upstairs. Kara removed her coat and shoes. Then she lay down fully dressed on the bed. Oskar lay down beside her. She felt strange lying beside him, nervous, and even a little uncomfortable. He'd promised he wouldn't try to make love to her, and she hoped he would keep his promise. But if he did try, she decided she would allow it. *He has done so much for me, and we are engaged. Perhaps it would help me to love him, the way he loves me.* Kara was relieved when he didn't try. In fact, he was asleep within minutes after he lay his head on the pillow. Kara was wide awake. She couldn't sleep. Every time she closed her eyes, she saw the photographs of Karl that had been in the packet. He'd been crying. She knew he was scared. *If only I could hold him and comfort him. Dear God, please let this be over. Please let my son be with me again before this day is out*, she thought, and her arms ached for the moment when she could hold him.

It seemed like forever until the sun rose on that crisp morning when the sky was the color of crystal-blue ice. Kara glanced over at Oskar, who was still asleep, and she felt a wave of tenderness come over her. *I believe that when the time comes, I will be able to make love to him. When I think of how kind and good hearted he is, I know I can learn to love him. Look at all he has done for me, putting his career on hold to help me. How many men would do that? Especially important men like Oskar?*

Kara took the key so she would not have to wake Oskar when she returned. Then she went downstairs to the lobby to see if the restaurant was open yet. It was. She ordered two cups of coffee, one for herself and one for Oskar. But when she got back to the room, Oskar was awake. He did not look like himself. His face was red, contorted, and angry.

"Where the hell were you?" he said, his voice harsher than she'd ever heard it. "I was worried about you."

"Why? Why would you be worried?"

"The truth, Kara? I am afraid you are not stable. I thought you might have run off and done something crazy, like trying to break into the Lebensborn home."

"I just went to get us some coffee," she said.

He took a deep breath. Then in his calm, regular voice, he said, "I'm sorry. It's just a very intense day for both of us. Can you forgive me?"

"Of course. We are both under a lot of pressure," she said, handing him the coffee.

He took a sip. Then a few moments later, he said, "I do love Munich, and as much as I believe that it is our duty as good Germans to colonize the East, I love being home in the fatherland."

She managed to smile at him, but she was a little taken aback by how quickly his mood could change. He had been so filled with rage, and in an instant it disappeared as if it had never been there at all.

"Perhaps we can get married here in Munich. What do you think? Do you like it here?"

She walked to the window, then looked out and said, "Munich is lovely." And she did think it was a beautiful place, so picturesque, but it was hard to concentrate on anything but Karl. "When do you think the Lebensborn home will be open for potential adoptees?"

Oskar looked at his watch. It was still only seven thirty in the morning. "An hour perhaps," he said. "Shall we go down for breakfast?"

"Yes, if you'd like." She knew he must be very hungry. But she wasn't. Even though the last time they'd eaten was yesterday morning, she couldn't bear to think of food. Her limbs ached. She thought of what it would be like if she tried to leave and run all the way to the Lebensborn home. *If Oskar knew my thoughts, he would definitely think I've gone mad.* In her mind's eye, she saw herself pounding on the door until someone opened it. *My son, my Karl is inside that building, and every minute that passes is another minute that I am apart from him.*

They were seated in front of a large picture window. The view was quaint and beautiful. Kara stared out the window trying to stay as calm as possible. *It's only another hour.*

Oskar ordered for both of them. Then he said, "It's called Steinhöring."

"What is?" she asked.

"The home for Lebensborn. The place we are going."

"Steinhöring . . ." she repeated.

"Are you all right?"

"I think so. I just wish we could go there already. I am overwhelmed with so many emotions, anticipation, worry."

"It will only be a little while now and they'll be open."

The food arrived.

"You should eat something," he said. "At least some toast."

She tried. But she couldn't swallow. Every few seconds her eyes traveled back to the clock on the wall: 7:45, 7:47, 7:50, 7:55. *We are so close now. I think I will go mad if we don't get there soon.*

Oskar ate quicky, then paid the bill. "All right. They should be open by now. Let's drive over," he said, taking Kara's arm. She leaned on him holding his arm tightly.

"I'm so nervous."

"Don't be afraid. I'm here with you."

"I am so afraid something will go wrong."

"Nothing will go wrong," he said. "Everything is going to be fine."

It was eight fifteen when they got into the car. Kara's hands were shaking. Oskar reached over and took one of her hands in his as he steered the car with his other hand. "My darling, you're so cold." He kissed her hand, then pulled to the side of the road and took the blanket he'd given her the previous day, to use as a pillow, and laid it over her. "There, that will keep you warm until we get there."

They parked in front of a group of buildings. As they got out of the automobile, a bunch of pretty young women, all of them blonde, and all of them pregnant, came strolling by. They wore heavy wool coats and thick scarves. A uniformed little brown sister, who was leading the others on their walk, saw Oskar and saluted: "Heil Hitler."

"Heil Hitler," he returned the greeting.

"Heil Hitler," Kara said as was expected of her.

They walked up a long walkway, then Oskar opened the door for Kara, and they entered the first building. "Sit down here, darling. I'll go to the desk and find out where we must go to find Karl."

"Heil Hitler." The girl at the desk smiled at Oskar. "Are you here to adopt a child?" Kara heard her ask.

"Yes," Oskar answered.

"The room you're looking for is right upstairs. Just go up to the second floor and then knock on the first door on the right. Someone there will be able to help you."

"Thank you, Fräulein."

Kara was trembling so hard that her knees felt weak as she climbed the stairs to the second floor. She almost fell, but Oskar caught her and held her arm tightly. "I've got you," he said. "Don't be afraid. I won't let you fall."

A warm feeling came over her. *I'm so thankful to have Oskar by my side.* And for the first time since she'd known him, she found that she was glad he wore that uniform. It made the people who worked at these institutions listen to him. She hated the Nazis, and everything they stood for, but right now, she needed them to respect him and to act on his behalf. Besides that, he'd never shown her anything but kindness. He was gentle and genuinely concerned about her son. *What more could I ever ask for?* The warmth and strength of his arm on hers gave her courage. *Perhaps, I have fallen in love with him,* she thought. *I would never have believed that I could feel this way about one of them. But he's not like the others, is he? He's different. He would never be cruel to another human being, the way the other Nazis are. I know he accepts their doctrine, but I also feel certain that there is no cruelty in him.*

They stood at the desk together, her arm tucked through his while he stroked her hand. It seemed to

Kara that they were waiting for hours, but it had only been five minutes. Then a woman in a crisp white nurse's uniform, with a white cap covering her brown hair, walked briskly up to the desk.

"Heil Hitler. What a beautiful couple you are," she said, smiling.

"Heil Hitler," Oskar replied.

"So, you have come to adopt a child? Have you filled out all of the forms?"

"No, we have not. I am Oberstrumführer Lerch. This is a rather unusual situation. You see, we are here looking for a particular child," Oskar said.

"Oh? I don't quite understand."

"It's a long, drawn-out story," Oskar said gently, and the nurse seemed to melt at the sound of his voice. Then he continued. "You see, Fräulein, we went to the children's welfare agency yesterday looking for the boy. But he was not there. Apparently, they accessed his records, and for some reason they sent him here."

"How old is the child?"

"He is only five. However, they may have sent him to the Lebensborn because he is an only child, and he has been very coddled all of his life. Because of this, they may have thought that he might need a bit more Germanization."

"I see."

"Yes, I was told by Frau Moller at the children's welfare agency to ask for Frau Altner; she's a brown sister. You may well know her."

"Of course, Oberstrumführer, I do know her very well. Why don't you both have a seat and wait here for just a moment, I'll go and find Frau Altner. She will be right with you."

A moment later, an attractive young woman with a serious expression came walking over to them. "You must be Oberstrumführer Lerch," she said, not bothering to address Kara.

"Yes, that's right."

"Of course. I'm Aloisa Altner." The woman smiled again. Kara watched her as her eyes combed over Oskar, and for a moment, Kara thought she was attracted to him. But then her expression was once again serious, and in a businesslike voice, she said, "Frau Moller called here yesterday and told me to expect you. Please, won't you both come into my office."

Oskar stepped back allowing Kara to go first, and he walked up beside her. They walked down a lengthy corridor, following close behind Frau Altner. The sound of crying babies came from the rooms on each side that were labeled, The Nursery. Another was labeled, Special Handling. And still another was labeled, Ready for Adoption.

Frau Altner opened the door to a small but well-organized office with two chairs on the opposite side of her gray metal desk. There were two clipboards in front of each chair. Frau Altner took the clipboards and put one of them into a drawer. Then she handed the other to Kara. "I'll need you to fill these out. They are just papers that are required to ensure that a child is being adopted by racially pure parents."

Kara nodded.

"I don't know if Frau Moller explained our situation fully. But we aren't looking for just any child. We've come here looking for a particular little boy. He is my fiancée's son. He was taken by mistake," Oskar said.

"Do you have a photograph of the child?"

Kara took the picture out of her handbag, and at the same time, Oskar handed Frau Altner the envelope he'd received the night before from the children's welfare agency. "There are several pictures in here," he said, "The one my fiancée is giving you is a little older."

Frau Altner laid all of the pictures out in a row on her desk. Then she shook her head as she looked up into Kara and Oskar's eyes. "I'm sorry, Oberstrumführer, but this child is not here."

"What? Of course he's here," Oskar said angrily. "His files are right in front of you. The files say he is here."

"I'm afraid he's been adopted. Would you like to see another child?" Her face was pale.

"Another child? Are you mad?" Oskar said.

"Adopted?" Kara said, "Adopted by who?"

"I'm afraid I can't tell you that. It's against the rules."

"Please, I beg you to help me. You can't do this

to me. Please, I am begging you to tell me where my son is!" Kara was screaming. She stood up and began pounding her fists on the desk.

Oskar put his hand on Kara's arm and tried to calm her. Her face was crimson, and she was breathing heavily as she looked up into his eyes. "Adopted. I was afraid of this," she said. "My son has been stolen from me. Now they won't tell us where he is."

"I'll find him," Oskar said. "No matter what it takes, I'll find him."

Kara felt her heart begin to race. She was dizzy. The room turned dark and began to spin. "Karl . . . dear God, help me. They've stolen my son," she said, then she fainted.

# CHAPTER TWENTY-EIGHT

"WHAT IS the meaning of this, Aloisa?" Oskar said when he returned to Frau Altner's office, after he'd carried Kara out of the room and put her into a bed in the women's section of the Steinhöring institute. A doctor had given her a sedative to calm her. For now, she was resting comfortably.

"I'm sorry, Oskar. There was mix up. I don't know how it could have happened. I knew you were coming, but the photographs I was sent were not of this child. We were sent photographs of the wrong child. What I am trying to say is we kept the wrong little boy for you," Frau Altner said. She was trembling.

"Well, that's a hell of a mistake, isn't it? I left you in charge of all this. You knew how much it meant to me that you carried out my orders. I told you to keep the child here until I arrived. He was never supposed to be adopted. Never even supposed to be considered for adoption. This was a plan that I devised to force his mother to become dependent on me. I thought I made that clear when I met with you the first time, even before he'd been kidnapped. Either you're stupid, or you didn't understand me. Either way, this is one hell of a mess."

"Yes, it certainly is." She was almost in tears. "Please, don't be angry with me, Oskar. I did my best."

"Well, your best was hardly good enough."

"I owe you a million favors," she said, begging for forgiveness. "Let me explain. Please. When the children were sent over here about two months ago, Frau Moller, who you said was also involved in this plan of yours, included pictures of another little boy. She sent them directly to me and told me not to allow this child to be seen by any prospective couples because he was the child you arranged to have kidnapped, and he was not to be adopted under any circumstances. Since you told me that she was also a part of your plan, I trusted her. I did what she asked. I kept him away from everyone who came. However, it turns out that he was the wrong child. Here . . . look." She took a picture of a frightened blond, blue-eyed little boy out of her desk. "I was told by Frau Moller that this is the child you would be coming to pick up. I was told that he was to be kept for you. The other little boy was not mentioned. So, it was all a terrible error. The child you are searching for was adopted."

"Where is he? Where has he been taken?"

"I don't know."

"Yes, you do. And if you don't, you had better find out."

"Oberstrumführer, please. I could lose my job. I am not at liberty to tell you." Her tone of voice told him that she was clearly afraid of him.

"Listen to me, and hear me good. If you are worried about your job, then you had better find that child. If you don't find him, I guarantee you will be out of work by nightfall, maybe worse. Now, you find him, and you call me within an hour and tell me where he is. Here is the phone number to my hotel. Now, Frau Altner," he said, growling, and not calling her by her first name in order to let her know just how angry he was. "I will be expecting a call from you, and if I don't receive one, there will be hell to pay. I promise you that." He picked up a pen that was on the desk, and with angry strokes of the pen he wrote down a number.

Frau Altner took the paper from him with trembling hands. Then she watched him, her eyes wide with fear as he walked out of the room.

# CHAPTER TWENTY-NINE

KARA AWOKE BACK at the hotel room. "How did I get here?" she asked Oskar, who was sitting by her bedside.

"I carried you," he whispered.

"Karl. Oh, Oskar. What are we going to do now? Someone has adopted him."

"It will be all right. I put in a call for the reichsführer. As soon as he gives them his permission, the staff at Steinhöring will release the address of the couple who adopted Karl."

"Are you sure? What if he refuses to help us?"

"Don't you worry. You have to trust me, Kara. Remember when I told you that I have influential friends?" Well, the reichsführer is an old friend of mine. I know he will help me. You'll see, everything will be fine."

"I hope so. A couple, probably a young, childless couple, have my son. They think he is their child. They won't surrender him to us easily. I know I wouldn't. And that's what is terrifying me."

"They will have to give him to us if the reichs-führer demands it of them. And I expect him to return my call any time now. You've had a difficult day. Why don't you just rest for a while." Oskar stood up and stretched. He'd been sitting beside Kara's bed for a long time, and his legs and back were stiff. Then he went into the bathroom and wet a washrag with cool water and wrung it out. When he returned, he put the cool rag on Kara's forehead, covering her eyes. "There, now, doesn't that feel nice?" She nodded and moaned softly. "Please, Kara, just trust me."

She nodded. "I'm trying."

Kara had almost drifted off to sleep when she was jarred awake by the ringing of the phone. Oskar answered it.

"Hello," he said, then he covered the mouthpiece and turned to Kara. "It's Reichsführer Himmler. You see? I told you he would call," Oskar lied; it wasn't the reichsführer. He didn't even know the reichsführer. But he wanted Kara to think he was important.

"Oberstrumführer Lerch." It was Frau Altner. "I've found the address of the couple who adopted the child you're searching for. I am going to give it to you. But you must promise me that you won't ever tell anyone where you got it."

"Of course. It will be our secret," Oskar said. He took a pen out of the breast pocket of his jacket and wrote down the information. Then he said, "Thank you." He glanced over at Kara who was lying on her side, looking out the window. He disconnected the call but still held the receiver in his hand. "You don't know how much I appreciate your help with this matter, Reichsführer." Then he hung the receiver back on its base.

"You have the address?" Kara asked incredulously.

"Yes, I have it."

"Really?" She sat up. "Where is it?"

"Berlin."

"Can we leave and go there now?"

"It's already late afternoon. It's at least a six-hour drive. We won't arrive until at least ten tonight."

"So, you want to wait until morning?" she said.

"I would prefer it."

She nodded. Then she began to cry. "I feel like we are never going to find him," she said.

"We already have found him."

"But what if these people don't have him, or they refuse to release him to us? Everything keeps going wrong, Oskar."

"I am certain that they have him. And you needn't worry, I'll make sure they release him to us. No matter what it takes," Oskar said. "I'm going to order dinner. What would you like?"

"I'm sorry. I know you mean well, but I can't eat."

"You must eat, Kara."

She nodded not wanting to argue. "Soup, then," she said.

"What kind?"

"Whatever they have."

When the food arrived, she didn't eat a bite. She just lay in bed staring at the wall. Oskar studied her. Then he took a packet of something out of his breast pocket, and when he was sure she didn't see him, he poured it into her water glass. Then he touched her shoulder. "Kara, if you won't eat, you must at least drink some water. If you don't, you're going to become dehydrated. You don't want to get sick. If you're sick, we won't be able to make the drive to Berlin tomorrow."

She obediently took the glass and drank the water. He sighed with relief when she fell asleep. *She should sleep until tomorrow afternoon. And that's just what I need because this is something I must do on my own*, he thought. *Just in case I have to become violent. I don't want her to see me like that.*

Oskar scribbled a quick note to Kara just in case she awoke before he returned.

Sweetheart,

If you should awaken, don't be afraid. Everything is going to be just fine. I promise you.

You fell asleep, and I know you need to rest. I realized how difficult this has all been for you. And you have had enough stress to last a lifetime. So I decided I would make the trip to Berlin on my own. I will bring your son back to you, my love. Perhaps then you will know how much I care, and you will find it in your heart to return my love willingly. I should be back by tomorrow evening.

Yours always, Oskar

# CHAPTER THIRTY

Kara never read the letter.

When she opened her eyes, she saw Karl sitting on the bed beside her. He was shaking her arm. Kara trembled; she thought she was dreaming.

"Karl?" Kara sat up in bed and reached out to touch her little boy. "Dear God, could it be? Karl? Is that really you?"

The child was much thinner than he'd been the last time she saw him. He wore a serious expression that somehow made his eyes looked older. He was pale and nervous. But there was no doubt about it, it was him. Oskar stood beside the bed watching Kara and smiling.

"Am I dreaming, Oskar?"

"You are not dreaming, love," he said, touching her cheek.

Kara was trembling; tears spilled down her face.

She grabbed her son and embraced him. Karl looked frightened and confused as he stared at his mother. But Kara didn't notice. Her hands were shaking as she touched his hair, his face, his hands. Oskar watched as he sat down on the bed beside her and Karl. For several minutes, Kara held Karl in her arms and rocked him. He sat rigid. Then in a small voice he asked, "Who are you?"

"You don't know me?" Kara asked.

"I don't know if I do or not," he said.

"I'm your mother, Karl."

"The other lady said she was my mother." He shook his head. "I'm not supposed to cry," he said, but he was crying. "They'll hit me for crying."

"No one is going to hit you," Kara said.

"They do hit me. If they hear one of us crying, they yell, 'Stop that right now,' and if we don't, then they hit us." Karl looked around frantically.

"I promise you; no one will hit you," Kara said. "I am your mother. I am your real mother. Your only mother."

"Who was that other lady, then? She got very angry if I didn't call her Mutti. She would shake me hard."

"You were taken away from me. I've been looking for you all this time, and I finally found you. This is Oskar. Do you remember him?"

"I don't know," Karl said, shaking his head.

"He helped me to find you, and then he brought you back to me."

Karl buried his head in Kara's chest. "I think I remember you. I remember you used to hold me and rock me like you're doing right now. There were mean people in that place where I was. They told me that if I didn't forget you, they would beat me until I did. They said they were going to make me strong no matter what they had to do. I told them I didn't want to be strong. I wanted to go home. That made them mad. When they got mad, they got even meaner. And they were grown-ups. Mean grown-ups are scarier than monsters. And I was scared, Mutti. I was so scared."

"Dear God. My poor child," she said, running her hands over his head. His blond curls were gone. His hair was so short, she could feel his scalp. "You're safe now. You're here with me and I will protect you. I promise." *Karl, my baby, you are finally here in my arms. I was so afraid I had lost you. My sweet little boy is home. The stolen child that Oskar turned the world upside down searching for is here, right here, in my arms. I've never felt such gratitude. I've never been so happy.* She was trembling as tears of joy spilled down her cheeks. She lay her head on top of his and inhaled his essence. She glanced over at Oskar, and her heart overflowed with feelings she had never felt before for this man who had brought back her precious son.

Oskar touched Karl's back. "Don't be afraid, son. I am here too. And I am bigger and stronger than any of those monsters. I promise you I will keep you safe."

"Are you my vater?"

"I am going to be. Your mother and I are getting married. You will be my son. And no one will dare try to harm you, then."

Karl looked up at Oskar. There was so much gratitude in Karl's eyes. And Kara knew he felt safe with Oskar. Kara melted. At that moment she decided she loved Oskar. She might not be in love with him the way she was with Abram. But she loved him. She reached for Oskar's hand and brought it to her lips. "Thank you," she said.

He nodded.

For several moments, Kara held Karl in her arms without speaking. Finally, she looked at Oskar and asked, "What happened? How did he get here?"

"I knew you'd had a hard time. I didn't want you to have to go through anything more. So, I gave you something to help you sleep. Then I drove to Berlin and picked him up."

"The couple who adopted him let you take him?"

"The reichsführer contacted them. They were told that they were to release the child back to me." He smiled. "And . . . they did. You see, sometimes it helps to have important friends. And . . . the man who will be your husband, yours truly, has very important friends," he lied. Although the adopted parents had only had Karl for a week, they refused to give him up. Oskar offered money, but they refused that too. Finally, Oskar had been forced to physically threaten the father until he agreed to release the child. Oskar held the man in a choke hold while he explained that he was ranked higher than the adopted father, and he would ruin him if he didn't give him the boy. "You can get another one. Just go back to the Lebensborn. Tell them what happened. Ask for Frau Altner. She'll give you another child," Oskar said as he picked Karl up and took him away. For the first half hour in the car, Karl lay on the seat and wept. Then he fell asleep.

"Oh, Oskar, I can't believe you have done this for me," Kara said.

"I promised you I would. I always keep my promises. Especially to those I love."

Her eyes met his. "I love you too," she said.

"Do you really?" he asked.

"I do."

"Shall I ask you again?"

"Ask me what?"

"Will you marry me, Kara? But not because you want my help to find your son. But because you love me?"

"Yes, I will marry you. And . . . yes, it's because I love you."

They kissed, and for the first time since she'd met him, Kara felt that she wanted him to come to her bed. She wanted to feel him lie beside her. Of course, it would not be that night because Karl would be there. But when the time came, she would welcome him physically.

Oskar stood up. He stretched for a moment. Then he winked and smiled at Karl. "You wait right here. I have something in the trunk of my automobile that belongs to you. I'll be right back."

Kara held Karl in her arms and kissed him all over his face. She looked at his hands and counted his fingers. She held his head in her hands and pulled him to her breast. "I thought I lost you," she whispered. "I thought I would never find you again."

Karl looked at his mother with confusion in his eyes. But she took him and pulled him close to her again. "My son. My son. My baby boy."

Oskar walked into the room with his hands behind his back. Smiling at Karl and then winking at Kara, whose face was covered with tears, he said, "Do you want to see what I have for you, Karl?"

"Yes, sir," Karl said.

Oskar pulled a charred teddy bear from behind his back. Karl's eyes shot open with recognition. He grabbed the bear and hugged it tightly.

"Little Bear," Karl said. "Little Bear. It's you. I never thought I would ever see you again." Karl hugged the bear to his chest. And Kara continued to wipe the tears from her face.

# CHAPTER THIRTY-ONE

OSKAR PLAYED on the floor with Karl while Kara telephoned Anka. She told her that they'd found Karl and that he was with them at the hotel. "Oskar brought him back to me," Kara said.

Anka screamed with delight. "Oh, Kara!!!! That's wonderful news."

"I know. I feel like I will never let him out of my sight again."

"I don't blame you."

"Oskar must return to work. He's been gone for several months, and he is fortunate to have good friends who have made it possible for him to take all this time off. I was wondering if it is all right if Karl and I return to your home to stay with you until after the wedding."

"Yes, of course. Ludwig and I would love to have you. When will you be returning?"

"Next week. If that's all right?" Kara said. All the annoyance she had been feeling toward her sister was gone. It was replaced by love. The world around was suddenly bright and promising.

"That's perfect. I am looking forward to it."

The following day, Oskar left the hotel for a few hours. When he returned, he had several different stuffed animals with him. Each of them wore a bow.

"These are for you, little man," Oskar said to Karl. "Remember? We had plans to go to the zoo before you went on your little adventure."

Karl stared at Oskar blankly. He didn't acknowledge the memory. He looked at the colorful stuffed animals. But he didn't reach for them. Karl held tightly to Little Bear.

"Well," Oskar continued, "it's still rather cold outside for the zoo. But I do promise we will go in the future. For now, however, I bought you these stuffed animals. This one is a zebra. Do you know why he is a zebra and not a horse?"

Karl shook his head.

"Because although he looks like a horse. He has black-and-white stripes. And that makes him a zebra. Zebras come from a land very far away called Africa."

"Africa," Karl repeated.

"This one is a lion. You see this thick mane? That means he is a boy lion."

Karl reached out one hand and touched the stuffed lion's mane.

Kara's heart melted. Oskar was already acting like a father. He was helping Karl cope with all that had happened.

"And look at this one. He is my favorite. Do you know what kind of animal he is?"

"An elephant?"

"That's right. You are such a smart little boy, Karl."

Karl beamed. Then Oskar hugged him. "These are all for you," Oskar said.

"What do you say?" Kara said.

"Thank you," Karl said. He lay Little Bear down beside him. Then he picked up each of the stuffed animals and played with them. But that night when Karl went to sleep, it was Little Bear that he held in his arms.

# CHAPTER THIRTY-TWO

OSKAR DROVE Kara and Karl to Anka and Ludwig's home. Karl moved back into his old bedroom which was adjacent to Kara's room. But he did not sleep well. Many times, he woke up at night and came running into Kara's room, gripping Little Bear tightly and shaking because he'd had a bad dream. She would allow him to stay. As the days passed, Kara was relieved to see that, although it was a slow process, Karl was regaining his memory.

The night before Oskar was to return to work, Kara waited until everyone in the house was asleep. Then she slipped into Oskar's room. He lay in his bed asleep, the moonlight that beamed through the window illuminating his face. Kara felt such tenderness for him that it surprised her. *He loves me so much. And he loves Karl too.* She sat down on the side of the bed and watched him sleep for a few moments.

Then she reached down and touched his face. He opened his eyes. His voice was hoarse whisper, "Kara . . ."

She nodded. Then she stood up and removed her nightgown. He gasped. "You are the most beautiful woman I have ever seen," he whispered.

She climbed into bed next to him. "I have waited so long for you to come to me," he said.

"I'm here," she whispered.

"I love you."

"And I love you too."

Gently, he kissed her, then he touched her face, and she surrendered to him.

But when it was over, Kara returned to her own room just in case Karl came looking for her.

# CHAPTER THIRTY-THREE

## Auschwitz

ABRAM EHRLICH SCRATCHED HIS HEAD; it was covered with open sores. The constant itching from the lice that lined the dirty straw where he slept was maddening. As if things had not been bad enough when he first arrived, he'd been moved to a new a location where he was assigned to the bottom bunk of a three-tier arrangement that had been set up in a horse's stable. *Well, at least I still have Moishe with me,* he thought as he looked at the bunk right above him where Moishe slept. The top bunk was occupied by a teenage fellow named Hersh. Although they didn't really know him, Abram and Moishe decided that Hersh seemed nice enough.

The entire camp had recently suffered from a bout of dysentery, leaving the stables where Abram slept permeated with the strong, noxious odor of diarrhea. When the dysentery first spread through the camp, Abram gagged and vomited often. But as time passed, he got used to the smell. Besides that, he was so exhausted from his day of working at the chemical plant, very little affected him. All he wanted to do when he returned to his block was lay down on his bunk and sleep.

Abram learned that it was best if the two men who slept above him were in their beds before he fell asleep. Otherwise, they would disturb him when they climbed over his bunk. Right now, he wished Moishe would return from the filthy hole in the ground that they used as a toilet, so he could go to sleep. Hersh was already snoring.

"Abram," Moishe said as he came walking over to the three beds. "You'll never guess who I saw?"

"Good or bad?" Abram asked.

"Worse."

"Oy, does it ever get better here?" Abram said, "Nu? So, who did you see?"

"I don't think this place ever gets any better," Moishe said, smiling a sad smile.

"Nu? So, tell me already. Who was it?"

"Lerch, the oberstrumführer."

"Oy, that sadistic bastard." Abram sighed. "I thought we got rid of him."

"Ali vie, from your mouth to God's ears. But no, we didn't. He's back. I heard him talking to one of the other SS. As soon as I heard his voice, I knew it was him. So, I hid around the corner and listened to see what he had to say. He was telling the other bastard that he had some business to take care of and that's why he's been gone. Something about a child and his fiancée. I couldn't make out the whole story. But, apparently, at least from what I could gather, he's getting married," Moishe said.

"What kind of a woman would marry a sadistic bastard like him?" Abram asked, shaking his head.

"One of them. Another Nazi just like him. She's probably some bitch who works in the women's camp."

"Well, well, isn't that just a perfect picture of domestic bliss? Two Nazi bastards married to each other. After work each day they cuddle on the sofa and say, "So, how many Jews did you kill today?" Abram said sarcastically.

Moishe nodded. "They should all rot in hell."

"I got some extra bread for us today," Abram said, taking a heel of hard bread out of the pocket of his uniform.

"How did you ever manage that?"

Abram laughed, "If I told you, you wouldn't think I was magical anymore. Remember I told you I'm a magician?"

"Don't be a nar, you fool," Moishe said affectionately. "Come on, tell me."

"One of the political prisoners gave me a few cigarettes in trade for writing a letter for him. He can't read or write, so he needs my help to write love letters. I feel like Cyrano." Abram let out a short laugh. Anyway, this fella is going to try to sneak the letter out to his girl who is in the women's camp."

"Nothing like a good old-fashioned romance in hell, huh?" Moishe said.

"Poor fella. I feel for him. I have to thank God that my Kara isn't here. I would be sick with worry every day is she was in that women's camp."

"Yeah, I know. Sometimes I think it's better not to know where your loved ones are. Rather than to know they are here in this miserable place," Moishe said.

"So, anyway, about the bread . . ."

"Yeah, about the bread," Moishe said.

"Since I don't smoke, I traded the cigarettes with a fella for his bread. See, it wasn't anything magical. And now I have lost my mystique." Abram let out a sad little laugh.

"Eh, you could never lose your mystique. I've never met anyone who could tell a story the way you do. And that sure is magic, especially here in this place, where all we have are your stories."

"You're a good friend, Moishe. That's why I share my bread with you."

"Are you going to tell us one of your stories tonight?"

Most nights after the prisoners were in their beds, Abram would tell them stories from the books he'd read. He was exhausted and longing for sleep.

But they would cry out to him. "Abram, please tell us a tale." And he knew how they looked forward to the half hour when they could escape into the wonderful stories he told by Hemmingway or Dickens. But, tonight, he was too exhausted. His chest hurt from breathing the chemicals inside the plant where he worked all day making synthetic rubber.

"Not tonight. I'm too tired."

"The fellows will be disappointed," Moishe said, taking a bite of the bread.

"I know. I wish I felt better. But I'm so tired. And now that you're telling me that Lerch is back, I feel even more miserable."

"Yeah, I'm sorry. I probably shouldn't have told you."

"It doesn't matter. I am sure I'll see his face at roll call in the morning."

"Just stay out of his way, Abram. He's one of the worst. I think his heart is made of stone. And I know for certain, because I have seen it, that he doesn't think twice about killing a Jew."

"Don't I know it."

Abram ate his half of the bread and then tucked the other half into his uniform. Then he lay down in his bunk.

"Ehrlich, are you going to tell us any stories tonight?" one of the prisoners whose bunk was on the other side of the room called out to Abram.

"I'm sorry. I can't. I promise, I'll tell you a story tomorrow."

"Yeah, if we live that long," the man answered.

"I really am sorry," Abram said.

After the room grew quiet, Abram closed his eyes and thought of Kara as he did every night before he fell asleep. It was important to him that he remember her face exactly as it was the last time he saw her. He traced the line of her jaw in his mind and looked into her eyes. She smiled at him, and he felt warm and safe. If he concentrated hard enough, he could hear her soft voice calling his name. And he could see her holding their son in her arms. Karl with his golden halo of curls and his chubby little arms and legs. He let himself drift into a dreamlike state where he could feel her hand on his arm. Her fingers glided over the muscles in his back, and he was soothed. *Dear God, please watch over my Kara and my son, Karl. And . . . my mother, my poor dear mother. Please, no matter what, don't let them end up in a place like this. I am begging you to protect them. I know I have sinned against you over the years. I've broken your commandments. I was wrong. I was so wrong. Now I am pleading with you for forgiveness. Please, Hashem, if you can find it in your mercy, please let me live and return home to my family.*

# CHAPTER THIRTY-FOUR

## Anka's house, near the lair in Poland

KARA DIDN'T REALIZE how much she would miss Oskar until he was gone back to work. They'd spent so much time together over the past several months that she had come to expect to see him each morning. But she understood that he had to return to work and could not help her plan their wedding. He'd taken too much time away from his job already. But Kara knew that Anka loved a celebration, and planning parties was her specialty. So she was eager to help. And since Karl's return, Kara found it much easier to have patience with her sister. They went through all the possible locations for the wedding. Anka insisted that the lair would be a wonderful option. "It's so much fun. There is so much to do," Anka said.

"Oskar and I would prefer somewhere quieter."

"I know, so he told me," Anka said.

"What about Cologne?" Kara suggested.

"I hear it's a beautiful place, but the recent bombings have all but destroyed the city."

"I think Munich is your best option," Anka said. "It's lovely and quaint."

Kara thought about her visit to Steinhöring in Munich, and she was a little unnerved. "I don't know about Munich. I was there recently."

"And you didn't find it absolutely charming?" Anka asked.

"It was charming. But . . ."

"Go on, but what?"

Kara sighed. As always, Anka left her with no choice but to tell her sister everything. And so Kara told her sister all about the home for the Lebensborn.

"I had never heard of such a thing," Anka admitted. Then her face lit up. "But, perhaps, Ludwig and I could consider adopting a child from there."

"Anka!" Kara said. "Those children are stolen from their parents."

"Are you sure that some of them aren't orphans?"

"Well, to be quite honest, I am not sure."

"I'll have Ludwig look into it," Anka said, then seeing the look on Kara's face, she added, "I'm sorry. I'm being thoughtless. Would it be all right with you if I had Ludwig look into it? I would never take a child away from its parents. You should know that."

"Of course, I know that, Anka. And it's me who's being selfish. I had a bad experience, but that's no reason for me to stop you from finding happiness. I know how badly you've wanted a child."

"Yes," Anka said. "Yes," then she added, "and you know what happened. So, the Reich owes me a baby. A healthy baby."

Anka's way of thinking never failed to shock and surprise Kara. Children were not like coats, or dresses; a new one could not replace the one that had been lost. At least not for Kara. She didn't know what to say. So she tried to smile.

Anka nodded. Then she continued speaking, "Now, I still say you should forget about the Lebensborn. I mean that part of your life is over. Now you and Oskar are about to embark upon the rest of your lives together. I say, the two of you should get married in Munich. It's so quaint and lovely. Besides, think about it, Berlin is too crowded. Nuremberg is not romantic enough, and it's also suffered its share of bombings."

"You can be convincing when you want to be," Kara said.

"I know." Anka smiled.

"Well, it seems you've worn down my resistance. So, Munich it is. We'll get married in Munich."

"And how about this: Ludwig and I will join

you. We'll make a long weekend of it. I am quite certain that you intend to bring Karl with you. After what happened, I know you would not leave him with a sitter. And, believe me, I don't blame you. You've been through quite an ordeal. So Ludwig and I thought that if we all went to Munich, you and Oskar could still have your honeymoon. We decided that Karl could stay with us in our room. That way, you and Oskar will have some time alone together. After all, every newlywed couple should have some time. Right?"

Kara nodded. *She's right. I would never leave Karl again, no matter what. Honeymoon or not. So this is probably the best idea. Otherwise, there would be no honeymoon. Karl would share the room with Oskar and me. And I certainly couldn't imagine making love with my son in the room.* "That's a wonderful idea. And so generous of you and Ludwig. Thank you."

"We adore Karl. You know that."

"Yes, of course, I know you do," Kara said, but she thought, *When he was missing, Anka didn't seem devastated. I don't understand her.*

"Then it's all settled." Anka winked. Then sensing Kara was not settled but not knowing why, she added, "Don't you worry. Ludwig and I won't let him out of our sight. I learned my lesson." A big smile came over her face.

# CHAPTER THIRTY-FIVE

EACH WEEK, on Sunday evening, Oskar telephoned Kara. The calls consisted mostly of small talk. He asked her how the wedding plans were going, and she told him that she and Anka were working on them. "We're still waiting for our application to be approved, but I am sure the approval will come through any day," he would say.

And she would answer, "I know." And although she never said a word, she was always worried that somehow the application was being held up because her relationship with Abram had been discovered. This caused her to be anxious, not because she was ashamed of Abram, but because she was afraid for her son.

On every weekly call, Oskar asked about Karl. His genuine concern touched her heart when he asked how Karl was doing after all he'd been through. Her answer was always the same—her son was adjusting. It was true that Karl had nightmares far more often than the average child. And if he happened to make a mistake, like spilling his milk, he would cower in fear as if he expected to be beaten. Kara knew he was too young to tell her what he'd experienced. But, from his timid behavior, she could see that he wasn't the confident little boy who had disappeared so many months ago. Even so, he was home. She convinced herself that in time he would forget.

At the end of each phone conversation, Oskar professed his undying love for Kara and told her how much he missed her.

Then on one such Sunday night, two months after Oskar had returned to work, he called, and in an exceptionally cheery and excited voice, he said, "My darling. I couldn't wait to call you. You see, tonight I have wonderful news!"

"Oh?" she said. "Tell me."

"Our application has been approved. We have been granted permission to get married. So, l am ready whenever you're ready to take the next step. Have you decided on where you'd like to get married?"

"Munich, I think."

"Very good choice. I can get a few days off in the late spring. Not long, though, because I took so much time away from work recently."

"I understand. I wouldn't expect any more,"

Kara said. "Anka and Ludwig would like to come to Munich with us. They can watch Karl, so we can have some time alone together. Anka said that he could sleep in their room."

"What a splendid idea."

"I hoped it would be all right with you."

"Whatever you'd like," he said. "That's not all I have to tell you. I have more good news."

"Well, don't keep me waiting, Oskar. Please, tell me," she said, his excitement contagious.

"The party has awarded me a house for us to live in. It's located right near my work, in a small town not far from Krakow, called Oswiecim. But don't worry, you won't be lonely. There are plenty of other German families in the area."

"Shall I bring Karl and come there to order some furniture so we can move in as soon as we are married?"

"No need. The Reich has thought of everything. This house is magnificent. It's already beautifully furnished. There is even a small library filled with lovely books. I know how much you love to read."

"Books." She sighed, thinking of Abram. "I do love books."

"And I'll make sure to stock it with plenty of good books for you to read to Karl as well. He'll have his own room. And I'll fill it with toys for him."

"It sounds wonderful. I can't wait."

"And . . . I can't wait to hold you in my arms again," he said. "How cruel that was to give me just a taste of your love knowing I would be forced to be away from you for a while."

"Are you angry?"

"Never. I am just hungry for more."

She felt her face flush. "Oh," she said, embarrassed.

There was a moment of silence. Then he said, "Ask Ludwig to help you find the hotel in Munich. Tell him I can take time off in the spring. Have him check if he can get the time off as well. Once you're sure he can, then tell him to book the room for the five of us for four nights. Tell him I will pay him back for it when I see him."

"All right."

"And when I call you next week, you can give me the dates."

"I will take care of it."

"I love you, Kara."

"Yes, I know," she said. Then she quickly added, "I love you too."

# CHAPTER THIRTY-SIX

## April 1942

ANKA INSISTED that Kara accompany her to the social gatherings that were given by the other
German hausfraus who lived in the area. Kara attended, not because she wanted to, but for Anka's
sake. Anka wanted so badly to fit in. She was pretty
and Aryan and everything a German woman
should be. But she was missing one very important
factor. She was childless. The other women had
plenty of children. The children ran around the
house while the mothers sipped coffee and shared
recipes. They reminded Kara of the girls in the
Deusche Madels. Even though these women were
no longer children, they were still narrow minded,
and they followed the Nazi doctrine blindly. It was
apparent in everything they said and did. They

openly and casually discussed their hatred for the Jews as if they were talking about how much sugar to add to a strudel.

Anka always brought a nice dessert, which she'd painstakingly prepared.

They attended one such luncheon in early April that was given by the woman who lived down the street from Anka. Her name was Gretchen, and she had five young children. When they arrived, there was an air of excitement in the room. Before the food was served, the hostess stood up and said loudly, "Please, ladies. Quiet down. I have an announcement to make."

The women quieted down, and Gretchen continued, "As you all know, next week is the twelfth of April. The birth date of our führer's mother. I am hoping I will receive a mother's cross. Because, as of this year, when Erich was born, I now have five children. Five children for the Reich," Gretchen said. Kara studied Gretchen; the woman was so young. She appeared to be in her early twenties.

They all cried out, "Congratulations!"

"Don't think you are so special. I have eight," another young girl said.

"Oh, please, I know a woman who has sixteen. She has been honored by the führer himself!" another offered.

*Sixteen children?* Kara thought. Then the woman said, "I've heard that women receive honors for having lots of children."

"Oh yes, the führer loves mothers; the more we have, the greater the honor."

Then someone said, in a loud singsong voice, "Kinder, kuche, kirche. Children, kitchen, church."

The other women all repeated the mantra: "Children, kitchen, church."

Anka turned away. She tried to force that smile that she always gave when her heart was breaking. Then she stood up and said, "It looks like the decanter is empty. I'll go and refill the coffee."

Kara wished she could do something for Anka. Even though she didn't care what the führer thought, she knew how much a child could enrich its mother's life. And she also knew that after what happened to Anka, her sister would never risk going through another pregnancy. So maybe an adoption was the best option for her. And perhaps some of the children at the Lebensborn were orphans, and Anka would be doing them a good turn by giving them a loving home.

# CHAPTER THIRTY-SEVEN

## Munich

OSKAR AND KARA were married on a crystal-clear day in the spring of 1942 in Munich, Germany. In the morning before they were to begin the ceremony, Oskar left Kara in the hotel room and went out to buy Kara a large bouquet of golden sunflowers, the official flowers of the Nazi Party, which was tied with a white ribbon. Anka looked lovely in a watercolor-blue silk dress and matching hat. Ludwig and Oskar appeared important in their perfectly pressed uniforms. Five-year-old Karl was charming in the suit Oskar had brought him. His hair had grown back just enough to curl slightly on the ends. Before she entered the room, Kara looked in the mirror. *This dress is beautiful. It's more than any girl could ask for. And I should be so happy.* But when she gazed into her own eyes, the mirror reflected such sadness that she had to look away. *I am so miserable. I should be eager to start my life with Oskar. And I should be grateful that I have found such a wonderful man. But I can't help but think of Abram, of all the dreams we shared. I know Karl looks just like me with his blond hair and blue eyes, but his mannerisms remind me so much of Abram that I could cry. The way he holds the book that Oskar asked him to hold.*

The book was a wedding edition of *Mein Kampf,* that had been sent by Adolf Hitler himself as a gift to the new couple. Kara had never read it, but she had heard that it was cruel, and it hurt her heart to see her innocent child holding it in his chubby little hands. As Karl walked up to his mother, so serious that it made her smile, she thought, *I see Abram in the way he tilts his head. But most of all, I see Abram in our son's smile.* Kara's heart ached for Abram when she looked at her little boy. And no matter how much she tried to be happy with Oskar, Karl brought back so many beautiful memories that were now painful. Kara loved Oskar; she had tender feelings for him and gratitude for all he'd done for her. But try as she might, she just wasn't in love with him. Oh, there were fleeting moments when she almost believed that she was. But they were gone too soon, and she knew that she would never love him the way she loved Abram. Not even at this moment. Not even as he looked into her eyes and they spoke their vows.

After the wedding, everyone went out for lunch.

Karl ate quickly. Then he was bored and had a hard time sitting still at the restaurant. The adults were busy talking, and since he wasn't the center of attention, he kept trying to get up and walk around. Whenever Karl started fidgeting, Oskar was able to control him by distracting and entertaining him. Oskar never got angry with Karl when he started acting up. In fact, he never seemed to mind caring for the child. As Kara watched Oskar and Karl together, she saw how wonderful Oskar was with her son. *I've made the right choice in marrying Oskar. He will be a good father to Karl.*

They spent the rest of the day walking around Munich, and looking in the shops. Across the street Oskar saw that there was a park. So he took Karl's hand and led him into a shop, where he purchased a ball. Then Oskar suggested that they all go to the park where he could play ball with Karl. At first Kara tried to discourage the ball-playing because both Oskar and Karl were dressed in their best clothes. But Karl begged, and Oskar gave her his brightest smile. So she finally agreed. Ludwig, Anka, and Kara sat on the bench and talked while Oskar gave the little boy his undivided attention. Every time Karl giggled, Kara felt like she might cry. *I almost lost him. If it weren't for Oskar, I would never have found him. I am so fortunate that Oskar loves me. Since Abram cannot be here to be a father to Karl, at least I have found the next best thing.*

That night as Oskar and Kara lay in bed in the

hotel room, she tried to give him her full attention. Although she went through the motions of making love to her new husband, she couldn't get Karl off her mind. She knew her son was in the room right down the hall. And she was fairly certain that neither Anka nor Ludwig would make the mistake of letting him out of their sight. Even so, there was still a twinge of doubt. What if somehow something happened, and Karl went missing again. Kara was afraid, nervous, and worried. It wasn't at all Oskar's fault; he was a good lover, not selfish or demanding. But her heart was just not in it. *I know Anka and Ludwig are watching him carefully. But when I can't see him, I can't relax. I am afraid that almost losing him has scared me forever. I don't know if I will ever be comfortable when he is out of my sight. I hope that when he grows up and becomes a man, I will feel more confident. Stronger. I can't help myself.* Her palms were wet with sweat and her mouth was dry.

Oskar didn't seem to notice Kara's detachment. He was madly in love. The object of his affection was now his wife. She lay in bed at his side, and for the first time in a long time, he was happy. The following morning, as soon as the sun rose, Kara slipped on the silk robe Oskar had given her along with her matching slippers, and quietly left the room. Oskar was still asleep as she made her way to Anka and Ludwig's room. Knocking on the door softly, she whispered, "Anka, open up, it's me."

Anka cracked the door open still half-asleep.

"Are you all right? It's still early. What are you doing awake? Did something happen between you and Oskar?"

"I'm fine. Oskar and I are fine. I'm sorry I woke you," Kara said, whispering so as not to awaken Ludwig, who snored loudly. "I really am sorry. I know you were asleep, but can I please see Karl?"

"Sure. He's right in here. He's still asleep. Try not to wake him." Anka led Kara into a small room adjacent to hers and Ludwig's. There Karl lay in his bed. His face was calm, and his breath was soft and even. As the sun was rising, rays of golden sunshine filtered through the crack in the window shade and illuminated his hair.

Kara looked down at her precious son who was sleeping soundly. "He looks like an angel," she said to Anka.

Anka rubbed Kara's arm. Then she whispered, "I know you're worried. But Ludwig and I won't let him out of our sight. I promise you. Look, he can't even get out of this room without passing through our room. So, once he's in bed for the night, he is completely secure. You see?"

Kara nodded. "Yes, I see. You're right. And I am sorry, but I can't help but be nervous. I lost him once. I have been blessed to have found him. I can't lose him again."

"You won't. We'll see to it," Anka said.

Kara hugged her sister. "I suppose I should go

back to my room. Oskar will awaken and wonder where I've gone."

"Yes, go on. Everything is fine. I promise you."

Kara kissed her sister's cheek, then she left and went back to the room she shared with Oskar. She slipped off her robe and slippers and climbed into bed beside him. He put his arm around her. *I love my sister, but I still don't feel that I can trust her. I know she wouldn't hurt Karl on purpose. But she isn't always responsible. Her values are skewed. Anka can easily become distracted by almost anything. Karl is just too valuable to me to put him at risk like this. And yet, at least for the time we are here on our honeymoon, I must. I would never admit this to anyone, but I can't wait for this to be over.*

The three days in Munich went by quickly. Each morning after breakfast, Oskar took Kara and Karl to the park where he played ball with Karl. He did this, he told Kara, in order to give Anka and Ludwig some time alone to relax. "Watching a young child is a lot of work, as you know, my love," he said that morning after breakfast as they walked to the park.

"Yes, I know. And I am glad you take him to the park each day," Kara said. "After all he's been through, he needs to feel wanted and loved. You are his father figure and his friend."

"I want to be that for him. I want to be the perfect husband and father."

"I know you do. And you're doing a wonderful job of it."

Oskar played ball with Karl for almost an hour. The sweet sound of Karl's delighted giggles filled Kara with a warm feeling of well-being.

"I am tired, Karl. You've worn me out," Oskar said as he picked up the ball and took the little boy's hand.

"Can we play again later?" Karl asked.

"We'll see. I do enjoy our ball game so much; however, don't you think we should spend some time talking with your mutti?"

"She's fine. She likes to watch us play."

"That she does. Still, I think it's time for a little break."

"All right," Karl conceded. Then he sat down on the bench beside Kara. Oskar sat down on Kara's other side. He took Kara's hand and said, "It's the last day of our honeymoon, and I truly hate to leave you, my love. How soon do you think you can be ready to move?"

"I've been packing. Perhaps another month? Have you moved into the house yet?"

"I have. It's really quite lovely. It's even nicer than I originally thought. I know you're going to adore the furnishings."

She smiled.

# CHAPTER THIRTY-EIGHT

AFTER LUNCH, Karl went to take a nap in Anka and Ludwig's room, leaving Kara and Oskar alone. As soon as Oskar closed the door to their room, he took Kara into his arms and began kissing her passionately. His hands caressed her. Then he slowly undressed her, planting kisses all over her body. Once she was naked, he took off his clothes and climbed into bed beside her. Oskar made love to her, savoring ever second, until finally he could hold back no longer.

After it was over, they lay side by side in bed. He stroked her arm.

"So, you know how much I love you?" he asked.

"Was that a question that required an answer?" she asked coyly.

"No, I just want you to be sure, you know."

"I do. And I love you too."

He kissed her. "We're going to have a good life together," he said.

"Yes."

"You will have everything you could ever need or want."

She smiled.

For several moments they lay in silence. Kara had been thinking a lot about Anka's being able to have a child of her own. She turned over on her elbow and looked at Oskar. "I know that I am changing the subject, but I have to ask you this before you leave."

"Yes, what is it?" He looked at her with concern in his eyes. "Is something wrong?"

"No, not really. I was just wondering if you could tell me a little about the Lebensborn. Are all of the children in there stolen?"

"Why would you ask that? Why now?" he said, sounding slightly annoyed.

"I'm not asking for myself. I'm asking for Anka. She and Ludwig can't have a child. They are considering adoption."

"Oh. I see," He sounded relieved. "Not all of the children have been stolen. In fact, it's rare, very rare, darling. Many of the children who are part of that program have been produced especially for adoption for pure German families who can't have children of their own. So, it would be a good choice for Anka and Ludwig to consider adopting a child through them."

"I really don't understand. What do you mean children are produced?"

"Why are you asking?" he said.

"Well . . ." She hesitated. "I don't know what that means."

"Very generous women agree to mate with SS officers in order to create more perfect Aryan children. The children are then adopted by couples like Anka and Ludwig."

"It sounds rather strange."

"I suppose. But it works. The children are only assigned to the finest of homes. As far as the stolen children. That rarely happens. It was a fluke really," he lied. The breeding aspect was true, but he also knew that plenty of blond-haired, blue-eyed children were stolen from their Polish families.

"I feel sorry for my sister. She had a very bad experience with her own pregnancy."

"Do you want to tell me about it," he said, his eyes filled with compassion.

Kara nodded, then she told him what had happened to Anka. How her sister had made the ultimate sacrifice for the Reich. "I don't agree with what she did. I could never have done that."

"I know, darling," he said, "and you'll never have to worry about it. Our child will be as beautiful and perfect as Karl."

Kara bit her lip. She'd become superstitious from Hoda, and she didn't want to tempt the evil eye. If Oskar had not been lying beside her, she would have spit three times. Silently she said a prayer: *Please God, let my future children be perfect and healthy.*

"Anka and Ludwig are young; they should try again."

"I believe she is afraid to try again."

"Hmmm. I understand," he grunted. "Poor thing."

"Yes," Kara said. "Can you tell me how this breeding process works? I'm very curious."

"All right, let me explain about the children in the Lebensborn."

"Go on," Kara said.

"There are many young women of pure blood who want to do what they can for our Reich. Many of them are single women who can't afford to care for a child. However, they want to contribute to the fatherland. So, they go to the home for the Lebensborn where they are thoroughly checked out to be sure their blood is pure. Then they are mated with a fine SS officer, also of pure blood. It is understood, even before conception, that the child will be given up for adoption. The mother is promised that only a good German family, which usually includes an SS officer, and his pure Aryan wife will be allowed to raise the child. That is, of course, unless the birth father changes his mind and decides that he wants to adopt the child. Then he is given the privilege. However, that rarely happens. Many officers I know have fathered several children at the home. It's an honor."

She cleared her throat, afraid of his answer, and yet knowing she must ask the question. "Do you have any children that you have fathered at the home?"

"Me? No. I'm too sensitive of a fellow for that, I'm afraid. I wouldn't be able to part with the child."

Kara took a deep breath. She was glad he hadn't participated in that strange program. The thought of children being bred like purebred puppies made her cringe. Yet this could be a good opportunity for Anka to find happiness. And how could she deny her beloved sister this opportunity? "How does one go about adopting a child?"

"Would you like me to make arrangements for Anka and Ludwig? As you know, I have connections, and I can arrange it for them."

"Anka and I have discussed it. However, before you arrange things, I suppose I should talk to Anka again, just to be sure that she and Ludwig want this."

"Yes, that would be a good idea. Perhaps you can speak to her today. Then if she decides that she and Ludwig would like to participate in the program, I'll make a call."

"You are so good to me," Kara said.

"Shouldn't a man be good to the woman he loves? You are my life, Kara. You and Karl. I am hoping you will eventually see fit to give Karl a brother or sister."

"You want a child of our own?"

"Karl is my son now. He is like my own. But yes, I would love to have more children. No child should grow up alone without a brother or sister."

"Once we are settled, we can talk about it again," Kara said. She glanced over at Oskar. He kissed her forehead. *Oskar is such a good, kind man. He deserves a wife who loves and appreciates him. A wife who wants to bear his child. After all, he's not like the other Nazis. He told me that he has no contact with Jews. I know him, and I know he would never mistreat an animal, let alone a human being. I should be more enthusiastic about our future together. Yet I am haunted by memories of Abram and Hoda, And I can't help but remember the faces of the Jewish people in the ghetto. I know Oskar loves me, but I still feel that it is not safe to tell him the truth about Karl. Why is that? Why do I feel that I can't fully trust him?*

"Yes, but we should get settled first," she said again.

# CHAPTER THIRTY-NINE

THE FOLLOWING MORNING AFTER BREAKFAST, Ludwig and Anka took Karl for a walk so that Kara and Oskar could say goodbye. Kara glanced at her son nervously as he left the hotel holding Anka's hand. Then she and Oskar went back up to their room. Kara sat on the bed while Oskar packed his small valise to leave for work, glancing up at Kara every few minutes as he folded his clothes. "I miss you already," he said in a husky voice. Then he added, "Frau Lerch. My wife."

Kara gave him a warm smile. "I'll miss you too," she said, "and so will Karl."

"Hurry and pack all your things, so you and Karl can move into the house with me. Every day without you there feels like forever."

"I'll finish as quickly as I can," Kara said.

He stopped what he was doing and walked over

to her. Then he kissed her tenderly. Gently he pushed her onto her back on the bed. Oskar didn't undress her. There was no time. He was late already. But his tender kisses turned to passionate ones, and before she knew it, he had lifted her skirt and was making love to her. When he finished, he touched her face. "I'll call you Sunday?" he said with a question in his voice.

"Yes."

"Please hurry with your packing, won't you?"

"I promise you, I will," she said. But the truth was, she was procrastinating, if only just a little. The idea of living in a compound of hausfraus whose husbands were Nazi officers sent chills down her spine. *Oskar is different. He's not like the others*, she tried to convince herself. *Isn't he?*

He closed his suitcase and picked it up. Then he walked over to where she sat and kissed her long and hard. "I'll see you soon," he said and walked out the door.

Kara waited a few minutes to be sure he was gone. For some reason she didn't want to have to see him and say goodbye again. *But I do love him. I do*, she thought.

Once she was certain he was gone, Kara went to Anka's room to see if she and Ludwig had returned with Karl from their walk. Anka answered the door. "Come in," she said cheerfully.

Kara's eyes searched the room frantically. "Where's Karl?" she asked.

"Oh, he wanted to go to the toy shop, so Ludwig took him."

Kara felt her heart pound in her chest. It was difficult to breathe.

"Are you all right?" Anka asked. "You look pale."

"Yes. I'm fine," Kara choked out the words.

Then the door opened, and Karl came running in carrying a toy gun in his hand. When he saw Kara, he ran to her. "Mutti, Uncle Ludwig bought this for me." She wasn't happy to see a gun in his hand even if it was a toy. But she was so glad to see him that she grabbed him into a bear hug.

"Where is Oskar? I want to go and play ball," Karl asked.

"He had to go back to work," Kara said, still holding Karl. He struggled a little to get away, and she finally let him go. Then he took the toy gun and ran into his room, leaving the door open. "I'm going to play with my new gun," he said.

"All right," Kara said. At least she could watch him while she and Anka talked.

"I spoke to Oskar about the home for the Lebensborn. Are you seriously interested in adopting?" Kara asked. She still had misgivings, but she decided that if the young women actually did willingly give up their children for adoption by childless couples, then perhaps it was all right for Ludwig and Anka to apply.

"Mutti, Uncle Ludwig is reading me a book

about Jews," Karl interrupted. "Do you and Aunty Anka want to come and hear the story too?"

"No, I don't think so," Kara said.

Ludwig was in the other room with Karl. Kara could hear him reading to Karl from one of the horrible children's books that was approved by the Reich. One of those books with the frightening pictures and messages about Jews.

"Do you remember the wonderful fairy tales I used to read to you?" Kara said to Anka, her voice a little curt.

"Of course."

"I wish Ludwig wouldn't read those books to him. It would be nice if he could tell him the story of Tom Thumb, or, well, anything but that." Kara took a deep breath. She was trying to contain her anger. It was a long ride back, and she didn't want to have a fight with Anka or Ludwig and then have to spend hours inside the small space of a car with them.

"You really hate these books, don't you, Kara?"

"I don't like them. They are too frightening for a child."

"Yes, they are frightening. But it is so necessary that we instill a fear of the Jews early in a child's life. They can be so dangerous to an Aryan child."

*I wish I could trust you enough to tell you the truth about Abram and Karl. You are my sister. My flesh and blood. But you have been so tainted by the Nazi ideology, that I can't trust you not to turn Karl in even though he is my son. If you could allow them to kill your own infant, I can't trust you. Not now. Not ever.* "Yes, well, I understand how you feel. But I would prefer that Karl grew up hearing stories that are less horrifying."

"The fairy tales we read when we were children were scary."

"I know they were. But this is different. These books cause hate. Can't you see that?"

Ludwig looked up. He must have overheard Kara. He stopped reading and handed Karl the book. Then he said to Anka and Kara, "I'm going downstairs to get a beer. Do either of you want anything?"

"Not me," Kara said.

"No, thank you," Anka said.

Ludwig didn't start an argument. But as he left, Kara could see that his face was flushed, and he was angry.

"Mutti," Karl called to Kara from the other room. "Do you want to see some pictures of Jews? They have big noses and black scary eyes. Did you know that they kidnap, then kill and eat children?"

"That's nonsense." Kara stood up. She shook her head as she walked briskly into the other room and grabbed the book, tearing it out of Karl's hands. "That's enough of this book. Enough of that gun too." Kara grabbed the toy gun.

"Mutti." Karl's bottom lip jutted out. He was almost in tears. Kara saw that she'd upset him. So she took him into her arms and held him. "It's all right. You didn't do anything wrong. It's not your fault. I know! Why don't you draw me a special picture? How about that?"

Karl nodded. He sat down on the floor, and Kara went over to the desk and got him some crayons that Oskar had purchased for him, and a few sheets of blank paper.

Anka walked into the room. "You are wrong to shelter him from the truth," Anka said.

"The truth? This is not the truth. These are propaganda-filled lies."

"What should I draw, Mutti?"

"What would you like to draw?" She was afraid he might say a Jew or something else that she would have to reprimand him about.

"A dog."

"All right. Draw a dog for me, then." She breathed a sigh of relief, then she added gently, "I want to talk to Aunty Anka alone for a minute, so we're going to go into the other room. I'll be right here where you can see me."

"All right," Karl said, smiling.

"You're such a good boy." Kara kissed the top of his head.

Kara and Anka sat side by side on the bed.

"Please don't tell me you want to talk more about how terrible you think these children's books are."

"Actually, no. I don't want to talk about it anymore. I've said all I need to say. But I really wish you would respect my wishes about the books."

"I think you're wrong, Kara. But he's your son, so I'll do as you ask. And I'll tell Ludwig to do the same."

"Thank you," Kara said. Then she took her sister's hand and continued. "Now, let's get back to our talk about the home for the Lebensborn?"

"Yes, let's get back to that."

"Well, as I said, I spoke to Oskar about it. And you have always wanted a child, haven't you?"

"You know how I feel. I would love to have a baby. But . . . you also know what happened. I refuse to get pregnant again. I can't go through that again."

"I understand. That's why I want to tell you more about the Lebensborn home. Do you know how it works?"

"Not really."

"All right. Let me explain." Kara told Anka everything Oskar had told her.

"So then, I wouldn't be stealing anyone's child?"

"Not according to what Oskar told me."

"I know Ludwig and I would qualify," Anka said brightly. "We are both of pure Aryan blood."

"I'm sure you would qualify," Kara said. "Oskar told me that if you are serious about it, he would make a call, and see to it that you were approved."

"Oh, Kara." Anka beamed. "That would be wonderful. Like a dream come true. Of course, I have to speak to Ludwig before you ask Oskar to call, just to make sure he agrees. But I have no doubt really that he will be happy. You know Ludwig. He allows me to do whatever I want. He's good that way. I am so glad he's nothing like our father."

Kara forced a smile. "Yes, that's a good thing. Our father, when I think about him, I still get chills. You know, it's kind of strange, but I haven't thought about our parents in a long time."

"I probably forgot to tell you this, but Father died during that year and a half that I didn't speak to you. The time when you disappeared for a while when you were living with Karl's father. Poor Mutti. She wanted to feel badly at his funeral, but I knew her too well, and I could see relief in her eyes. Who could blame her the way he used to beat her? Then she surprised me, about two months after Father's death, I heard from one of my old classmates, who still lived in our neighborhood, that she'd remarried. So, I went to see her to see how she was doing, you know?"

Kara nodded, a little surprised at all of this news.

"When I went to our old flat, she was gone. I asked the landlord if he knew where she'd moved to. He said he had no idea. One night she just disappeared. She left all of her things behind. Not that we ever had much, if you recall."

"Yes, I recall," Kara said. She was thinking about her mother and feeling such a mix of emo-

tions that she couldn't define them all. She was remembering the old apartment, and how hard her
mother worked, and how sorry she'd felt for her.
The poor woman had worked from sunup to sun-
down. But she was also remembering how her
mother had ignored it when her father had sexually
abused her and tried to abuse Anka. And for a moment she remembered why she'd left and how much
she had hated her mother at the time. A sick feeling
came over her.

"You know what? The landlord thought that
Mutti ran away with some Jew. That would be just
like her, wouldn't it?"

"Mutti?" Kara said, shaking her head. "Why
didn't you tell me any of this before?"

"You never asked."

"I had to ask you? I would think you would have
told me on your own."

"I didn't think you wanted to talk about our
parents anymore. You ran away from them too, just
like I did. Besides, all of this is rather upsetting
news. I didn't see any point in telling you."

"So why tell me now?"

"I don't know. Maybe because you're married,
and I know you have someone in your life who
loves you. And, well, I thought our past couldn't
hurt you anymore. When you were living with that
married man, Karl's father, I never felt certain
about your future. After all, he was married, and I
didn't know if he would ever leave his wife. So, I

was always afraid you might still be attached to our past."

"Why would I ever feel that way?"

"Because, you didn't have a solid relationship. Karl's father wasn't your husband. I don't know. Perhaps I should have told you."

"It doesn't matter," Kara said. "I only hope Mutti has found happiness."

"If she's with a Jew, she's probably in some kind of trouble."

"We don't know anything for sure."

"No, we don't, and I can't find her. So, all we can do is hope she's all right. Besides, I never felt close to either of them. You were my only real family when we were children. When we were little, I would sometimes pretend that you were my mutti. Did you know that?"

Kara shook her head.

"I still feel so close to you, Kara. And I am going to be so sad when you move away. But at least I will know that we can still spend holidays together," Anka said, "and if I can adopt a baby, I won't feel so lonely."

"You have Ludwig."

"Ludwig," Anka said, sighing. "Yes, I have Ludwig. I only wish he was more of a man. More like Oskar. He is so wishy washy."

"He does love you, Anka. I can see it."

"That he does. I just wish he were more. Do you know what I mean by that?"

Kara shook her head, but she did know.

"I wish he were more handsome, more manly, stronger, more of the kind of man who takes charge, I guess."

Kara reached for Anka's hand. "You wouldn't be happy with a man who didn't give you your own way. You've always been a little headstrong, Anka," Kara said, then she squeezed Anka's hand. "Believe it or not, I think Ludwig is a good match for you."

That afternoon they packed their things and drove back to Anka and Ludwig's home.

The following morning, Anka was sitting at the kitchen table sipping a cup of coffee. She was smiling with excitement as Kara walked into the room. Karl was already awake and sitting on the living room floor playing with a bunch of blocks that Ludwig had gotten him.

"Mutti," Karl said, "I want a dog."

"You what?"

"I want a dog."

"Where did this come from?"

"One of Aunty Anka's friends came over to visit this morning. She had a little puppy. She said her husband got it for her. I liked it so much. I want one too."

"Yes, well, we're moving soon, and I don't know how Oskar will feel about that." Kara couldn't bring herself to refer to Oskar as Vater.

"I'll ask him," Karl said.

"We'll see," Kara said, pouring herself a cup of

coffee and then sitting down at the table next to Anka, who was grinning from ear to ear.

"I talked to Ludwig about adopting a baby. He thinks it's a good idea. The more I think about it, the more excited I feel. I can't wait to do it, Kara. I want a child. I always have."

"I know that." Kara touched Anka's hand. Then she took a sip of coffee, "And this is a good opportunity for you."

"How soon can we do it?"

"I'll speak to Oskar when he telephones on Sunday, and see how soon he can set something up." Then she added, "Who came by this morning?"

"Just one of the women I know, who lives in this little compound. Her husband works at the lair."

# CHAPTER FORTY

ON SUNDAY WHEN OSKAR TELEPHONED, Kara told him that she'd spoken with her sister and that Anka and Ludwig would very much like to adopt a child. "Can you set things up for them soon?"

"I'll make some calls tomorrow morning and I'll arrange everything," he said. "I can't tell you how much I miss you. How's the packing coming?"

"Fine. I'm almost done."

"Ahhh," he sighed softly, almost as if he were starting to make love to her. "I'll be holding you in my arms again very soon?"

"Very soon."

Then Karl began screaming, "I want to talk to Oskar."

"What's this?" Oskar asked Kara. "Is that Karl?"

"Yes, he wants to ask you something."

"Oh? Well, put him on the phone," Oskar said.

"Are you sure? It's long distance."

"Positive, I'd love to talk to Karl."

"Come here," Kara said. Karl ran over to her. "Don't talk too long, all right?" she said, handing Karl the phone.

"Oskar!" Karl said in an excited voice.

"Hello, Son!" Oskar's tone was warm.

"I want a dog. I really, really want a puppy."

"Do you now?"

"One of Aunty Anka's friends came over and she had a puppy. I loved it. I want one too."

Oskar let out a laugh. "Would that make you happy?"

"Oh yes! Very happy."

"I see. What does your mother say about it?"

"She said I had to ask you." Then Karl turned to Kara and said, "Mutti, can I have a puppy if Oskar says it's all right?"

"I suppose so."

"I heard your mother," Oskar said, "and so . . ." He hesitated for effect, then he added, "it seems that I'll just have to find a way to get you a puppy."

"So you mean you'll get me one?"

"That's what I said."

"I love you, Oskar."

"Call me Vati?"

"I love you, Vati," Karl said.

After Karl hung up the phone, Kara watched him run into the living room to play. She leaned back in her chair and thought about her son calling Oskar "daddy." At first it had rubbed her wrong. She felt almost as if it was a betrayal to Abram, and it made her sick. *But Karl needs a father and Oskar loves him, and he is so good to him and to us. If Abram cannot be here, isn't this what is best for my son?* she thought, and even though there was a pain in her heart, she decided to be as enthusiastic as possible. *I am fortunate that a wealthy, successful man is willing to adopt my son and take care of us. I must remember that. And the fact that he is in the SS will guarantee Karl's safety. After all, no one would ever suspect Oskar of having a half-Jewish son.*

# CHAPTER FORTY-ONE

A WEEK LATER, Kara knew she'd procrastinated long enough. It was time to make the move into her husband's home and her new life. She had waited as long she could because she knew that once she moved in with Oskar, she must give up the dream of Abram ever returning to her. In her heart, she felt certain that Abram was gone, but until now there had always been just a tiny flicker of light, of hope, that someday he would find his way back to her. *It's so hard to accept that he's probably dead. If he wasn't, I would have been able to find him when I went back to the Mitte to search for him. And Karl needs a father. Just look at the way he was so excited when I told him yesterday that we were going home to live with Oskar. His face lit up. He couldn't wait. Oh, dear God. I hope I am not making a mistake. I pray I am doing what is best for my son,* she thought as she closed the final suitcase.

Ludwig drove Kara and Karl to the train station. Anka went along with them to say goodbye.

"I am going to miss you and Karl so much," Anka said, hugging her sister as they stood on the platform.

"Yes, I will miss both of you too," Ludwig said.

"I know. And I will miss you. But I suppose a wife should be with her husband, no?"

Anka nodded. "Yes, it's only right."

"Well, anyway . . ." Kara smiled. "I must tell you that I am so excited for you about the baby. The next time I see you both, you'll probably have a child."

Anka smiled broadly. "I can hardly wait."

A week prior to Kara's leaving, Ludwig and Anka had received a telephone call from a woman. Her name was Aloisa Altner; she worked in the home for the Lebensborn. She explained that Oskar had contacted her and asked her to call them. Aloisa made arrangements with Ludwig for he and his wife to travel to Munich where they were to be screened at the Steinhöring institute. "It's just a formality," Aloisa Altner said. "I have no doubt you will pass. After all, Oberstrumführer Lerch is a personal friend of mine and he recommended you. Still, it's protocol, and we must do this in order to ensure that all of our couples are of pure blood."

"I completely understand," Ludwig said, "and I look forward to meeting you."

Anka was so excited. She had asked Kara to go with them, but Kara refused. "As much as I would love to go, I have to go home to Oskar," she said. "He would be so disappointed if I went to Munich with you. He's been waiting for Karl and I to come home for so long now." But that wasn't the real reason Kara didn't want to go with Anka and Ludwig. The truth was she couldn't bear to walk into that place again. Even thinking about it brought back horrible memories. In her mind's eye, she could see each of the rooms, and just the thought of being there made her shiver. All she could think of was how desperate she felt when Karl was missing. But she didn't want to go into all of that with Anka. She didn't want to spoil her sister's excitement.

"I know. He has been waiting a long time for you. I still wish you could come with us. But I do understand, and I'll call you as soon as we are approved," Anka said. "Are you eager to see your new home?"

Kara nodded and smiled. *I'm happy. Well, if not happy, I'm content. I am as happy as I can be,* Kara thought.

Ludwig helped the porter to load Kara's luggage. Then he gave Karl a hug and awkwardly hugged Kara.

Kara turned to Anka again and pulled her into her arms. "I'll talk to you soon," she said. Then

Kara picked Karl up and carried him onto the train.

The motion of the train put Karl to sleep, and he slept most of the way while Kara thought about Abram, and her heart ached as she remembered.

# CHAPTER FORTY-TWO

WHEN KARA and Karl arrived at the train station, Oskar was standing outside his black automobile waiting to take them home. He chose not to ask his driver to pick them up because he had a surprise for Karl. In the back seat was a little black-and-tan shepherd puppy. When Oskar opened the door and Karl saw the dog, he let out squeal of delight.

"Vati!" he said, remembering to call Oskar daddy. "You did it. You got me a dog."

"Of course, Son. I always keep my promises."

Kara looked at the furry little thing already licking Karl's cheek, and she smiled and shook her head. Then she let out a short laugh. "You got him a puppy."

"I hope you're not angry."

"How can I be angry when you are so good to us?" Kara touched his arm.

"You are my family; I love you," Oskar said as he started the car.

Kara reached over and patted Oskar's hand. He smiled at her.

*I made the right choice. I know I did,* she thought, but then her eyes fell upon the death-head symbol on Oskar's hat, and she felt a shiver run down her spine.

"Is it all right if I call him Patches, Vati? I want to call him that because he has two different colors in his fur," Karl asked.

"You can call him whatever you want. He's yours," Oskar said.

The strangest thing about the little town called Oswiecim, where they were going to live, was the odd, unpleasant odor that permeated the air. It was a sickly-sweet smell, nauseating. But Kara could not figure out what it was. She had never smelled anything like it before. Sometimes bits of ash blew through the air.

Kara asked Oskar about what the smell and ash were.

He replied, "There is so much industry here. There are chemical plants, medical plants, and a factory that makes rubber. In fact, Germany is currently in the process of opening a coal mine. It's all part of the colonizing in the east."

"What exactly do you do at your job?" Kara asked. "You've never told me."

"I never told you because you never asked," he

said, smiling. "I don't do anything exciting. How-ever, it is top secret. So, I am afraid I can't tell you," he said.

"Is it difficult?"

"Yes, sometimes. The employees get out of hand and must be reprimanded. And it's my job to keep them in line and see to it that they do their work. Sometimes I am forced to be harsh."

"I can't imagine you reprimanding anyone harshly. I see how you are with Karl. You have so much patience, and I know he can be a handful," she said, then smiling at him, she continued, "You're such a gentle soul." But then she thought, *I do remember how furious he was with that woman at the children's welfare agency who had transferred Karl. And how he'd responded when I was arrested. There is another side of him. A side I sometimes choose not to see. But we had been searching for Karl for so long, and we were both so frustrated. I can't blame him for losing patience. And then when I was arrested, he was unnerved when he saw that I'd been beaten. I can't hold that against him either.*

"I am a gentle soul with you and Karl because you are my family and I love you. However, when I am at work, I must be firm. It's the only way to get things done."

She nodded. "I understand," she said.

Unlike her sister and Ludwig, Oskar and Kara didn't spend much time with the other German families who had moved into the area. Kara as-sumed that Oskar preferred to be alone because they were newlyweds. But on the rare occasions when they attended a party at someone's home, none of the men ever talked about their jobs, and no one asked them any questions either.

Karl went to kindergarten at a school that had been set up within the German community. The teacher was a young, vivacious girl from Heidelberg. She played piano and sang. And all of the children, including Karl, loved her. The students, the faculty, and the officer workers at the school were all of pure German descent. And by the drawings that Karl brought home, Kara could see he was being taught to be proud of his Aryan heritage. He loved to sing the songs he learned, to Oskar. They were children's songs, but they spoke of the glory of the fatherland. In the pictures he drew there were stick figures with short mustaches that he told Kara were Adolf Hitler, and beside Hitler were crude drawings of the Nazi flag. Kara didn't mind any of this until Karl began to spew hatred of what he'd learned were inferior races. Then one afternoon, while he was sitting down for his afternoon snack, he began to tell Kara about the superiority of the Aryan race.

"What did you do in school today?" she asked him as she placed a cut-up apple and a plate of cookies on the table.

"Mutti, we are going to make all of these people who live in Poland our slaves. They will do all of the work for us and we Germans will rule them. Do you know why?"

Kara sucked in a deep breath and poured Karl a glass of milk.

"It's because we are Germans, and we are better than they are. And pretty soon there will be no more Jews for us to be afraid of. Our führer is protecting us from them."

Kara felt a shiver run up her spine. She couldn't tell him the truth, that he was half Jewish. He was just a child. If she told him, he was bound to say something to the other children at school. And yet it was painful to hear him spouting the horrible Nazi rhetoric he was being taught.

"Don't talk like that, Karl. I don't like to hear you talk like that," she said weakly, not knowing how to explain why.

"But Mutti, it's true. My teacher told us."

Karl brought children's books home from school that were filled with hate propaganda. At night he asked her to read them to him. She always made an excuse. But when he went to sleep one night, she thumbed through the books. They all had the same messages of German superiority and hatred for Jews, Gypsies, and anyone else Hitler saw fit to despise. One of the books had frightening pictures of mentally and physically handicapped people with captions that read, "They are sucking the life out of our fatherland. It is your responsibility to get rid of those not fit to live." Kara felt sick as she read this.

"Come to bed, darling," Oskar said when he glanced over and saw Kara reading the books. "It's late, and I want to hold you for a while before we sleep."

That was his way of telling her he wanted to make love. She put the book the down and stood up.

"Do you know that you get prettier ever day?" he said.

She smiled at him.

"You do," he continued. "Each day you grow more and more beautiful. And . . . do you know that when I take you to a party and everyone stares at you, I am so proud that you are my wife."

"You embarrass me."

"You shouldn't be embarrassed, my love. You should be delighted. You're a stunning woman."

She shook her head and followed him into their bedroom. He had been right when he told her that she would love the furnishings in this house. How could she not love them? They were beautiful beyond anything that she'd ever seen before. Until she had moved into this house, she thought that Anka and Ludwig's home was magnificent. It was so much nicer than where she and Anka had grown up. But this house was even more elegant than Anka's home. In fact, to Kara, it was like living in a castle.

They made love. Oskar was a generous and considerate lover, but the passion she had once felt with Abram had still not developed with Oskar. As they lay side by side in the darkness, she said, "I was looking at the books that the teacher gave Karl. They are so harsh and frightening for a young child."

He patted her hand. "I understand how you feel. You're his mother and you want to protect him. However, the lessons in these books are important lessons that he must learn. And what better time to start teaching him than when he is young."

"You've looked through the books?"

"I have."

"And you didn't think they were a little too frightening for a child?'

"Perhaps. Frightening, yes. But also necessary."

She'd never asked him before, but she felt compelled to ask him now. "Do you hate Jews?"

"Hate them?" he repeated.

"Yes, do you hate them?"

"I don't trust them."

"But you told me that you have never had much to do with them. How do you know you don't trust them?"

"I haven't had much to do with them, and quite frankly I'm glad. But I have heard stories of things that happened to other people, friends of mine."

"Things that happened with Jews?" Kara pressed.

"Yes, dear. Why are we talking about this?"

She was suddenly silenced. *Yes, why am I asking him all these questions. I am lucky that Karl and I are safe.*

"I don't know why I am asking. I suppose I just wanted to know your thoughts."

"Shall I tell you my thoughts?"

She trembled. "No, it's all right."

He took her hand and kissed it, then he said, "My thoughts are that I am one happy man. I am married to the most exceptional woman." Then he leaned over and kissed her. "I love you, Kara. Do you love me?"

"Of course I do," she said, but she lay awake long after he was asleep.

# CHAPTER FORTY-THREE

**January 1943**

KARA WAS SIPPING a cup of coffee when the phone rang.

"We passed all of our tests. We are registered as a pure Aryan couple, and we've been approved to adopt a child!" Anka's voice was high pitched and excited.

"Where are you? At home or in Munich?"

"At home. I just received the approval a call from Steinhöring, and as soon as I hung up, I telephoned you."

"I'm so happy for you," Kara said.

"Oh, so am I. We could have gotten an older child right away, but Ludwig wanted a baby. I suppose I did too. So, we are waiting for the mother to give birth."

"There is a mother at the home who is pregnant and about to give birth?"

"She is expecting the baby in March."

"If the child is born in March, when are you permitted to pick it up?"

"Usually, the infant stays at Steinhöring for a year after its birth. Then he or she is given a name. After the baby has been named, it can be taken home. But I was hoping, perhaps, Oskar might be able to help us bring our child home sooner."

"As soon as he returns from work this afternoon, I'll ask him if there is anything he can do to help speed up the process."

"You're such a dear sister," Anka said. "By the way, how do you like it there?"

"It's all right. I don't really know anyone. And Oskar isn't very social. So we spend most of our time just the three of us. That's fine on Oskar's days off. But most of the time Oskar works all day, and with Karl in school, it does get lonely." Then Kara took a deep breath and said, "I miss you."

"I miss you too. I have lots of friends here, but there is no one who knows me as well as you do. You're my sister, after all."

"Yes, after all we have been through, we are still sisters."

"Tell me though, Oskar treats you well, yes?"

"Yes, very well."

# CHAPTER FORTY-FOUR

## Auschwitz

"MOVE FASTER, YOU FILTHY PIGS!" Oberstrum-führer Lerch yelled at the men who were returning to their blocks from their jobs at the chemical plant. It was cold, and even though he wore a warm wool coat, he hated being outside. Snow had begun to fall. The pure white powder dusted the already dirty, gray slush mixed with ashes that was scattered all around the camp.

Abram and Moishe shivered as they ran back toward their block. Moishe was barefoot. Someone had recently stolen his shoes while he slept. He'd been so tired and fallen into such a deep sleep that he hadn't felt the shoes being removed from his feet. And now, Abram knew, that if he didn't find a way to get Moishe another pair of shoes, Moishe would probably die. Abram felt sick as he looked down and saw the bloodstained snow under Moishe's feet.

"Good-for-nothing Jew pigs. I said move faster. It's cold out here," Lerch shouted. "If I didn't have to watch over you, I could be inside where it's warm. Now move."

A young man, who Abram had spoken to once or twice, was running in front of him and Moishe. The man slipped on the ice and began to fall forward. Abram grabbed him and slipped his arm beneath him to keep him from plummeting. But the man had turned his ankle and could hardly walk. Moishe came over and put his arm under the man's other arm. Then Moishe and Abram tried to run while carrying the man between them.

"This piece of dirt is slowing you down," Lerch said, indicating the young man who had just turned his ankle. Shaking his head, Oskar Lerch drew his gun, and without another thought, he shot the young fellow in the face. The man went limp in Abram's arms. Abram glanced at Moishe. There was no point in holding on to a dead man. They let him fall. His blood was dark and rich against the white snow. Abram stood staring at the young man; he was paralyzed for the moment. But then Moishe grabbed Abram's arm, and pulling him, the two of them began to run toward their block.

# CHAPTER FORTY-FIVE

THAT NIGHT when Abram closed his eyes, he saw the young man as he lay dying in the snow. He shivered. Then he saw the oberstrumführer's eyes.

"Are you awake?" Abram whispered to Moishe.

"Yes."

"I can't sleep. I can't stop thinking about the man who broke his ankle. The one that the oberstrumführer shot today. He was alive one minute and dead the next. We were holding him. He died in our arms."

"I know," Moishe said.

"I don't understand these guards. How can a human being be so heartless? Lerch is one of the worst. He seems to have no feelings at all. He murdered a man without even thinking about it," Abram said.

"That's because they're not human beings, Abram. They're Nazis."

# CHAPTER FORTY-SIX

## Spring 1943

EARLY ONE MORNING, Oskar got up and was getting dressed for work while Kara was still lying in bed. She had a few minutes before she had to get up and prepare Oskar's breakfast and then start getting Karl ready for school. She stretched and wished she could go back to sleep at least for another hour. The bed felt heavenly. But then the phone rang. Kara looked at the clock. It was too early for a casual call. And the nervousness that she'd developed when Karl had been missing still haunted her. She jumped out of bed, suddenly very awake and grabbed the phone.

"Hello," she said breathlessly.

"Kara?" It was Anka. Her voice was high pitched and excited. "The baby was born a few hours ago. Our baby, my baby. I just got the call from Steinhöring. It's a little girl. The brown sister who telephoned told me that Oskar had made arrangements for Ludwig and me to take the baby immediately. So we're leaving for Munich today. Can you meet us there?"

"Of course. I won't be able to leave until Oskar gets home from work. But I'll speak to him then, and see if he can come too. If he comes, he'll drive me, and I'll leave tonight. If not, I'll catch the next train which will probably be sometime tomorrow. I'll have to arrange for Karl to take time away from school. Shall I go to Munich or go to your home?"

"Come to our home. We are just driving directly to Munich, picking up our little girl, and then driving right back. Oh, Kara, I am so excited. And both Ludwig and I will be forever grateful to your wonderful husband for all he's done for us. You do realize that it was Oskar who made this possible."

"He's a very good man. I am very fortunate," Kara said.

"I have to go."

"Have a good trip. I'll see you soon," Kara said.

Oskar came out of the bedroom in his underwear. He took a clean uniform out of the closet and laid it on the bed. "Is everything all right, liebchen?" he asked. "I heard the phone."

"It was Anka. The baby was born. It's a little girl. She and Ludwig are going to pick her up in Munich today."

"Do you want to go?"

"Yes, very much. But Anka said that I should come to her home rather than trying to meet her in Munich. She didn't mention it, but I think that once she gets the baby home, she might find that she needs me to stay for a while and help her with the baby. She has no experience with children."

"I'll arrange for a driver to take you to Anka's house. Then I'll come as soon as I can."

"I can take the train."

"Shall I arrange for someone to come here to the house to watch Karl while you're gone?"

"No, I'll take him with me," Kara said. "I'm going to call the school right now and tell them that he will not be in school for a while. I don't expect it will be a problem. He's only in kindergarten."

Oskar smiled. "I knew you would choose to take him with you, but I wanted to give you the option of going alone if you preferred."

# CHAPTER FORTY-SEVEN

KARA ARRIVED at Anka's home two days after Ludwig and Anka had returned with the baby. She was a cherub of a child with rounded cheeks, short golden curls that framed her tiny head, and bright-blue eyes. They named her Gretel. But Gretel hardly slept. All night long she cried unless someone rocked her in their arms. Kara, Anka, and Ludwig took alternating shifts of rocking the baby and sleeping. A week later, Ludwig needed to return to work, and he could no longer help. Kara and Anka were awake most of the night because Ludwig needed his rest.

Karl was jealous of the baby when his mother held her. He would cuddle up to his mother and de-mand that she paid attention to him too. He nagged because he missed school and all of his friends. But most of all he missed Patches and Oskar too. And he constantly told Kara he wanted to go home.

Kara loved the precious little girl. Still, she couldn't help but wonder how the child's birth mother was doing. Even if she'd agreed to this adoption, she must feel so empty without the baby. After all, she'd carried the child in her body for nine months. *There is a special bond that forms*, Kara thought as she remembered how she'd felt after Karl was born. She couldn't imagine how she would have felt if she had given him up.

Kara knew she should return home, but Anka begged her to stay. Oskar had been trying to get away and come to see the baby, but so far, he had been unable to leave work. Months passed. Ludwig helped Kara to enroll Karl in the kindergarten program at the German school.

Spring turned to summer and with it came relentless heat. Oskar telephoned weekly begging Kara to come home. She was tired, and she wanted to go, but the baby was still not sleeping through the night, and she couldn't leave Anka. It became more and more apparent to Kara that Anka was not as strong a person as she was. Ludwig hired a woman to come in each morning to prepare their food and to keep the house clean. He asked Anka if she would like a nurse to come in and help with the baby, but Anka refused. She said she didn't want a stranger caring for her child. Kara wondered if that had something to do with Karl's having gone missing. But she didn't ask because Anka was overly sensitive lately. Perhaps it was because she hardly got enough sleep.

Sometimes in the afternoons, Gretel would sleep for an hour or two. When the child fell asleep, Anka looked longingly at her bed. Sometimes Kara noticed that Anka could hardly keep her eyes open. She had grown pale and was losing weight. While the baby slept, Kara insisted that Anka get some rest too. Anka protested. She tried to share the nap time with Kara. "You take a half hour, and then I'll take a half hour," Anka said.

But Kara shook her head and smiled. "I'm not tired," Kara lied. "You go on up to your room and get some sleep. If Gretel wakes up, I'll be here to take care of her," Kara promised. After Anka went to bed, Kara sat in the living room sipping coffee and looking out the window. She couldn't help but remember how she, Hoda, and Abram had taken turns caring for Karl when he was small. There had been no outside help. No one to hire. They had worked as team. Together they kept the house, did the cooking, maintained the bookstore that the family owned, and cared for Karl. Hoda had been working outside the home, at the butcher shop. But she never complained. When she was at home, she was always there to help with her grandson. It was a struggle, but they managed. Kara knew Anka could never have done it. Anka was delicate. It was apparent in everything she did. Over the years, Anka had become accustomed to the comfortable lifestyle Ludwig provided. And although Kara knew her sister was not in love with Ludwig, she also knew that he was the best husband for her.

In many ways, Anka was like another child, a teenager: carefree, and often frivolous. Kara took on all the responsibilities, and she often felt as if she were the only adult female in the house.

# CHAPTER FORTY-EIGHT

**August 1943**

WHEN THE TELEPHONE rang on Sunday evening, Karl ran to answer it. "Vater?" he said, then he turned to Kara and said with a big smile, "It's Vater."

Kara nodded and smiled back. She wanted to be happy. She wanted to feel good about Karl thinking of Oskar as his father. But she didn't. Inside, she was cringing as she heard him say the word Vater. She sat quietly and waited, listening as Karl excitedly told Oskar everything he'd done that week. Finally, he said, "I miss you too, Vati." And handed the phone to Kara. "Vati wants to talk to you, Mutti," Karl said.

"Hello," Kara said into the receiver. "How are you?"

"Mine liebchen," Oskar said in a hoarse voice. "I am fine. As fine as a man can be without his wife. I miss you terribly." He sighed, then continued. "And, you must admit, I have been very patient. However, you have been gone for such a long time. I know you care for your sister. But Anka must learn to be a mother on her own. I need you. And Karl wants to come home too. I mean, don't get me wrong, Patches is a wonderful companion. But he certainly can't take your place."

"I know. You're so right. It's not fair to you that I stay here. I should be there with you. I'll speak with Anka in the morning."

"I love you," he said.

"Yes, me too."

The following day, Gretel awoke at four in the morning. She had started sleeping for several hours at a time, but she still did not sleep through the night. At the slightest cry, Kara took the baby out of her crib and folded her into her warm arms. Then she carried Gretel into the kitchen where she warmed the baby's formula. Once it seemed ready, Kara tested it on her wrist to be sure it was not too hot. "Your bottle is ready, little one," she said. Then she carefully sat down in the rocking chair and gently began to rock Gretel in the dimly lit living room, humming softly as Gretel sucked on her bottle. There was a calm to the early hours that Kara loved. Sometimes she would stay awake with the baby sleeping in her arms just to watch the sun rise.

Kara heard Ludwig in the bathroom getting ready for work, and she knew it was five thirty. He walked into the kitchen and started a pot of coffee. Then he prepared his own breakfast. He never complained that Anka did not get up with him.

"How's our little girl?" Ludwig asked as he looked down into Gretel's sleeping face. "She looks so peaceful."

"Yes, she does, doesn't she?" Kara said.

"Can I bring you a cup of coffee?" he asked.

"That would be lovely," Kara said.

Ludwig poured two cups of coffee and brought one over to Kara. She sipped the hot liquid.

"There's nothing like that first cup of morning coffee," he said.

"I agree."

They sat together for a few minutes watching the baby. "I'm going to have some bread and cheese; would you like some?" he asked.

"No, thank you. I'll wait for Anka," Kara said.

After Ludwig finished eating, he left for work. And, as always, about fifteen minutes later, Anka came out of her room. It was as if she waited to get up until she was certain Ludwig was gone.

"Good morning," Anka said to Kara. Then she went into the kitchen and poured herself a cup of coffee. She brought it into the living room and placed it on the coffee table. Then she stretched and plopped down on the sofa. Even in the morning, without her makeup, Kara could see how pretty her sister was. She had no lines or wrinkles. In fact, she seemed not to be aging at all.

"Have you been awake a long time?" Anka asked as she did every morning.

"Gretel woke up at about four. I've been rocking her since."

"I didn't hear her."

"I know, Anka." Kara sighed. Then a few moments later, she said, "I have something I must speak with you about."

"What is it? Is something wrong?"

"It's just that I must go home now. I've been here since spring; now summer is almost over. Oskar has grown impatient. It's time I return."

"I wish you could stay with us forever. I need you, Kara. Having a child is much more difficult than I ever anticipated."

"I wish I could be two people, one here with you and the other at home with Oskar," Kara said as gently as possible. "However, I need to go home."

Anka bit her lower lip. She looked like she might cry.

"You'll be fine. I promise you. You have Ludwig to help you. And Marta comes in every day to clean and prepare your dinner," Kara said. Then she tried to smile. "And, look, Gretel is sleeping longer now. Soon she'll sleep until morning."

Anka nodded. "When will you come back?"

"I don't know yet. Perhaps the three of you can

come to see us for Christmas?"

"Yes, that would be wonderful. Even if Ludwig can only get away for a couple of days."

When Anka and Karl were leaving with Ludwig, who was driving them to the train, Anka embraced Kara. She held on tightly to her and began to cry. Then she said, "Please come and see us soon."

Kara touched her sister's cheek. "Don't cry, Anka. You have a beautiful baby girl and a wonderful husband. You'll be fine."

"I don't think I can do all of this without you."

"You must try. I will see you at Christmas?" Kara asked, then she glanced at Ludwig, who nodded.

"I'll get a few days off so we can come and visit," he said.

Kara had to gently pry Anka's arms off her so she could leave. "I'm sorry. But I really can't stay," Kara said, but she thought, *I sometimes can't believe just how selfish Anka is. Then again, I have always known it, but I chose not to see it.*

Oskar was thrilled to have his wife back home. He brought her sunflowers made from silk to put in a vase on the dining room table. He brought her chocolates from Switzerland and toys for Karl. When Oskar made love to Kara the night she arrived home, he did so with such tenderness that it brought tears to her eyes. And so it was that she came to decide that she did love him.

# CHAPTER FORTY-NINE

## End of Summer 1943

I T WAS EARLY on a warm summer morning, and the birds had just begun to sing outside, that Oskar Lerch could hear the prisoners being interrogated during roll call. He was busy working in his office when there was a knock on the door.

"Yes?" he said.

"Oberstrumführer, I have a message here for you. May I come in, please?" It was Ursula, the new secretary he'd recently hired.

"Yes, come on in," he said.

"Heil Hitler," she said.

"Heil Hitler." He smiled.

"You received a message from Sturmbannführer Saur a few minutes ago. The message said that he would like to see you," Ursula said.

"Thank you," Oskar said. He hated going to the offices of his superior. It was never about something beneficial for Oskar. Still, he knew he must go, and the sooner the better.

When he arrived, the sturmbannführer's sexy, young secretary ushered him into the office. She winked at Oskar before she left.

"Heil Hitler," Sturmbannführer Saur said.

"Heil Hitler," Oskar replied.

"Sit down, Lerch. I want to speak with you."

"Yes, what is it?"

"I've always indulged you, doing favors for you whenever possible; have I not?"

"Yes, you have been very kind, Sturmbann-führer," Oskar said. *I have been very helpful to you too,* he thought. *I rented rooms for you and kept them secret from your wife and family. Then I found young girls for you and covered for you when you brought them to those rooms, including this secretary who is working for you right now.*

"I need a favor."

*Another favor. What now?* Oskar thought, but he asked, "Of course, what can I do for you?"

"We acquired a coal mine a couple of years ago. It will supply hard coal for the IG Farben factory here at Auschwitz. The mine isn't too far away from here. It's located about thirty kilometers away in a town called Wesola. In case you haven't heard of Wesola, it is rather close to Myslowice."

Oskar nodded his head, listening.

"You would not be required to move from your home."

"Forgive me, but I don't understand what you are asking of me, Sturmbannführer."

"Then I'll be blunt." The sturmbannführer leaned forward in his chair. "We must set up a sub-camp there in order to work the mine. I am getting older, and the last time I saw the doctor he said my heart is weak. I cannot take on this job. I am asking you to do it for me."

*This is the last thing I want to do. Saur is a liar; he's always been a liar. He says he has a weak heart. Well, I wish he would just die already. If he did, all my secrets would die with him. But I dare not refuse to help him with this mine. He knows too much. He knows everything I did with Kara and Karl. He was the one who arranged for Karl to be kidnapped in the first place. He made all of the arrangements with the Lebensborn too. I have no choice but to do what he asks even though a mine is the worst possible place for me because of my background. A background I've worked so hard to forget.* "Of course, I would be more than happy to do it for you," Oskar said with a smile.

Saur let out a sigh of relief. "I knew I could count on you, Lerch."

# CHAPTER FIFTY

OSKAR WAS in a foul mood after he left his meeting with Saur. He knew coal mining was a filthy and dangerous business. In fact, he knew all too well because, unbeknownst to anyone, his father was a coal miner. He grew up with all the misery of the life of a coal miner. As a young child he'd listened to his father's incessant coughing. Death from lung disease was overly common in the small village in the Ruhr valley, where he'd lived.

Had it not been for the generosity of his Hitler Youth leader, he would have spent his life working and dying in a mine just like his father. However, as a child, Oskar showed promise. He was a powerful athlete, handsome and strong. More importantly, he was well liked. He was charming, and he knew how to flatter his superiors. And this ability had taken him far. By the time he was nineteen and returned from working on a farm, where he'd completed his six months of required field service, he was not only an outspoken devoted party member who was being introduced to all the right people, but his friend and Hitler Youth leader told him in confidence that he was being groomed for the SS. When an offer came to leave his family behind and travel to Nuremberg for a job, Oskar jumped at the chance. He left the Ruhr valley, with its poverty and death from lung disease, and never looked back. He'd risen in the ranks by accepting and excelling at every position that was offered to him. He was careful to make the right friends, and he never refused to do anything they asked him to do. No matter what was required.

When he'd been offered the job at Auschwitz, he knew what was going to be expected of him. He would be surrounded by Jews and other undesirables, along with plenty of filth and disease. However, the job came with a huge promotion. He, Oskar Lerch, the son of a miner, was now an oberstrumführer for a Reich that would reign for a thousand years. He readily accepted the job. From the day he started work at the camp, the Jews sickened him, constantly scratching from the lice that festered in their beds and on their bodies. The bloody, oozing sores on their bodies made him shiver. Like most of his colleagues, he feared disease. And the camp was overrun with it.

Before Oskar had started work at Auschwitz, he had never had much to do with Jews. He'd seen them on the street, and he found them strange and disgusting. Especially the obvious ones, with their odd hats and long sideburns. Dr. Goebbels had made it clear that they were treacherous people. And Oskar believed it. But he knew there were also other Jews. Jews disguised themselves to look just like everyone else. And those were the ones who scared him even more. They were far more dangerous because they were undetectable. Oskar wasn't surprised to learn that they were thieves. They stole bread whenever they were given the chance and could not be trusted to carry out a job unless they were closely watched. He hated them even more because it was his responsibility to make sure they stayed in line and followed the rules. It was a constant struggle, and if it was not done properly, if one of them escaped, it was his head that was on the chopping block. So on days like today, when he felt extreme pressure, he took his anger and frustration out on the prisoners. There were no consequences. He could do whatever he liked to those men. Sometimes he would vent his anger by beating one of the men to death. By the time he'd finished clubbing a man with the butt of his rifle or a metal bar, he found that his rage was spent, and he could face his superiors with that winning smile he used to get what he needed. He also found that he could turn on the charm again at the end of the day when he returned home to his beautiful wife with a bunch of flowers or a box of chocolates. And as annoying as little Karl could be, he could find the patience to act as the strong Aryan father figure his wife expected him to be.

Oskar walked back to his office and took the heavy, black metal pipe from under his desk. Then he went out into the camp to find a victim.

# CHAPTER FIFTY-ONE

ABRAM AND MOISHE were on their way back from their respective jobs when they saw the oberstrum-führer strolling through the camp patting his black metal pipe against his thigh. They exchanged glances. Both of them knew what this meant. They'd seen the oberstrumführer in this mood before. "Make sure he doesn't see you," Abram said. "Stay back."

Moishe nodded, sweat beading at his brow.

They were behind the oberstrumführer when they saw him walk up to a skinny teenage boy who was filling up the soup cauldron. From where they stood, they couldn't see the boy's face. The Oberstrumführer tapped the boy on his shoulder with the pipe. Abram and Moishe couldn't hear the boy, but they saw him fall to his knees and grab the oberstrumführer's pant leg. They knew the boy was begging for his life. Next, they saw the oberstrum-führer kick the boy and then grab him by his arm and lift him onto his feet. Then he pushed the boy into the center of a crowd of prisoners already lining up for dinner. Abram swallowed hard, then he looked over at Moishe.

Everyone seemed to have been frozen, they stood staring with dark terrified eyes. This time they heard the teenage boy when he let out a scream as the metal pipe came down on his back. "I wonder why he's beating him," Moishe said, wincing.

"You know those Nazi bastards don't need a reason."

The pipe came down again. The boy's screams unnerved Abram.

"Come on." Abram grabbed Moishe's arm. "Let's get out of here. Hurry up. Let's walk quickly behind the crowd and get back to our block."

"Yes, you're right," Moishe said, but he seemed glued to the ground. He couldn't move. His mouth hung open in horror. "Abram, I think it's Hersh."

"What?"

"Hersh, the kid who used to sleep in the bunk above ours. I think that bastard Lerch just killed him."

"Come on, let's get out of here."

"I can't move, Abram."

"Moishe, wake up. Snap out of this. Come on. Who knows if he'll grab another fellow. We have to get out of here." Abram shook the sleeve of his friend's uniform. Then the oberstrumführer brought the pipe down hard and fast on the back of the boy's skull. Abram and Moishe were too far away to hear the skull crack, but Abram imagined that he heard it. Even from where he stood, he could see the blood and brain matter fly across the camp and hit another prisoner in the face. The boy fell to the ground like a broken toy.

Now Moishe and Abram were moving. They raced behind the others, and as they did, they heard Lerch say, "You," as he pointed to another prisoner, "the boy's blood landed on your face, so that makes you next."

"No, please," the man begged.

Abram and Moishe were frozen again. They both knew that the begging was of no use.

Lerch grabbed the inmate and threw him to the ground. Then Lerch raised the already bloody pipe and brought it down hard on the back of the second prisoner. Moishe shook Abram hard. "Let's go," he said.

This time when Moishe and Abram's eyes met, their feet began to move. Moishe grabbed Abram's arm. Then together they began to run.

# CHAPTER FIFTY-TWO

Oskar was spent. His rage was gone, and he was
ready to go home.

He walked back to his office where he wiped the
metal pipe clean of blood and brain matter. Then
he went into the closet where he kept a change of
uniform. He did this so that he never had to explain
to Kara why he was wearing a blood-splattered uniform when he went home. After he changed his
clothes, he handed the soiled uniform to his secretary who was sitting at her desk, and told her to
have it cleaned. Her eyes fell upon the spots of
blood, but as always, she didn't ask him any questions, and he didn't provide any information. The
girl just took the uniform and nodded. "Yes, Ober-
sturmführer." That was what he liked about her.
She understood that it was not her place to ask him
anything.

Ursula was his young secretary, who had come into his employ about six months prior. He thought of her as not only a pretty young girl, but also as a brave little thing who had traveled from Germany to Poland alone after graduating secretarial school. Oskar believed she did this because of her love for her country. She hated the camp and the Jews; she had already confided as much to him. However, she told him that she wanted to be of service to the war effort and even more importantly to the cleansing of the east. They had eaten lunch together a few times. He'd even taken her out for a beer after work once. Oskar was no fool; he acknowledged that he felt an attraction to her. But he was also a disciplined man who loved his wife. He planned to bed Ursula because he could. And he would keep her as a pleasant distraction as long as she didn't give him any trouble. But in his heart, he knew he loved Kara and would never leave her. She had been too difficult of a prize to win.

Over the last year, the murders of the prisoners at the camp had risen. The crematorium ran constantly to dispose of the bodies. Oskar had worked at Auschwitz for several years prior, and he'd grown accustomed to the noxious odor that was always present at the camp. But since the gassings had increased, the smell had become overpowering. The increase in killings had begun after the conference in the winter of 1942 at Wannsee. Oskar had not been invited to attend. He wished he had, but he was not that high of an official in the party. However, rumors had penetrated the camp, and he knew what had taken place at that meeting. Several very high-ranking officers had decided that the best way to deal with the Jewish problem was to exterminate the Jews as quickly as possible. And since they'd given those orders, the camp was required to fill a quota every day in order to achieve this goal. Ashes constantly vomited like gray snow out of the chimney of the crematorium and landed on Oskar's clothing. He hated the smell of it, and the look of it. Once when he'd come home covered in it, Kara had asked him what the gray ash was from. He'd lied and told her it was from the chemical plant. Oskar was relieved that she seemed to accept his answer.

To cope with the increased demand at his job, Oskar had taken on two new habits. He'd begun keeping a bottle of schnapps in his desk drawer, and he'd also started smoking. It was common knowledge that the führer was against smoking. But Oskar didn't care. He reasoned the führer is sitting at his desk pumping out his demands. He's not here. He doesn't have to cope with the Jews, with the smells, and with the disease. He isn't subject to constant threats of betrayal from his fellow officers who want to be promoted and don't care whose back they must climb over to get to the top.

Oskar leaned back in his chair and lit a cigarette. The hot smoke filled his lungs and calmed him even further. Then he took a swig from the bottle of schnapps. *That bastard Saur demands that I build a camp near a coal mine. I grew up the son of a poor coal miner. I have spent my entire life trying to escape those memories and now they are coming back to haunt me. The men, the faces black with coal dust. The coughing. The constant threat of explosions. Even the mine itself. As if this camp wasn't bad enough. Why me? Why did that bastard choose me?* He drank for a while and smoked two cigarettes. Then he got up and walked outside. Oskar looked around him. He sucked in his breath. *I am a powerful man. Look at the faces on these Jews. They're terrified of me. They know that if it suits my fancy, I can end their lives with one shot. I like knowing that I am like a god to them. Even so, this work is dirty, and I am always afraid of getting some vile disease from these filthy vermin. Sometimes, I must admit, I envy Ludwig. He goes to work at the lair every day. His job requires him to run a pleasure palace for SS officers. What could be better? What could be more civilized? I could request a transfer to work there with him. And yet if I did, I would have to give up this power, and there is something deep inside of me that thrives on it. When I am here at Auschwitz, I'm no longer that poor, pathetic boy doomed to work in the mines until the coal dust sucks the air from his lungs. I am an Aryan god.*

# CHAPTER FIFTY-THREE

THE FOLLOWING MONDAY, when Oskar arrived at the mine, he found that it was already operating. Slave labor which consisted of Jews and Soviets was already in operation. He learned that Rudolf Hoss was behind this operation. It was he who had negotiated with the IG Farbenindustrie AG and Fürstengrube GmbH to build this additional camp which was to house six hundred prisoners, bringing the total number of workers in the mine to twelve hundred.

Jews from Lager Ostland, a forced-labor camp, had been brought in to build the new facility.

Looking around him, Oskar felt his heart sink. He already knew he was going to hate this job of setting up the camp for the prisoners that would work in the coal mine. But he was a master at hiding his feelings, and he would never let his superior officers know what he really thought. He knew how to follow rules. But most importantly, Oskar also knew how to flatter his superiors while hiding his hatred and resentment for them, which was constantly growing. *The oberstrumführer is always in control.* He wore a mask that no one could see through, not even Kara. And he decided that was his greatest asset. As a child, Oskar had learned how to manipulate others. It made him a good poker player and an even better SS officer.

On a warm day in September when the leaves had begun to fall, covering the ground in brilliant colors, the SS began moving the group of prisoners they'd brought to the new camp surrounding the coal mine, among them Moishe and Abram.

"Where do you think they are taking us?" Moishe asked.

Abram shrugged as they were loaded at gunpoint onto open trucks. Once the truck was filled to capacity, two armed guards boarded, and they were on their way. As the truck headed out toward its destination, Abram raised his head and glanced over at his fellow inmates. They were painfully thin, skeletal, and weak. Their eyes were deep, black holes. He could see how frightened they were; he was frightened too. It was no secret at Auschwitz that transfers were never a good thing for the prisoners.

The contrast of the beauty of the fall day, the golden rays of the last days of summer, and the horror of what awaited them at the end of this ride, struck Abram like a blow to the stomach. So many of the men had lost their fight. The starvation, the hard work, and the cruelty had sucked all of the will to live from them. They'd quietly, simply given up. But not Abram, not yet. He thought of Kara and Karl, and he forced himself to be strong. I must continue to live so I can return home to my family. They will need me. Then he thought of his mother, and he hoped that Yitzar, her new husband, had been able to protect her.

The ride to the mine took less than an hour. But with every bump in the road, Abram felt his stomach flip, and he prayed he wouldn't vomit. Vomiting could get a man killed.

Once they arrived at their destination, the men were forced to jump off the truck quickly and get into a single line for a roll call. After the guard who had ridden with them finished the roll call, Oberstrumführer Lerch came out of a building and walked to the front of the line.

"Welcome to Fürstengrube, subcamp of Auschwitz," he said, his voice sarcastically cheery. "You have two jobs to complete here. You will be extracting coal from the old mine, and at the same time you will be in the process of building a new mine. The work will continue around the clock. Each of you will be assigned one of three shifts. And you had better know it now; laziness will not be tolerated."

The oberstrumführer walked back and forth surveying the lineup of prisoners. Then he gave each of the men an assignment. Some were sent to the older mine where they worked in eight-hour shifts around the clock. The others were sent to the new mine where they worked ten-hour shifts, but no nights only days.

A young, enthusiastic guard followed Oberstrumführer Lerch as he assigned each of the men to their jobs. The young guard wrote down the prisoner's number along with his assignment, so there would be no confusion later. As Lerch strolled through the line, he stopped and pointed to Moishe. "This one, to the old mine, extracting coal, five a.m. to one p.m." Next in line was another man. "This one, old mine, one p.m. to nine p.m." Then Lerch stood before Abram. For a moment he hesitated, then the oberstrumführer said, "Old mine, nine p.m. to five a.m. After they were given their assignments, Abram and Moishe stole a frightened glance at each other. Abram knew that working in a coal mine was going to be grueling and potentially very dangerous.

# CHAPTER FIFTY-FOUR

OSKAR HAD BEEN DREADING IT, but he finally told Kara that he'd been assigned to work at a coal mine. "It's only temporary," he said with a smile. Then he went on to explain everything: where the mine was located, the resources it would provide, everything except that he would be working with the men who were unpaid slave labor. Jews who would otherwise be on their way to gas chambers and crematoriums. He tried to make the job sound important, explaining that the IG Farben factory was working with the Reich, and that they needed coal. She listened but not with great interest. To her it sounded like work and nothing more.

However, once he made the transfer, she began to notice that each day he returned from work exhausted and unhappy. It was unlike him to be so quiet and moody, and she was concerned. One

Sunday, about a week after he'd been sent to the mine, she tried to arrange a picnic for the family in the hope that the fresh air would help Oskar find some relief from his job. It was brisk outside, but she hoped it would be warm enough in the sun for them to be comfortable. She'd never seen him so distracted. He hardly listened to her when she talked to him. And the last several times they'd made love, he'd been unable to perform. The picnic did very little to brighten his spirit. Even as Oskar tried to play with Karl, tossing a ball back and forth, Kara could see that his heart wasn't in it. Finally, that night as they lay in bed, Kara asked him what was wrong.

Several moments passed before he answered. "My father was a miner. I spent my entire life trying to escape from that life, and yet here I am back again. The mine brings back horrible memories from my childhood. My father, the black lung, the explosion. So many things . . ."

"Oh, Oskar," she said, touching his arm. In all the time that she'd known him, he'd never told her much about his past.

"It's miserable to be there."

"Can you get transferred?"

"I don't know. Originally, I was only going to stay until everything was set up. Now, Saur wants me to stay on and make sure that things are running properly. He's talking a year perhaps. The very idea of that makes me sick."

"Does he know how you feel? Have you told him? Does he know about your father?"

"I am too ashamed to tell him. I was ashamed to tell you."

She sighed. "You don't have to be ashamed of anything with me. I'm your wife. I love you."

He let out a small, choked sob. "You do? You really do?"

"Yes. Of course, I do." She leaned into him and ran her hand over his forehead. In the moonlight that filtered through the window, he looked younger, vulnerable. "Oh, Oskar, of course I love you."

Oskar turned over and took her into his arms. She felt that his cheeks were wet when he kissed her, and she knew he'd been crying. Then tenderly, he made love to her. It was the first time he was able to make love since he'd been transferred to the mine, and it gave Kara hope that their relationship would be all right.

# CHAPTER FIFTY-FIVE

THE MINE WAS A DARK NIGHTMARE, filled with danger, coal dust, bosses, prisoners, and civilians as well as the Nazi guards who were cruel and demanding. The foreman and civilians were given protective clothing. But the prisoners were not. They worked the mines in their striped uniforms, their Stars of David covered in dust. Working without protective gear made this already dangerous job even worse. By the time Abram had been at the mine for six months, he'd already witnessed eight fatal beatings of prisoners by civilian staff.

Inside the mine the underground passages were narrow, and the ceilings were low. Water covered the ground. It was so dark that a man could not see his own hand in front of him. It was stiflingly hot, and each deep breath became a chore. At the end of Abram's shift when he emerged from the mine, he gave thanks to see the world again, to taste the fresh air and feel the wind on his face. He was glad that the sun had not yet risen when he came up from the darkness of the mine; he needed a little time to adjust to the light. Moishe told him that when he came up from the mine at one in the afternoon, the bright sunlight felt like a knife stabbing his eyes. The men who had been assigned to work in the old mine were dying like flies, and Abram prayed that he and Moishe would somehow be transferred to the new mine.

And then something akin to a miracle happened, and Abram was certain that it had saved his life. He was on his way to the mine one evening when the oberstrumführer stopped him. "You," Oberstrumführer Lerch said, pointing to Abram. Abram stopped walking. He was shivering with fear. The oberstrumführer went on to say, "I need you in the new mine. For tonight, go to work at your regular shift in the old mine. Then tomorrow morning at nine, I want you to come to work at the new mine. You'll be working there from now on."

It would be brutal to work the entire night in the deep darkness of the old mine and then be forced to return to work at the new mine a few hours later without much rest. However, Abram was certain that although it would be a hard night, followed by a hard day, in the long run he would be better off. And that proved to be right.

Building the new mine was not easy work. But it

was still far better than working at the old mine extracting coal. He was assigned work as a bricklayer. It was backbreaking work, but at least he was able to breathe the fresh air. And he'd made friends with a young, strong man named Samuel, who was teaching him to weld. The welding was hot, and it hurt his ears, but it was a trade, and for Abram, a man who offered no skills that the Nazis might find useful, it was a godsend.

The camp that was set up to house the Jewish slave labor should have been hell, but Abram marveled at the resilience of some of his fellow Jews. In their prior lives they'd been musicians, actors, dancers. And they loved their craft so much that at night they performed for the other prisoners. One of the men, who Abram came to know, had once been a comedian. And even with all he had suffered at the hands of the Nazis, he still had the desire to make people laugh. When Abram asked him about it, he said, "The sound of laughter is like air to me. I can't live without it."

# CHAPTER FIFTY-SIX

**Winter 1943**

WHEN WINTER ARRIVED, the men were dying at an even faster rate. The ones who were in the old mine were sweating all day and then exposed to extreme cold when they came up from the mines in their thin uniforms. Those who worked outside in the new mine struggled against the winter chill all day long. And with the lack of sufficient food, their bodies were far too weak to fight the elements. Moishe and Abram stole food whenever they could, even though they knew that if they were caught, they would be punished severely. They'd seen men shot to death for stealing a heel of moldy bread. It was a tightrope that Abram and Moishe walked every day of their lives. If they wanted to stay alive, they had to eat, and since the food that was provided was not sufficient, they had to steal. Not only did Abram fear for himself, but he was always afraid for Moishe. Moishe had become like a brother to him, and Abram was terrified of losing him. He was the only person in the camp whom Abram felt close to. Sometimes when they huddled together to stay warm through the brutally cold nights, Abram thought he would rather die than lose Moishe. Every day and every night was a challenge to stay alive. It seemed as if the winter took a thousand years before the ice began to melt and spring brought new life.

It was announced that Hauptscharführer Otto Moli was officially named the camp's first commandant. The occasion was celebrated by giving each of the prisoners an extra piece of potato in their soup.

"Does that mean that the oberstrumführer will be gone?" Moishe asked as he gobbled a bite of his potato.

"I don't know." Abram shrugged. "I think the oberstrumführer is a higher rank than the hauptscharführer. But I'm not sure. Maybe he'll come and go, leaving the hard work to the hauptscharführer."

"Maybe he'll go back to the main camp permanently, and we'll never have to see his face again," Moishe said.

"Ala vie. From your mouth to God's ears," Abram said.

"Ala vie," Moishe repeated. "Maybe this one will be better."

"I doubt it. They're all no good. Especially for us because we're Jews," Abram said, shaking his head.

"Stay hopeful."

Abram shook his head. "I wish I could. But I am losing hope every day that we're here. Sometimes I can't even remember what Kara looked like. I can't remember my son's face and how it felt to hold him in my arms. Or my mama's chicken soup. Sometimes, Moishe, I just want to give up."

"Don't you dare even think that way. If you do, it's for sure that you're going to die here. Now, eat this lousy soup, and pretend it's your mother's chicken soup. All the while keep on thinking about the future and how we are going to get out of this hell. Think about how I am going to come to eat by you. Think about how we are going to laugh and reminisce. Yes? This is what you must do, Abram. This is the way to survive," Moishe said as he devoured the rest of the potato.

# CHAPTER FIFTY-SEVEN

**Spring 1944**

THE PRISONERS LINED up outside for roll call one cool spring morning. The air smelled fresh as tiny blades of grass peeked their heads through the once frozen ground.

The oberstrumführer stood on the sidelines watching. He seemed to be in a good mood as he was speaking with a foreman. Then the foreman turned to the lineup of prisoners and said, "I need two of you." He walked in front of the line and continued, "Two of you with a good eye for beauty and color. Do any of you have experience building a garden?"

Moishe nudged Abram "Raise your hand," he whispered as he raised his own.

Abram glanced at Moishe. *Volunteering for anything*

*at this place is a mistake*, he thought. But Moishe pulled Abram's hand and raised it into the air.

Several men had their hands up. But the foreman looked directly at Moishe. "You two," he said, indicating Moishe and Abram. "You two look like a couple of homos who would know how to plant flowers. Step forward and follow me. The rest of you, get on your way. It's time to start your shift at the mines."

Moishe grabbed Abram's arm and led him to the foreman.

"Get in the truck. I have a job for you two."

Abram shook his head. "This doesn't look good. They could be taking us anywhere," he said.

"I know. I'm sorry," Moishe said.

"Yes, well, we'll have to hope this isn't our last ride. And if it is, then it's God's plan."

"No matter what happens, it's God's plan," Moishe said.

Abram and Moishe were led to an open truck. A guard got into the back and pointed a gun directly at them.

They drove for several minutes, and the guard laid his head on his arm. It looked as if he were taking a nap.

Abram looked at the guard certain that he wouldn't hear him. "I don't know anything about gardening," Abram whispered to Moishe. "I grew up in the city. My family owned a bookstore."

"Keep your mouth shut," Moishe said. "You

don't want them to hear you. I'll tell you this much, I know enough to know that creating a garden is a lot easier than working at either of the mines. It will be like having a couple of days off."

"Unless it's not really a garden. Maybe it's just a massive grave and they want us to dig it."

"Yeah, these sick bastards would call a grave a garden."

"We might end up at the bottom once we've finished," Abram said.

"Stop talking. This isn't helping."

They arrived at the house. It was a large, sprawling red-brick home with a well-maintained lawn. The guard stood up and stretched; he rubbed his eyes and then said, "Get off the truck, you swine."

Abram and Moishe jumped down from the bed of the truck and stood waiting for orders.

"He wants the garden right here: sunflowers, roses, you know, flowers. Just make sure it's beautiful," the guard said.

Abram shot a glance at Moishe, who didn't look back at him. Instead, Moishe nodded to the guard as if he had been a landscaper all his life. "I'll send the driver into town to get you any supplies you need. Just tell him what you want."

Then the guard went over to the side of the house and picked up two shovels that were leaning against the building. He walked back and handed them each a shovel. "You'll need these to turn the soil," he said.

Moishe began to turn the soil. Abram followed Moishe's lead.

"The Oberstrumfuhrer wants lots of flowers. Preferably roses. His wife loves roses." The guard said.

"Then we're going to need rosebushes, lots of flowering rosebushes," Moishe said to the guard, who nodded, and then he sent the driver to pick up the supplies.

It was not long before the driver returned with several bushes, and by afternoon, they'd cleared an area and were ready to plant. The rosebushes had thorns, and the men had no gloves. So by the time they'd put the bushes into the ground, their hands were cut and bleeding. "Still, it's better than the mines," Moishe whispered.

Abram nodded. *At least it's not too hot or cold outside*, he thought.

Then Moishe, as if reading Abram's mind, said, "The weather is beautiful. We're out in the sunshine. The guard is busy writing a letter to someone, probably his girl. What more could we want? So, a little blood to water the soil? Could be worse. Could be a lot worse." Moishe smiled.

For the next three days, Abram and Moishe were transported to the home immediately following roll call. Abram began to enjoy seeing the garden take shape. The beauty of the flowers made him think of Kara. *I wish I could build a beautiful garden like this for my wife.* The fresh air and sunshine renewed his broken spirit. He saw Kara's eyes in the purple color of the sterling-silver roses. He saw her face when he looked up into the sun. He imagined he heard his child's laughter as he poured water on the newly planted bushes. For lunch, Abram and Moishe were each given a heel of bread and a cup of water. Moishe had no shoes. But at noon, when they finished eating, he suggested that Abram take his off and feel the earth beneath his bare feet. The foreman was not paying attention, so Abram took his friend's suggestion. The earth was cool and pliable between his toes. And for the first time in a long time, Abram felt the presence of God.

# CHAPTER FIFTY-EIGHT

IT WAS the last day that Abram and Moishe were scheduled to work on the garden. They'd been informed that everything must be complete by the time the officer returned, or there would be hell to pay. *Somehow Moishe and I pulled this off,* Abram thought as he looked at the work admiringly.

"Go and pick up an array of large, colorful garden rocks. Hurry, and get yourself into town to purchase them because the officer wants the rocks to be placed so they are surrounding the garden, setting it off from the rest of the yard."

"I'll be right back," the driver said.

A half hour later the driver returned with the bed of the truck loaded with giant stones. Abram stared at the heavy rocks and his heart sank.

"Get these off the truck and place them around

the garden," the guard demanded. "And mach schnell!"

Abram headed over to the truck with Moishe to begin unloading the heavy rocks. Then the guard walked over to Abram and Moishe. His face was red, and he was shaking because he knew that he was also on the clock, and if he didn't produce the desired results in time, not only would the prisoners suffer, but he would suffer as well. He nudged Abram with his rifle butt. "Move. Mach schnell!" he yelled. "This is no time to be lazy. There is no time for eating today. You only have a couple of hours to get this job done."

The stones were so heavy that Abram and Moishe had to roll each one individually to its destination. The sweat poured down their dirty faces, but they rolled each stone with great care so as not to let it drop on the other man.

# CHAPTER FIFTY-NINE

Sweat poured down Abram's face. His uniform was stuck to his body with perspiration. He and Moishe were out of breath, struggling to move the last stone to its place in the garden. As they rolled the heavy stone, a jagged edge caught Abram's finger. He felt his skin tear. But there was no time to stop, not even for a moment. The foreman was yelling at them to hurry. "I can see the car coming down the street. We must be gone before he arrives, or there will be hell to pay. Mach schnell, I tell you. Mach schnell!"

Abram's heart was beating so hard that his left arm hurt. But the stone was finally in place. "Come on, we must get out of here. Get into the truck," the foreman said.

Abram and Moishe walked to the truck as quickly as they could. The guard who had been waiting in the back of the truck held his gun on them. Abram climbed in, then he helped Moishe up.

Abram had been looking down at the nasty slash on his finger which he'd gotten from the stone. It was deep. He would have to borrow a needle from one of the men and pull a thread out from his uniform to sew it. The driver closed the truck, then got into the cab and started the vehicle. The engine turned over with a roar just as the black automobile pulled up in front of the house. The chauffeur got out of the black auto and opened the door.

The truck driver hesitated for a single moment to admire the work the men had done on the garden. And then he shifted the truck into gear.

"This is for you, my darling. Your birthday present from me," the officer said loud enough for Abram to hear.

Abram heard female laughter. The voice was so familiar that Abram looked up from his bleeding hand to see the oberstrumführer and his family. There they were. The cruel and terrible oberstrumführer holding the hand of a blond-haired little boy. Then he saw the woman. Her golden hair, the slender shape of her arm. Abram's heart sank as he looked at her face. *How is this possible?* It was the face of the woman he loved. *Am I hallucinating? Is it really her?* His breath caught in his throat. *Kara. This monster is married to my Kara.* The truck began to pull away. Shaking, Abram stared at the scene.

Abram's eyes went to the boy. *That's my son. That's my Karl.* Abram had to stop himself from jumping off the truck and calling out her name. He tried to call out to her, but his voice was gone. It was as if God was protecting him, because if he did call out, he would be shot on sight. *I don't know how this happened. The Nazis have stolen my life. That oberstrumführer bastard has taken enough from me. Now, I know my family is alive. And I know where to find them. No matter what I must do, I will find a way to come back here and claim what is rightfully mine.* The truck turned the corner and picked up speed as they pulled onto a main road that headed back toward the camp. Abram watched as blood dripped down from his finger, staining the bed of the truck red. Then he looked up to the heavens, and in his mind, he vowed to God, "I will not give up. I will never give up."

# AUTHORS NOTE

I always enjoy hearing from my readers, and your thoughts about my work are very important to me. If you enjoyed my novel, please consider telling your friends and posting a short review on Amazon. Word of mouth is an author's best friend.

Also, it would be my honor to have you join my mailing list. As my gift to you for joining, you will receive 3 **free** short stories and my USA Today award-winning novella complimentary in your email! To sign up, just go to my website at www. RobertaKagan.com

I send blessings to each and every one of you,
Roberta
Email: roberta@robertakagan.com

# A WEB OF SECRETS

## The Final Book in Jews, The Third Reich, and A Web of Secrets

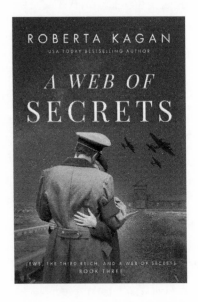

His given name was Walter Lerch, but everyone called him Lucky, a nickname he earned by cheating death more times than he could count. For a boy who worked in the coal mines, this was a gift which his mother gave thanks for in the small Lutheran church she attended every Sunday. In a mining town such as this one, it was not uncommon for women to pray daily as their husbands and sons left their homes and walked down the dirt path to enter into the dark belly of the mines.

Walter's father had not been as lucky as his son. He had worked in the mines for years and had been hurt several times. But he came to a terrible end when he was trapped with five other miners by an explosion. The mine bosses came, and they made a slow effort to dig the men out. But the time they were unearthed, they were all dead. Although his mother despised the mines, she and her son had to eat, and in this small village, there was little else for a man to do to earn a living. So Walter was forced to begin his career as a miner at twelve. He was a happy-go-lucky sort of boy, who tried to make the best of things, always putting on a good front for his mother. He told her he wasn't scared and reminded her, with a smile, that his nickname was Lucky. But that night before his first day at the mine, when he was alone in his room, he wept.

The following day he got up and ate the breakfast his mother had prepared for him. He could see her face was red from crying. "I'll be all right, Mutti," he promised her. "I just know it."

She nodded. "I packed you a lunch," she said, handing him one of his father's old lunch pails.

"Thanks, and don't you worry," he said, forcing a smile until she closed the door behind him.

Then he joined the other miners walking toward the beast of a mine that morning.

When he arrived, there was an old man standing in line outside waiting to enter the mine.

"You're a young one. Not the youngest I've seen though," the old man said. "What's your name?"

"Lucky," Walter said.

The old man let out a loud burst of laughter. Then he said, "Well, Lucky. You'd better hope that your name holds out for you. Because I been around a long time, and I'm going to tell you right now that the mine is a cruel mistress. She will take you one way or another. You mark my words, son," the old miner said, then he patted Walter on the back as he walked into the dark cavern, his lunch pail in his hand. Before Walter could get away from him, the old man added, "Either it'll get you by turning your lungs black, so you suffocate and can't take a breath, or it'll snuff the life out of you in an explosion. There's just no way around it. Can't say when it'll happen, but it will. I'm sick. I got lung disease. But I would say I'm one of the lucky ones. You see, I lived a long time. Fellas I know died much younger."

Walter turned to look at the old man, who coughed blood into a dirty, white handkerchief. But he didn't say anything. Instead, he forced himself to walk on into the darkness.

That night when Walter returned home, he hid his fears from his mother. She adored and doted on him. His dinner was always ready when he returned from the mine, and his clothes were always washed.

The years passed, and his mother began to relax. It seemed that Walter was truly lucky. He was
never injured in the mine, and so far, there had not
been any serious accidents. To his mother's disappointment, he was growing into a man. If it had
been her choice, he would have stayed a young boy
and hers forever. But he was growing, and his
mother knew that the time was coming when he
would want a woman. When the other boys his age
began to court local girls, his mother had something
bad to say about every one of the girls in town. She
needn't have bothered because none of them
piqued Walter's interest. He'd known them since
they were children, and he couldn't see them as
anything but friends.

Then when Walter was seventeen, a pretty
blonde with sparkling blue eyes moved in with his
neighbors. Listening to his mother talk to her
friends, he learned that the girl's name was Hedy.
She'd come to live with her uncle and aunt when
her parents and two siblings were killed in a fire.
She was a petite, pretty little bit of girl. And he
found himself thinking about her a lot and wondering what she was like. Then he took to watching
her from his window when she walked by. He loved
the way her hair bounced and her hips swayed.
Walter decided he had to get to know her better,
and so he must find a way to speak to her.

That Sunday, although he was exhausted, he

got up and went to church with his mother, who was elated to have him. Most Sundays he complained that he was too tired and refused to get out of bed in time to go with her. But that particular day, he rose early and worked vigorously to ensure he'd removed any trace of the coal from his face and hands. He diligently scrubbed under his nails to remove as much of the black soot as possible. Then he put on his only suit. It had been his father's and was still too big for him, but when he looked in the mirror, he nodded his head. *I guess I do look pretty good*.

When his mother saw him, she let out a sigh. "Don't you look handsome?" she said.

He smiled, quite sure that he was a handsome young man, and he would find a way to speak to Hedy. His confidence was strong, and he was very sure of himself until he saw Hedy sitting beside her aunt. She was by far one of the prettiest girls he'd ever seen. *Far too good for me,* he thought. As he eyed her from across the room, Walter began to lose his confidence and feel that his attraction was nothing more than a hopeless fantasy. Even so, he couldn't take his eyes off her.

After the church service ended, Walter accompanied his mother home; he watched Hedy walking just a little way in front of them. She held her four-year-old cousin's hand as she followed her aunt and uncle quietly. Her full hips swayed in the flirtatious way that made his heart beat fast and heat shoot through his body. *Hedy looks like she is sad*, he thought as she kept her head down. *I'm sure she must still be heartbroken at the loss of her parents*, he thought, feeling a wave of sympathy come over him, and with it came a strong desire to comfort and protect her.

When Hedy and her family turned the corner to head down a street to their house, Walter watched. *I don't know how I am going to do it, but I have to find a way to talk to her.*

Each week Walter gave his mother his pay envelope and then took out a few coins to spend as he pleased. It wasn't much, but it was enough to purchase a pretty hair comb when he went into town that afternoon. He sighed as he handed the Jewish store owner his coins. *Jews*, he thought, *they have all the money.* The store owner wrapped the hair clip for him, then he stopped and looked into Walter's eyes. "A gift for your girlfriend or your mother?"

Walter nodded. "Yes," he said, but he didn't say whether it was for his mother or his girl.

The shop owner nodded too and didn't ask any more questions. Smiling, he took a pretty white hair ribbon from the shelf. "My gift to you," the shop owner said. "If you give the comb to your girlfriend, give the ribbon to your mother. They are both very important people in your life, no?"

Walter nodded. He suddenly felt ashamed for having had those bad thoughts about the Jewish shop owner. "Thank you," he said.

The shop owner smiled. "Zie gezunt, be well," he said.

*Available now!*

To Be An Israeli

Forever My Homeland

**Michal's Destiny Series**

Michal's Destiny

A Family Shattered

Watch Over My Child

Another Breath, Another Sunrise

**Eidel's Story Series**

And . . . Who Is The Real Mother?

Secrets Revealed

New Life, New Land

Another Generation

**The Wrath of Eden Series**

The Wrath Of Eden

The Angels Song

**Stand Alone Novels**

One Last Hope

A Flicker Of Light

The Heart Of A Gypsy

# ACKNOWLEDGMENTS

I would like to thank my editor, proofreader, and developmental editor for all their help with this project. I couldn't have done it without them.

Paula Grundy of Paula Proofreader
Terrance Grundy of Editerry
Carli Kagan, Developmental Editor

Manufactured by Amazon.ca
Bolton, ON

25356843R00215